'I'm having ... hands off you ...'

His words ign ... ... she immediately felt breathless and light-headed. 'Marty!' Nat closed her eyes and shook her head. 'Don't say things like that.'

'Why not?'

'Because…we're friends.'

'You *are* attracted to me, aren't you?' He brushed her hair back from her face. 'You do feel this...this *thing* between us?' His hand brushed her neck and she gasped, unable to break eye contact.

'Marty.' His name was a tortured whisper and she was desperately losing control. 'I do want to, but—'

Marty shook his head impatiently and within an instant had covered the distance between them, pulling her into his arms and pressing his mouth to hers in one swift motion.

Dear Reader

Christmas is one of my absolute favourite times of year, which is why I wanted to write a book set around that time. From the early morning wake-up and opening of presents, to the rich food and eventual contentedness of the day, it's certainly one for sharing with people you love.

In *Christmas-Day Fiancée,* Marty and Natalie go through a lot—wearing Santa hats, hanging dusty Christmas decorations, poor Natalie ruining more than one outfit—to finally get their happily-ever-after Christmas.

I hope you enjoy getting to know them and have a wonderful Christmas.

Warmest regards

Lucy Clark

Recent titles by the same author:

DR CUSACK'S SECRET SON
CRISIS AT KATOOMBA HOSPITAL*
COMING HOME TO KATOOMBA*

*Blue Mountains A&E

CHRISTMAS-DAY FIANCÉE

BY
LUCY CLARK

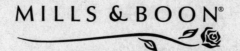

MILLS & BOON®

For the people I went to school with. We grow, we change,
we eventually find ourselves, but a part of us will always
remember those days in the old school yard!
Phil 4:19

First published in Great Britain 2005
Harlequin Mills & Boon Limited,
Eton House, 18-24 Paradise Road, Richmond, Surrey TW9 1SR

© Lucy Clark 2005

ISBN 0 263 84350 5

Set in Times Roman 9½ on 10 pt.
03-1205-65459

Printed and bound in Spain
by Litografia Rosés, S.A., Barcelona

CHAPTER ONE

'I'VE changed Alysha's medication to an immunosuppressant as the corticosteroids didn't seem to be working too well,' Natalie Fox said to the nurse looking after Alysha. 'Monitor her closely and let me know how she is in a couple of hours.'

'Will do, Natalie.'

'I'll do a serum electrolyte count then.' She finished writing the notes for her six-year-old patient before picking up her stethoscope from the desk. When her pager beeped, she groaned. 'What now?' She checked the number, her Santa hat almost falling off her head. She pushed it back on impatiently.

'Who is it?' Cassie, the ward clerk, asked.

'Radiology. Hopefully, they have those films I've been bugging them for all morning.'

'Impatient as ever, I see,' a male voice drawled behind her, and Natalie turned, her glare already fixed in place to scare off her annoying colleague, Andrew...but it wasn't Andrew who'd spoken. Her eyebrows lifted in stunned surprise.

'Marty?' Natalie gaped at him.

'One and the same.'

The smile that lit her face was sincere as she leaned forward to hug him. Although the contact was brief, his body felt firm where she touched him and the fresh aftershave he wore was natural but very nice. Not like Richard's expensive brand, which always seemed to give her headaches. She pushed the thought away and quickly stepped back from the embrace. 'What are you doing here?'

'In Sydney?'

'Well, yes, and here at St Gregory's. Visiting a patient?'

'Nope. I'm your new ward round buddy and, by the looks of things, another of Santa's little helpers. I love the hat. It suits you.' Marty's grin was wide and gorgeous and causing a strange reaction deep down inside her. She shifted, trying to keep her thoughts on track.

'You're working here?'

He held up the stethoscope in his hand. 'Certainly am. Lucky you, eh.' He waggled his eyebrows up and down and Natalie laughed, as did Cassie.

'Oh, sorry,' Natalie said. 'Marty Williams, meet Cassie Adams— ward clerk *extraordinaire*. Marty and I went to high school together.'

'Wow.' Cassie held out her hand and Natalie didn't miss the hungry look the other woman gave the new doctor. It had been nine years since she'd last seen Marty when they'd met quite by accident in Fiji, but even since then he'd changed. His hair had been longer and unruly whereas now the dark brown cut was short but not too short. Not army short like Richard's. It suited him, especially as his face was creased with laughter lines and a touch of afternoon stubble.

His eyes, though, were what she recognised the most. The laughter was still there, the joker he'd always been, but as she watched him making small talk with Cassie, Natalie also saw a hint of reserve.

'So that's settled, then,' Cassie was saying. 'Meet us there when you've finished your shift and we'll take it from there.'

Natalie frowned. 'Where are you going?'

Marty smiled and the reserve she'd witnessed disappeared. 'Still a daydreamer, eh?'

'Impatient and a daydreamer.' Natalie shook her head, her smile instantly matching his. 'Are those the only things you remember about me?'

He raised his eyebrows teasingly. 'Well, there is a memory of you streaking through the school naked.'

'I was not naked,' she retorted indignantly.

'You did *what?*' Cassie demanded. 'We've been friends for over five years and you've never told me about that.'

Natalie groaned. 'I was wearing a skin-coloured body suit, which had bright feathers sewn on it,' she explained to Cassie, but her gaze never left Marty's. 'I was in the school play and I'd changed into my costume at one end of the school and the rehearsal was at the other end of the school so I—'

'So she ran through the school, looking just like a streaker.'

'With feathers.'

'Yes.' Marty's teasing was now in full swing. 'All the guys loved it. The costume was very...form fitting,' he said in an undertone to

Cassie. 'And my darling Nat was what we called an early developer.'

Natalie's jaw dropped open for the second time in ten minutes, although this time it was from embarrassment rather than shock. 'Martin!'

'Ooh. See, now I'm in trouble because she called me Martin. She only ever uses my full name when I'm in trouble.'

'When was the last time you two saw each other?' Cassie asked.

Marty frowned a little. 'Must be about nine years ago.'

Natalie nodded in confirmation.

'We caught up with each other in Fiji but that was a real quick visit. Before that, it would have been about six or seven years earlier,' Martin said, his gaze meshing with Natalie's again. 'My parents moved to Darwin to live at the end of grade nine. We kept in loose contact for a while and have been exchanging Christmas cards since Fiji.'

'Do I get a Christmas card this year?' Natalie asked. 'Or do you want to leave that out as we'll probably be working together on Christmas Day?'

He grinned, his smile making her feel special. 'You never know your luck, Nat.' Their gazes met for a moment and the smile slowly slid from his lips, his eyes becoming serious. Natalie had only seen that expression on him once before and it had been when he'd said goodbye to her on the last day of school. He'd given her a Christmas present, stared at her for a few minutes then hugged her and left, his hands in his pockets as he'd walked to catch his bus home from their last day of school.

The following year hadn't been the same without Marty around.

Natalie's pager beeped again and she broke eye contact, startled that she'd just been standing there, staring at him. The phone on the desk rang and Cassie went to answer it, giving them a few moments together.

'Radiology again?' he asked.

'No. It's...Richard.'

'Richard?'

'Orthopaedic surgeon. I need to discuss the X-rays with him.'

'There's more to it than that, Nat. Is he blond?'

'What?' She stared at him in disbelief, then relented a little. 'How can you possibly know that?'

Marty shrugged. 'Is Richard your boyfriend? I'm presuming you're not married as you're not wearing a wedding ring.'

'No.' Natalie looked down at the floor and shuffled her feet. 'I'm not married and Richard is...' She shrugged. 'Well, we've been dating for a while.'

'You don't sound too enthusiastic about him.'

Natalie shrugged again. 'Aren't all relationships complicated?'

'I guess.'

'What about you? Taken any more chances with matrimony?'

'No. Once bitten, twice shy. I'm footloose and fancy-free and intend to stay that way, thank you very much.'

'Same as the old Marty from high school. From one girl to the next.'

He grinned. 'You can talk. How many guys did you date in year nine?'

Natalie frowned but Marty continued.

'Tell me, is Richard a better kisser than Neville O'Grady?'

Natalie gave a shout of laughter. 'Oh my gosh. I'd forgotten about him.' She shook her head in bemusement as the memory returned, her Santa hat falling off. 'Nev O'Grady.'

Marty stooped to pick up the hat and placed it gently back onto her head, the scent of him whirling around her once more. Natalie sucked in a breath, ignoring the frisson of awareness she felt between them. He stepped back, thankfully putting more distance between them. 'Nev O'Grady. Alias the *licker*.'

She laughed again, glad the previous moment had disappeared. 'I still can't believe I told you about that. You teased me the entire time I went out with him.'

'From what I recall, you got me back twice as bad when I dated Missy the Hissy.'

'Oh, yes.' Natalie laughed again, the feeling of life in a simpler time returning to wash over her. 'Ah, nostalgia.'

'It's good for the soul.' They shared another meaningful look before returning to reality. 'I'll let you get to Radiology while I sign my life away on three thousand different forms—all in triplicate, mind you—to keep the pencil-pushers happy.'

'When do you officially start?'

Marty checked his watch. 'In about twenty minutes, if I can write that fast.' He grimaced.

'You're doing clinic this afternoon?'

'That's the current plan.'

'Excellent. Someone to help with the workload.' Natalie pointed to the forms. 'Write fast, my friend, and I'll see you in clinic.'

'See you there, Nat.'

She started walking out the ward but turned to face him. 'Oh, and don't forget to get a Santa hat from Cassie.'

'Will do.'

Natalie headed out of the general paediatrics ward and down the stairs to Radiology, unable to believe she was going to be working with Marty. 'It's a small world,' she whispered. She went directly to the radiologist's office and was glad to find her friend there.

'Here you are, Natalie.' Lisa handed over a packet of films. 'All reported on and ready to go.'

'Thanks, Lise. I appreciate the rush.'

'Ah, you'll pay. So tell me all about your old schoolfriend.'

'What?'

'From what Cassie says, he's gorgeous *and* single.'

'How did you know?' Natalie raised her eyebrows, surprised at the speed of the hospital grapevine.

'I called the ward just a few minutes ago and spoke to Cassie. She said you were just about to leave but were chatting to a gorgeous hunk you went to school with.'

'Marty? A hunk?' Natalie thought for a moment. He hadn't been back then...but now? 'Yeah, I guess he is.'

'You sound surprised. Can't you see it?'

She shrugged. 'I guess I still see him as he was in school.'

'Definitely not hunky?'

Natalie smiled and shook her head. 'Nerdy yet cute and very funny is how I'd have described him.'

'Well apparently he is now *hot*.'

'I guess we've all changed since high school.' She took a deep breath. 'Enough yammering. I have to meet Richard. Thanks for these.' She took the X-rays and headed towards the orthopaedic department. She was stopped along the way by Jim, the orderly.

'You're looking very happy and bright today, Dr Natalie.'

'Am I? Maybe it's the hat.'

'Could be, but there's a spring in your step and a smile on your face. It's good to see.' He paused and then snapped his fingers. 'I know, have you broken it off with that brisk orthopaedic doctor?'

'Jim. You know his name is Richard and, no, we haven't broken up.'

'Pity. He's no good for you.'

'Jim. Let's not go there.'

'No. You're right. Not when you're looking so happy. I'd just like to meet the man who's put that smile on your face and shake his hand.'

'How do you know it's a man? Perhaps one of my patients is better and has gone home?'

'No.' Jim shook his head emphatically. 'You have a different look when that happens—a look of pleasure and relief. This one...' he waggled his finger at her '...is one of unabashed joy.' He gripped the empty wheelchair he was pushing. 'I need to get this to Maternity. Stay happy, Dr Natalie.'

'I'll try, Jim.' Natalie continued on her way to meet Richard, mulling over Jim's words. She did feel happy and it was because she'd seen Marty. She sighed and hugged the X-rays to her chest. It was always nice to share a positive memory from the past and Marty had provided plenty of those.

She walked through the orthopaedic department, smiling at the secretaries who guarded the surgeons' privacy. 'Hello. Is Richard in?'

'Yes. He's expecting you, Natalie.'

'Thanks.' She knocked once and waited for Richard's reply before going in. Richard didn't like too much familiarity from her at work. He liked keeping their professional and private lives separate, which meant he usually ignored her if they were in a meeting together. He'd not long graduated as an orthopaedic surgeon and where Natalie had thought the pressure would lift once his exams were over, it had become even more intense than before. Richard had territory to mark out—at least, that's what he'd told her.

'Come in.'

Returning to the present, Natalie went in and Richard instantly stood up and held out his hand for the films.

'Do you really have to wear that hat, Natalie?'

'Yes, Dr Scrooge, I do. You could do with a bit of Christmas cheer in here. Shall I ask your secretary to put some tinsel up?'

Richard gave her a withering look.

'Anyway, you're forgetting I work in Paediatrics and the children expect more Christmas cheer than on other wards.'

'I suppose so, but it looks ridiculous.'

Natalie ignored his comments, deciding she liked Marty's reaction better, and focused her attention on the X-rays Richard had hooked onto the viewing box.

'Quite a clean break, but she'll still need plates and screws.'

'What about an external fixator?' Natalie asked.

Richard frowned and pondered the thought. 'Hmm. I don't think so in this instance. How old is she?'

'Almost twelve.'

'I think inserting the metal will be the best way to go.'

'You're the surgeon. Shall I have your secretary book Laura onto your operating list?'

Richard pulled down the films and gave them back to Natalie who put them in the packet. 'I'll do her tomorrow afternoon. I'll probably finish late in Theatre but it can't be helped.' He sat behind his desk and picked up a pen. He glanced down at a piece of paper before scribbling his signature on it.

'I guess that means we won't be having dinner—again,' she muttered.

'No. Sorry, Natalie. You'll have had a busy day and I don't want to make you wait in case you get low blood sugar, so it's easier to cancel. Besides, you know how things can go in surgery. One minute every thing's fine, the next I'm stuck there for a few extra hours, fixing a complication.'

'But you've missed the last three Friday nights. Our scheduled weekly date is the only time I really get to spend with you, Richard.' Natalie's tone was firm and she once more realised that her relationship with Richard was becoming too hard to work at. When that had happened in her previous relationships, she'd take it as a sign to break it off.

'I know but work comes first. I told you things would be different once I graduated. We'll have dinner next Friday.'

'I have a Christmas party to go to, unless you've changed your mind about coming with me.'

He paused and gave her a thoughtful look. 'I'd forgotten about that. Do you have to go?'

'Yes. It's fundraising for my unit, Richard, not to mention the department's annual Christmas dinner.'

'So it is.' He came around and placed a hand on her shoulder.

The gesture was benign and would have been impersonal if she hadn't seen the sincerity in his eyes. 'We'll find time. I promise.'

'OK.'

He dropped his hand and headed back behind his desk. 'The offer is still open to move in with me, Natalie. That way you'll be able to see me all the time.'

Natalie smiled, not taking him seriously at all. 'We've already discussed this, Richard, and my answer hasn't changed since last time.'

He returned her smile. 'Can't blame a guy for trying.' He was a handsome man—tall and blond with brown eyes. A lot of the female staff liked him but his reserved manner was what put most women off. Natalie had known Richard since medical school but they'd only been dating for the past six months. She'd chosen him because he'd been 'safe'. He was career orientated and didn't seem to want anything too permanent from her. Since he'd qualified, however, she had to admit he'd changed a lot and the things they'd had in common were becoming few and far between. She frowned as she picked up the X-ray packet and headed for the door. 'Have a good afternoon, Richard.'

She headed out of the orthopaedic department, shaking her head at his continuing insistence that she move in with him. That was something she wasn't even willing to contemplate. She was traditional at heart even though her parents' marriage had ended in divorce and she still wasn't willing or even ready to commit to another person on such a deep and intimate level.

Natalie checked her watch and realised she had a whole ten minutes before afternoon clinic began. She raced to the cafeteria in the hope of finding something left over from the lunch rush. Marty was standing in line, his tray piled high with a plate full of food. 'Surely you've stopped growing by now and don't really need to eat that much,' she said softly from behind him.

He turned and looked over his shoulder. 'My darling Nat, I may have stopped growing but I still need to fuel this gorgeous body of mine.'

Natalie laughed. 'Still as vain as ever.'

'And just as cute.'

'I'll say.'

'Really?' He seemed surprised.

'Oh, sure. I've already heard two women gushing about you, wanting me to spill every little detail.'

'O...K,' he drawled slowly, as though he was grasping what she meant. 'Hungry?'

'That's why I'm here.'

'Salad roll still the favourite?'

'Oh, my gosh. Am I that predictable?' She watched as Marty grabbed the last salad roll from the tray and placed it with his own food. 'Have I honestly been eating the same lunch since the ninth grade?' She followed him to the cashier where, to her surprise, he paid for her food. 'Thank you.'

'You're welcome and, yes, I guess you are that predictable—but only to those who know you so well.' They went over to a table and sat down.

'I have actually changed in the last fifteen years or so, Marty,' she said firmly as she put the X-rays down.

'We all have, Nat, but some things stay the same. Your hair, for instance. I'm so glad you haven't cut it short.' As usual for work, she wore it tied in a bun at the nape of her neck. 'How long is it now?'

'Halfway down my back.' She closed her eyes and shook her head. 'Exactly as it was in the ninth grade.' She quickly opened her eyes and unwrapped her roll. 'I have changed it but I seem to have come full circle. I've had it coloured, streaked, cut up past my shoulders, even curled.'

'Curled? Did it actually stay in?'

Natalie shook her head, thinking how her dead straight hair had refused to curl. 'For about two weeks. It was bliss. I paid a fortune to have curls for two weeks but haven't done it again. Actually, I had it curled not long after I returned from Fiji.'

'Felt like a change, eh?'

'Yeah.' She met his gaze and nodded. They'd had some serious discussions during their brief meeting in Fiji, as well as some of the best fun she'd had in years.

'I'm glad you don't have a colour through it now,' he murmured. 'Chocolate brown suits you—matches your eyes.' He forked in another mouthful and she was surprised to realise he was close to finishing the mound of food he'd heaped onto his plate. She bit into her roll, realising there was no way she was going to finish before clinic started but something in her stomach was better than nothing.

'How are your parents?' she asked.

'Good. They've moved back to Sydney, which is part of the reason why I've come back.'

'They're both well?'

'Yes, and still as blissfully as happy.' He smiled but it didn't reach his eyes. Before Natalie could say anything, he continued, 'They have a hectic social life and spend a lot of time with my aunt and uncle. Remember my cousin Ryan?'

'Vaguely.'

'His parents live down the road from them so my mum can spend lots of time with her sister.'

'That's great. I'm happy they're still together and doing well.'

'What about your folks?' Marty asked softly.

Natalie sighed and shrugged. 'My dad has remarried twice and the last time he even had a couple of kids.'

'How do you and your brother feel about that?'

'Dad's in Perth so I don't get to see them that often but we're in contact via email. Davey sees them now and then and tells me what's going on.'

'And your mum?'

'She became a career-woman and is living in Melbourne, running some giant corporation. Again, email contact but that's about it. I think she's happy.'

'I guess that's what counts in the end.' He paused. 'What about you? Are you happy?'

She thought about the question for a moment and Marty laughed. 'If you have to think about it, Nat, what does that tell you?'

'Hey, I was just trying to come up with the right words.' She took a bite of her roll, chewed and swallowed. 'I'm...content.'

He nodded slowly. 'Content. Right.'

'Hey, just because you like to live life in the fast lane, that doesn't mean there's anything wrong with the rest of us settling for contentment, *Martin.*'

'I never said there was, *Natalie.*'

She saw the barely veiled pain in his eyes and reached over to take his hand in hers, giving it a squeeze. 'Sorry. I didn't mean to snap.' Her words were soft and she remembered the pain he'd felt when his marriage had ended in divorce. 'It's been about nine years since your divorce. Are you still not willing to chance a long-term relationship?'

He squeezed her hand back then let go, picking up his drink and taking a sip. The subject of his ex-wife had been off-limits to everyone—except Natalie, who had been there when his depression over his failed marriage had been at its worst. He glanced around at their surroundings, indicating it wasn't the time or place to get into a deep and meaningful discussion. 'I guess not.'

She checked her watch. 'Two minutes until clinic. You know you can't play the field for ever, Marty.'

'Want to make a bet?'

She shook her head. 'The last time we bet on something, I ended up carrying your schoolbag to school for a fortnight. No bets.'

He grinned, the seriousness gone. 'Ah, that was the life. I should have upped the stakes and made you my personal slave for the fortnight.'

Natalie's eyes widened at his words. The vision of being Marty's personal slave was something she didn't find at all unappealing. She took another bite of her roll.

'We should pick another time to catchup and also a different place.' He glanced around the cafeteria once more.

Natalie swallowed. 'How about tomorrow night?' The words were out of her mouth before she could stop them. 'We could have dinner. Catch up some more. I can patronise you. You can tease me.'

He grinned. 'Just like old times, eh? You have no plans for Friday night? What about your orthopod?'

'He has surgery.'

'All night?' Marty shook his head. 'He'd rather spend time at the hospital than with you? Don't tell me you're still dating losers. The guy you told me about in Fiji sounded like a loser as well. I mean, who'd prefer to work rather than accompany their girlfriend to Fiji?'

Natalie glowered at him. 'Richard's not a loser,' she stated.

'Break the cycle, Nat. Since high school you've chosen one wrong guy after another.'

'They weren't wrong. Just because you didn't give your stamp of approval to any of them—'

'Hey,' he interrupted. 'I was just trying to protect you because that's what friends do. Those jerks either made you think you were beneath them or didn't pay enough attention to you. They made you feel as though you weren't as smart as they were and they took you for granted. And you let them!'

'You don't even know Richard.'

'He sounds like the same sort of man you've been dating for the past sixteen years, Nat. Honestly, it's time to break the cycle and find a man who treats you the way you deserve to be treated. If this Richard guy wants to spend his hours in Theatre rather than with you, the guy needs his head read.' Marty held her gaze for a moment and Natalie knew his words made complete sense.

Why had she been going out with the same sort of man since her schooldays? The answer—she was too scared to take a chance on someone good. If someone she really cared about broke her heart, would she ever recover? She'd seen it happen to her parents and they'd taken a long time to get over that lost love.

'Sorry to come down so hard,' he said by way of an apology. He grinned and raised his eyebrows in the teasing gesture she remembered so well. 'Besides, won't your orthopod think I'm encroaching on his territory?'

Natalie laughed, her previous uneasiness gone. 'You and I are colleagues and friends, Marty. We're not going to tumble into bed the instant we're alone.'

'We're not?' He feigned disappointment. 'And here I thought my luck was changing.'

She laughed, her previous heaviness lifting instantly. 'It is *so* good to see you again. Anyway, tomorrow night. Come around for dinner. Beth and I live in a town house two blocks from here.'

'Beth?'

'Orthopaedic registrar. Come around. We can have dinner, chat and maybe even catch a rugby game on TV.'

'It's cricket season,' he said automatically as he ate the last of his lunch and swallowed. 'Hang on a minute. You like rugby?'

'Ah-ha. So you haven't remembered everything about me. Of course I like rugby. You're the one who taught me how the game was played.'

'I did?'

'Sure.' Her pager beeped and she checked her watch again. 'Oh, man! We're late for clinic. Andrew and Sister will have a hissy fit.' She rewrapped her roll and stood.

Marty stood and pushed his chair in, snagged the X-rays she'd left behind and followed her out of the cafeteria. 'Her name isn't Missy, is it?'

'Missy the Hissy? No. You're safe.' She laughed again and took the X-rays he held. 'Oops. Thanks for grabbing them. So, tomorrow night?' she pressed. Now that she'd voiced the idea, she really wanted him to come. 'You can choose what we talk about,' she ventured, so he'd know she wasn't going to pressure him into a deep and meaningful conversation.

'Really? Interesting. OK.'

'Good.'

'Wait a minute.' Marty stopped in the middle of the corridor, pulled a Christmas hat from his pocket and put it on. 'Let me straighten yours. It's starting to slip—like your halo.'

'Hey!'

He grinned. 'There. Now Santa's helpers are ready to go to work.' Then, to her surprise, Marty linked his arm in hers and they set off down the corridor towards clinic. Natalie desperately tried to ignore the way his friendly and hardly intimate touch made her feel weaker in the knees than she'd ever felt before.

CHAPTER TWO

THE outpatients clinic was decorated with tinsel and had a smallish Christmas tree in the patient waiting area. Andrew, who was the senior registrar on the paediatric ward, was a stickler for red tape and liked the clinics to run on time. In some ways he reminded her of Richard but as Richard had pointed out on previous occasions, in a hospital as big as St Gregory's it was usually best to do things by the book.

She finished writing up a set of notes and went to call in her next patient. 'Jaiden. Come through.' She held the door and waited for the seven-year-old boy and his mother. 'You're managing those crutches like a pro.'

'It didn't take me long,' Jaiden told her as he manoeuvred to a chair and sat down. 'My big brother couldn't even do it. He got the end stuck in the chairs and he fell over. It was so funny.'

Natalie looked at Jaiden's mother. 'Sounds as though there's been a lot of...er...extra noise in your house over the past two weeks.'

'And then some,' his mother groaned.

'All right, Jaiden. Have you had X-rays taken today?'

'Yes. They cut my cast right off with a saw and it didn't even hurt! And then I sat very still for my X-ray. See. I got a sticker that says "I sat still for my X-ray". And then they wanted to put me in the wheelchair but I'm super on my crutches so they put this splint thing on so I could come and see you. See, Mum, I remembered it was called a splint.'

Natalie listened patiently to the child, admiring his sticker and oohing and aahing at the appropriate places and praising him for a good memory. 'OK. Do you have the X-rays?'

'They said they'd send them up,' Jaiden's mother said.

Natalie nodded. That meant Radiology was running behind but she couldn't do much for Jaiden until she'd seen the X-rays. She called Radiology but was told the films had been sent to the clinic. 'I'll be back in a moment,' she told mother and son as she headed for the door.

The instant she opened it, she was faced with a hard, muscled chest. She glanced up into Marty's sparkling blue eyes. 'Hello. You scared me.'

'Sorry. Was just about to knock. I have some X-rays here for you.'

'Delivery boy?'

'No. Our packets were mixed up. I pulled out an X-ray of an arm only to find it had changed to a leg.'

Jaiden giggled as he listened and Marty came into the room. 'Hello, mate. Let's get these films sorted out so Dr Natalie and I can look at the right ones.'

'I didn't break my arm.' Jaiden laughed. 'I broke my leg.'

'I can see that.' Marty gestured to the crutches as he and Natalie figured out which films went with each of their patients.

'I was on my new skateboard that I got for my birthday and I was getting better and then I went over a bump and fell off and Mum said it was lucky I was wearing all my safety gear or I could have hit my head really hard.'

'Your mum's absolutely right. I remember falling off my skateboard all the time,' Marty said.

'You used to ride a skateboard?' Jaiden was impressed.

'Dr Marty,' Natalie said, 'is a great sportsman. Cricket, rugby and soccer are just a few of the sports he loves to play.'

'Really?' Jaiden's eyes went wide with delight. 'I've played soccer *and* cricket,' the boy said proudly. 'And I haven't even hurt myself in those games.'

'Thank goodness,' his mother murmured, and both doctors smiled.

'That's the last one,' Marty mumbled as they put the X-rays into their respective packets. He turned his attention to the seven-year-old. 'Do you like playing soccer?'

'You bet, and I love playing in the rain and getting all muddy. But Mum hates it.'

Marty grinned. 'Playing in the rain and getting muddy is half the fun. Well, it was nice to meet you.' He shook hands with the boy and then his mother. 'I have to get back to my patient now that I have the correct X-rays.' As Marty headed out of the room, he grinned and winked at Natalie.

'Bye, Dr Marty.' Jaiden waved then turned to look at Natalie. 'Is he your husband?'

Natalie was taken aback by the question. 'Er...no.'

'Jaiden,' his mother scolded.

'It's all right,' Natalie insisted. 'Actually, Dr Marty and I are very old friends. We went to high school together.'

'Wow. You must be really old, then.'

Natalie laughed. 'I guess we are. All right.' She hooked the films up. 'Let's take a look at these X-rays.'

'Will I be on crutches at Christmas?'

'Yes, I think you will,' Natalie replied gravely, hoping Jaiden wouldn't worry about being unable to run around on Christmas morning.

'Awright!' He pumped the air with his fist. 'That's so cool.'

'Oh. Well...good.' She glanced at Jaiden's mother who just shrugged and smiled. 'Let me turn your chair around so you can see how well your bones are behaving. Look. They're starting to grow back together but they're not quite done yet.'

Jaiden was amazed—for about thirty seconds—and then started asking questions about Dr Marty and what other sports he played and if he was any good at cricket and what his highest score was and whether he like to bowl or bat. Unfortunately, Natalie couldn't provide many answers.

'I'd like you to come back just after Christmas for me to review his leg,' she told his mother, before turning her attention to Jaiden. 'I'll ask Dr Marty if he can come and see you when you're here, and you can ask him all the questions you want.'

'Cool.'

'Would you like a candy cane?' she asked as she took the jar from her desk and held it out to him.

'Aw, yeah. These are the best.' Jaiden took one and Natalie held the jar out to his mother, who also took one.

'You weren't the patient, Mum,' Jaiden complained.

'True,' Natalie replied. 'But I can see she's been *very* patient.' Both women smiled while Jaiden only frowned at them. She left Jaiden-the-chatterbox with the plaster orderly, who would put another cast on the boy's leg.

Clinic continued to progress and just as she was writing out her last patient's notes, the phone on the desk rang.

'Hi, Natalie, it's Cassie.'

'What's the problem?'

'There's only been a slight improvement in Alysha's condition.'

'I'm done here. I'll be right down.' She replaced the receiver and as she wrote the last few words in the notes she stood and edged around the desk.

'Heading off?'

She looked up and smiled at Marty. 'Only to the ward.'

'Problem?'

'I hope not.'

'Mind if I tag along?'

'No. Not at all…but aren't you due to meet Cassie at the end of your shift?' She raised her eyebrows questioningly, a teasing glint in her eyes.

'So?'

She shrugged. 'Nothing. It's good to see you settling into a new working environment so quickly.'

'The best way to get to know your colleagues is to see them off duty. Besides, it's not just Cassie I'm meeting. Apparently, there's a group of people who go out after work.'

'Stuie's.' She nodded. 'It's a popular place to wind down at the end of a shift.'

'Not your scene?'

Natalie shrugged again, this time feeling a little self-conscious. 'Sometimes. I've never been good in crowds.'

'No.' He studied her for a moment. 'No, you weren't. Neither were you in the ''in'' crowd.'

'Ha. You can talk. Why do you think we both became friends in the first place? Neither of us were joiners.'

'We definitely enjoyed more…individual company.'

Natalie laughed. 'All those girls you dated in such a short time.'

'Exactly.'

She closed the case notes, put them on top of the completed pile and headed for the door. 'Although now it seems you've changed, taking on more than one at a time. Remember not to be greedy.'

Marty chuckled and slung his arm about her shoulders, giving her a quick squeeze. 'Ah, Nat. How I've missed you.' He let her go and she looked at the floor, trying to get rid of the tingles that had flooded her body at his touch. 'Besides, it would be boring to stay the same so why not see them in a group and then weed out the ones that don't interest me?'

'Oh, the ego. Save me from the ego!' They walked out of clinic, chuckling.

'Hey, why are there Christmas decorations up all around the hospital but not in the paediatric ward? I thought that would have been one of the first wards to be decorated.'

'They'll be going up some time this weekend. The children have been busy making lots of decorations, but you're right—we're a bit later this year than we have been in the past.'

Marty paused and restuck a Christmas picture that was coming away from the wall. He nodded with satisfaction, then caught up with Natalie. 'So what's the deal with your patient?'

'Alysha. She's six years old and has been admitted with Crohn's disease.'

'Really? That sort of inflammation of the intestines isn't that common in kids. Corticosteroids?'

'She's been on them for two days but she's not responding as quickly as I'd hoped. Just before I bumped into you this morning, I changed her to an immunosuppressive agent, but Cassie just called to say there hasn't been much change. I'll check her electrolytes and we'll see where we stand.'

'Perhaps the immunosuppressive agent needs a bit longer to act. What about her diet?'

'The dietician is monitoring it closely. You know, the usual high-calorie, high-vitamin, high-protein, low-residue and milk-free diet.'

'And she's still not responding as you'd have liked?'

'No. I just feel if I don't get this under control quickly, she'll end up in surgery.'

'What tests has she had done?'

'On admission, she had complete blood-cell count, serum chemistries, stool to check for occult blood. She presented with complaints of diarrhoea, fatigue and abdo pain.'

'No fever?'

'Not when she came in, but her temperature's gone up since then. Nothing too crucial but—'

'But you want to get things under control.' He held the door for her to enter the ward. 'What about fish oil?'

'Pardon?'

'Fish oil. I saw a case a few years ago where fish oil worked brilliantly.'

'In a child?'

'Yes. We stopped all drug therapy, gave her a course of fish oil and, *voilà*.'

Natalie looked at him. 'Really? Fish oil?'

'Sometimes the natural remedies are the best. First, though, let's look at your patient's electrolyte levels. I presume she's had a sigmoidoscopy or colonoscopy?'

'Yes. No obstructions were noted at that stage.'

'But they can happen quickly if not controlled. I'm with you. Lead the way, Nat.'

They both reviewed Alysha, who was understandably upset and irritable. After taking another blood sample for electrolyte testing, Marty personally took it to the pathology lab, telling Natalie he'd be back with a result as soon as possible. As Cassie had already left for the day, Natalie contacted the dietician, hoping to catch her, and was successful. 'Alysha's not responding too well to the medication and I wanted to discuss with you the pros and cons of giving her fish oil.'

'I was going to discuss that option with you yesterday, but the corticosteroids appeared to be working then.'

'They're not now and, although I've put her on an immunosuppressant, I'm not hopeful. Tell me about the fish oil.'

'As Crohn's disease is an inflammatory disease, we need to cut the inflammation. Fish oil works because of two key components—eicosapentaenoic acid or EPA and docosahexaenoic acid, or DHA. These are both omega-3 fatty acids, which have been shown in early tests to help reduce the inflammation of the bowel walls. You can monitor the effects through a white blood cell count, which should show the decrease.'

'Can I keep her on the immunosuppressant or should I take her off?'

'If the immunosuppressant isn't doing any good, take her off and try the fish oil. How are her electrolyte levels?'

'I'm waiting on the results now.'

'OK. See how she goes and let me know.'

'Will do.' Natalie rang off and went to make herself a soothing cup of tea. It just wasn't fair. Alysha was only six years old and now that she'd contracted Crohn's disease she would have it for the rest of her life. She would eventually need surgery but Natalie still hoped to hold it at bay for the time being. With a well-controlled diet and proper treatment, she'd be able to lead a full life, but there would always be restrictions.

While she waited for the kettle to boil, she pulled her salad roll from her pocket and looked at it. Where before it had been firm and tasty, it was now soggy and unappealing. She tossed it in the bin, preferring to get something later.

She'd finished her cup of tea by the time Marty came back into the ward, a wide grin on his face. 'Have you got the results?'

His answer was to smile smugly and hand over the report. 'The ol' Marty charm works again.'

'Let me guess. A female pathologist was on duty?'

'Would I have been this quick if it was a male?'

'I guess I should be glad.' Natalie read the report and shook her head. 'Fluids are more decreased than I had expected and potassium and chloride concentrations are also down.' She stood and headed to Alysha's bedside with Marty right behind her. She introduced Marty to Alysha's mother. 'Dr Marty's had some experience with Crohn's disease in children,' she explained, before going on to tell the girl's mother about the fish oil and how she expected it to help Alysha's condition. 'We also need to increase her fluid intake, which we'll do via the IV drip.'

Marty smiled at the woman and Natalie saw her relax instantly. The man had charm in abundance and he wasn't afraid to use it. Thank goodness she was immune to the Marty Williams brand. 'I've also seen how fish oil can be of benefit in these circumstances,' he told Alysha's mother, who continued to ask both doctors questions. Even Alysha had a few good questions of her own.

'But I don't like fish. It tastes yuck!'

'It comes in the form of a tablet.'

'But I can't swallow tablets. I'm not good at it.'

'We'll figure out a way,' Natalie reassured her, pleased the little girl was being adamant about something. A sign that children were either getting better or coping with what was happening to them was when they started to argue or debate.

'All right. I'll get things organised, then.' Natalie felt a little better as she walked back to the nurses' station. If Alysha was willing to try the fish oil, surely that was good. With the boost to her fluid and electrolyte levels, hopefully she'd be able to avoid a bowel obstruction and therefore not require surgery.

Marty was hard on her heels and Natalie turned to face him. 'Thanks for staying, Marty. I appreciate it and the fish oil suggestion. I'm feeling more optimistic about the whole situation.'

'Glad to be of assistance.'

She pointedly looked at the clock. 'You should go. Cassie and the others are waiting for you.'

'It's all right. I don't mind staying.'

She tilted her head on the side and raised her eyebrows. 'Are you really the joiner you think you are?'

He smiled but didn't answer.

'Go enjoy yourself.'

'I always enjoy myself, even if I'm just chatting with another colleague at the nurses' station. However, you do have a point.'

'Your harem might not wait all night.'

Marty shrugged as though he didn't really care, then closed his eyes and stretched. Natalie's gaze widened at the sight of him. His torso was lean and firm, the muscles easily defined beneath his white cotton shirt, which had come untucked from his designer shorts. The shorts dipped down and the shirt went up and a small section of skin covered with a thin smattering of dark hair was revealed at the base of his washboard stomach. She couldn't believe he looked so good and simply drank her fill. He had incredible, long legs, his height was well over six feet, and as her gaze travelled up his body once more, briefly lingering at that glimpse of skin, she marvelled at how wide his shoulders were. He was definitely an incredibly sexy man now and not just her teenage high-school friend.

When he cleared his throat, Natalie's gaze jerked up to meet his and she realised she'd been caught. 'Oh, no.' She covered her face with her hands. 'I'm so sorry.' Embarrassment flooded through her and she wished the floor would open up and swallow her.

'Don't be. I enjoyed it.'

She dropped her hands and glared at him. 'Marty! You're not supposed to say things like that.'

'Why not? An attractive woman just checked me out. Why shouldn't I enjoy it?'

He thought she was attractive? She brushed the thought away, focusing on her own humiliation. 'Because we're friends and...and you're my colleague.'

'So?' He laughed, then shook his head. 'Nat, Nat, Nat. You've got to loosen up, honey.'

'Don't call me honey.'

'Why not, honey?'

'Because I'm not your honey.'

He laughed again. 'It's just an endearment that I'm sure two old friends like us can share. Surely your Richard wouldn't object to that.'

'Richard? What's he got to do with it?'

'He is your boyfriend, isn't he? You told me so yourself, although I must say the hospital grapevine gossip says you're far too good for him.'

'What? You've been here a whole afternoon and you've already heard the gossip about me?'

'Hey—I was *told* the gossip, honey, I didn't ask for it. Word got around that we were at school together and people were all too happy to give me the gossip.'

Natalie frowned then shook her head. 'Are you leaving?'

'If it's going to make you happy, yes, I'll go.'

'I think you should.'

'Are you on tomorrow? I haven't had a chance to have a good look at the rosters yet.'

'I'm here. When aren't I here?' she mumbled.

'Well, hopefully now the hospital has employed another registrar for this unit, you'll be able to take a day off. Just one, though. No more. We don't want you thinking you can have a holiday or anything like that,' he finished with mock sternness, shaking his finger at her.

'You sound like Andrew.'

'Now, there's a fun guy,' Marty drawled sarcastically. 'Is he always so strait-laced?'

'Yes.'

'Well, isn't it just as well I'm here to lighten things up a bit? Good ol' Marty—ward jester.'

'You're well qualified, after being classroom jester.'

'Thank you for the recommendation.' He glanced at her. 'I'll see you tomorrow?'

'Yes. Do you know the way to Stuie's?'

'I go out the hospital's main entrance and turn right. Keep going to the end of the block and if the noise doesn't tell me which way to go, I need to have a hearing test.'

Natalie chuckled. 'I see Cassie was the one to give you directions. She's right, though. Thursday and Friday nights seem to be busier than any other night of the week at Stuie's.'

'I thought you didn't go?'

'I said I don't go regularly.'

'You're more into quiet, intimate nights, eh?'

'Definitely. Like tomorrow night. You, me, Beth and probably Beth's latest boyfriend.'

'Changes them regularly, does she?'

'She ditches them when they get serious.'

'Interesting.'

'Why?'

Marty didn't answer but said instead, 'I'll leave you to it, Dr Fox. See you tomorrow.' He placed a hand on her shoulder and squeezed reassuringly. 'Don't hesitate to call if you need extra help.'

'Ha. You can tell it's your first day on the job.'

Marty grinned and waved as he left. As she watched the doors to the ward close behind him, she was surprised at the melancholy feeling that swept over her. Martin Williams. He was back in her life and she wasn't sure how she felt about it. It was quite strange to run into someone from your past and find they were going to be part of your future.

And that's why you've asked him over for dinner tomorrow night, she reminded herself. Catching up would be fun but they also needed to set down some ground rules if they were going to have a successful working relationship. He knew things about her no one else did, and while these things weren't bad in any way they were personal. Then again, she knew things about him and she was certain he wouldn't want them broadcast around the hospital—not that she'd ever do that, but already today she'd been pumped for information about him.

Yes, tomorrow night would be good. She must remember to mention it to Beth in case her friend was busy. Then again, even if Beth was busy, would it matter if she was alone with Marty? They were friends, for heaven's sake, so why did the thought of being alone with him make her feel as though she were cheating on Richard?

When she finally arrived home, Beth was in the kitchen, eating leftover Chinese. 'You're later than usual.'

'I had some things to get organised.'

'There's a message on the machine from Richard. He said he's had a cancellation on his list for tomorrow and will be able to keep your usual Friday night date.'

'No!'

'No?' Beth was surprised. 'Trouble in paradise again?'

'No. When Richard said he couldn't make it, I made other plans.'

'So? Give Richard a taste of his own medicine and stand him up for a change.'

'But it's my only time to actually sit down and talk with him.'

'Include him in your plans.'

'Ha. That won't work.'

'Why?' Beth's eyes twinkled. 'You don't want him to meet the absolutely scrumptious registrar you went to school with?'

'You know? About Marty?'

'Sure. He was at Stuie's and when he found out my name he asked if I was the Beth who worked in Orthopaedics and shared a town house with his beloved *Nat*. I can't believe he called you Nat. You don't like people calling you Nat.'

'That's not true. I just prefer Natalie from most people. You've called me Nat before and that doesn't bother me. Besides, Marty's always called me Nat. It would be strange to hear him call me anything else.'

'So, anyway, Marty told me he's been invited around for dinner tomorrow night.'

'Yes and now Richard's free.'

'I'm sorry, *Nat*.' Beth smiled at her. 'It's a no-brainer. Hunky, gorgeous, blue-eyed doctor who makes you laugh, or staid, boring Richard who will do more talking about the intricacies of internal fixation than he will listen to anything you say. I guess if you do end up inviting Richard around, it'll give me a clean crack at Marty.'

'I thought you were dating John.' Natalie frowned, surprised she found the idea of Beth and Marty completely unpalatable.

'Not any more.'

'Well, at least John lasted longer than the others. What? Two weeks?'

Beth shook her head, indicating she didn't want to talk about John. 'As I was saying, Marty looks like fun.'

'He's a love 'em and leave 'em type.'

'Interesting.' Beth eyed her friend closely. 'What's up? Want him for yourself?'

'No!' Natalie answered a little too quickly. 'We're just friends,' she clarified.

'Sure.' Beth nodded and shrugged nonchalantly. 'So why can't I hook up with him? He's the love 'em and leave 'em type and so am I. Sounds like a perfect match.'

Natalie shook her head and ground her teeth, then started pulling the pins from her hair. 'We can talk about this later.'

'I still think you should stand Richard up and keep your date with Marty,' Beth called as Natalie headed up the stairs to her part of the town house.

'It's not a date,' Natalie called back, before continuing up the stairs. She stripped off and headed for the bathroom. As she stood under the spray of the shower, glad of its warmth and soothing massage on her shoulders, she realised how sad she would feel, telling Marty she'd have to cancel. Of course they could arrange another time but she had been looking forward to it.

After she'd dressed and brushed her hair, she headed out. 'You really think I should tell Richard I have other plans?'

'Yes.'

'Richard and Marty are like oil and water. They just won't mix.'

'Then I guess you need to choose.'

'You're right.' Natalie surveyed the contents of the fridge and grabbed some more leftovers. 'So, come on, tell me, what happened with John?' Natalie reheated the contents and sat down to listen to her friend describe her latest dating failure. 'I don't know how you do it,' she said with a sigh.

'It's easy.' Beth shrugged. 'I have a wall and I don't let anyone past it. I refuse to get hurt again.'

Natalie frowned, wondering whether she herself had really been hurt in affairs of the heart before. If she broke it off with Richard, how would she feel? She pondered the idea for a moment, then realised she'd probably be disappointed another relationship hadn't worked but that was about all. If she was honest with herself, what did she and Richard actually have in common, other than the fact they were both doctors? Why was she still with him? Habit? Companionship? Or was Richard still a safe bet?

She found it difficult to get to sleep that night, thoughts of Marty and Richard keeping her awake. Marty had jumped back into her life with a well overdue splash of colour. He knew what made her happy, how to make her laugh, how to listen when she needed to talk. He'd been her best friend and even though she'd been curious about what it would be like to kiss him, they'd never let things go that far, preferring to enjoy what they had. Besides, he'd been the

most determined flirt she'd ever met and she hadn't wanted to join
the long line of girls on his discarded pile.

'Some things don't change,' she murmured to her ceiling. She
could recall with perfect clarity their time spent in Fiji. She'd been
wandering around a market when she'd accidentally bumped into
someone. She'd turned around and come face to face with an enormous backpack hanging from a tall man's shoulders.

'Sorry,' she'd mumbled automatically.

The man had turned around at the sound of her voice, not seeming at all put out that he'd been jostled, and there she'd stood,
looking up into the blue eyes of Marty Williams. To say she'd been
surprised was an understatement and Marty, it seemed, had obviously felt the same.

'Nat? Natalie Fox? Is that really you?' Marty put his hand on her
shoulder as though to prove to himself it was really her. She felt a
tingle of awareness pass through her at his simple touch but put it
down to the unexpected but pleasant surprise at seeing him again.
'What on earth are you doing in Fiji?'

'What most tourists do here...holidaying.' She laughed. 'How
about you? Just arrived or just leaving?'

'Just arrived, only I'm not here as a tourist. I've come to help
out at the medical clinics run by a world aid organisation.'

'You're a med student?' At his nod, she smiled. 'So am I. Isn't
that amazing?'

He shrugged. 'Sure is. Guess we're both smarter than we look,'
he said lightly. Natalie was just about to tease him back when she
realised that although his blue eyes were the same as they'd been
when they'd been teenagers at school, this time they were not filled
with laughter but sadness. 'How's your life been going?' she asked,
a little cautiously.

He shrugged again and tried a nervous laugh—he failed and it
came off as a moan. He looked down at the ground for a moment,
then finally raised his gaze to hers, his gaze now intent. 'Terrible,
actually. I got divorced this morning.'

Natalie was heartsore at seeing her old friend so down. 'Oh,
Marty.' It was her turn to reach out and touch him, taking his fingers
in her hand. 'I'm sorry to hear that.' She glanced around them
before asking, 'Where are you staying? Maybe once you're settled
in, we can get a drink and talk.'

Marty thought it over for a moment, wondering if he really

wanted to burden Natalie with the gory details of his divorce. If she had been any other woman, he'd have played it cool and worked hard at masking his current pain, but this was Nat...his *friend*, and right now he needed a friend.

He must have been thinking for too long because she quickly said, 'But if you'd rather not, that's OK. I understand.'

'That would be great,' he said sincerely, cutting off her last words. They stared at each other for a moment and he realised just how incredible she looked. He'd always known she'd grow into a beautiful woman and he was glad to have been proved right. For a moment, the mood between them shifted to one of awareness and it seemed to startle them both. Surely those old feelings he'd felt for her when he'd been a gangling teenager weren't still there? He shut the thought away as quickly as it had come. He was depressed, he was distraught and he was recovering from a messy divorce. This was not the time, although the glorious setting might certainly have been the place.

Marty forced himself to smile and say brightly, 'Then again, unlocking my psyche may be hazardous to your health.'

Natalie paused for a moment before returning his smile. 'I think I'm strong enough to risk it. Besides, you helped me when my parents got divorced. That was a tough time for me and you got me through. Marty, if you need an ear, chew mine. I owe you one.' She gave his hand a final squeeze before releasing him. 'Do you want to meet in half an hour?'

'No.' He took her hand back. 'Come with me. It won't take long to check in.'

They talked about the world aid organisation as they headed to his hotel and went through the rigmarole of settling him into his room. 'I'm only here for a week, then I move to wherever they need me,' Marty explained.

'Best enjoy that comfy bed while you can, eh?' she said as she stood by the door. The room felt small with the two of them in it and for some reason she felt more comfortable by the door. Stop it, she told herself. This is *Marty,* for heaven's sake. But Marty had changed since school. His shoulders were broader, his legs were longer and his hair was darker. And there was her road block. She only dated blonds and preferred men with either green or brown eyes. He wasn't her type, and even if she *was* interested in Marty, he was her *friend* and right now she sensed he needed friendship above all things.

'Where shall we go to talk?' she asked when he was finally settled, if you could call dumping his backpack on the floor and using the bathroom 'settled'.

Again, those broad shoulders shrugged. 'You've been here longer. Know anywhere we can get a drink and talk privately?'

Natalie thought for a moment. Sunset would be in an hour and she was starting to get hungry. 'I have an idea.' Within another half an hour, after dragging him to some of her favourite food places, she'd assembled a rough picnic, including a bottle of cheap wine, and carried it to the beach. 'We don't have any glasses, so we'll just have to take turns swigging from the bottle,' she said with a small chuckle, but he didn't respond. She'd noticed he'd become more and more withdrawn as time had passed but finally they were sitting on the sand, most of the people heading back to their hotels and homes for their evening meal.

Wordlessly, she handed Marty some food, insisting that he eat. 'Mmm,' he said after his second mouthful. 'Thanks.'

She wasn't sure if he was thanking her for the food or something else. He still didn't seem inclined to blurt out whatever was bothering him and, being the impatient person she was, it certainly wasn't easy, cooling her heels.

'Have you been in Fiji long?' he asked as he unscrewed the lid on the wine bottle. He took a swig, then grimaced. 'This stuff is bad.'

'Bad but potent,' she offered.

'And you figured I'd need potent tonight?'

Natalie shrugged. 'Don't you?'

Again he just looked at her and she felt as if she was sitting on shifting sand. Finally, he spoke. 'Probably.' He took another swig. 'Second mouthful isn't as bad as the first.'

Natalie laughed. 'Glad to hear it.'

'Answer my question.' He put more food in his mouth and waited.

'I've been here for two weeks and I leave tomorrow evening.'

'What? So soon? Can you extend your stay?'

'I'd really like to but I can't. I'm due back at work the day after I get back.'

'Work?'

'I work part-time in a lab at the medical school.' She shrugged. 'It pays the bills.'

'Same old independent Nat.' He took another swig. 'Actually, this isn't too bad at all.'

'Glad to hear it. So, divorced this morning, eh?' she blurted, now too impatient to be tactful. She knew she didn't need to apologise for her behaviour. This was Marty and he knew her of old. True, they hadn't seen each other for years but there was a bond between them...one that seemed to help them pick up where they'd left off at the end of year nine.

Marty chuckled. 'Same old Nat,' he said again.

'Hey. Not so much of the *old*.' She took the wine bottle from him and took a swig herself, coughing a little. 'What exactly does "divorced this morning" mean?'

'I signed my divorce papers first thing this morning. Then I jumped on a plane and came here, running away to a world aid organisation. I know it will look good on a résumé and the people here need help, but honestly, Nat, my motives are as selfish as they come.'

'I think they'd appreciate the help, whatever the driving force is that brings people here in the first place. Besides, it sounds as though you need space and a complete change in routine.'

'You've got that straight.'

Natalie waited a beat before saying, 'Divorce, huh? Doesn't sound like fun.'

Marty took the bottle back from her and took a long drink. 'Nope. No fun at all...and you know how much I like having fun.'

'Your ex-wife wasn't fun?'

'Gloria?' He paused for a moment. 'Fun isn't a word I'd use to describe her.'

'What word would you use?'

'Stunning, poised, gentle.' He sighed and looked out over the water to the setting sun. 'At least, that's the way she was in the beginning. I have a revised set of adjectives.' Another drink. 'Vapid hits the top. Conniving, untrustworthy.'

'How long?'

'How long was I a sucker?'

Natalie nodded.

'One year and eight long months. Well, we've been separated for a year but we were officially married for eight months before I filed for separation.'

'Eight months? That's it?' Natalie was surprised. 'That's not long, Marty. It's less time than it takes for a baby to form in its mother's womb.'

'The fact that I was taken in at all irritates me.' He picked up a handful of sand and let it slowly sift through his fingers. 'I was a fool.'

'No,' she countered. 'You're not a fool, Marty. She's the fool, and don't you know that only fools are ever satisfied? You *weren't* satisfied. You saw through her in eight months! It took my parents almost eighteen years to see through each other and there was a lot of bitterness and anger all the way through that. Your marriage failed, Marty, but that doesn't mean *you're* a failure.'

'How...?' He stopped, had another drink and then shifted so he was looking straight at her. 'How am I supposed to trust my judgement again?'

'As dumb as it sounds and as clichéd as it sounds, the answer is time.'

'Time? That's all you've got for me?' He picked up another handful of sand and let it slowly drain away. 'Come on, Nat. Think back to your psych classes. I need more than just *time.*'

She took a deep breath and thought. 'First of all, let go of all the revenge you feel like inflicting on her. That's not going to happen. *Know*—for a fact—that there are plenty of other fish in the sea and some lucky woman is going to one day see you for who you are. Don't give up on the fairer sex...at least, not just yet.' She smiled but he didn't reciprocate.

He looked at her again, then asked in a quiet voice, 'Who am I?' He wasn't fishing for a compliment—he was genuinely asking the question, and in that one moment Natalie realised the depth of his hurt. She cared for him, he was her friend and she desperately wanted to help him in any way she could.

'You're a caring, honest man.'

'How can you know that? You haven't seen me for years and years.'

'It's what's deep down inside that counts, Marty. You were there when I needed help all those years ago when my parents got divorced and, in fact, you were the one who told me time would heal my hurt.'

'And did it?'

Natalie thought for a moment, knowing he deserved her complete honesty. 'My dad and I are at least talking now. *Time* is healing that wound but I've learnt not to rush it.' She smiled.

'Well, that's new. Natalie Fox not being impatient. Never thought I'd see the day.'

She gave his shoulder a friendly punch. 'Seriously, Marty, you're a terrific person and Gloria was wrong to do what she did to you. It will change you but ultimately what's happened will make you a better, stronger person. Don't try and fix everything immediately. Allow yourself the opportunity to grieve, to let go of what's happened. I mean, you only signed the papers this morning.'

'The whole of this last year I've been asking myself how I could have been such an idiot. Why I didn't see through her in the first place. None of my friends were comfortable around her and I didn't heed the warning signs.' His speech was starting to slur and there was a highly charged emotion to his words. 'I bet you're not that dumb. You've probably not been stupid enough to tempt marriage.'

'Stupid? Scared out of my wits is more like it.' Natalie emphatically shook her head. 'I'm seeing someone but I'm not looking to get married, I have medical school to finish. But we're not talking about me.'

Marty frowned at her. 'You're seeing a guy? Where is he?'

'He's not here in Fiji, I mean. He's back in Sydney.'

'Your boyfriend let you come to Fiji all by yourself?'

'I'm a big girl, Marty.'

Marty laughed without humour. 'You're a *beautiful* big girl, Nat. You've really grown into a stunner.'

'Thanks, but I'd rather be thought of as smart than pretty.'

'Too late.' He grinned and drained the bottle. 'This stuff is... Whoo!' he yelled, making her jump.

'Let's get back to your psychoanalysis.'

'Hit me, babe.'

'Slow down and get to know the new *you*. You're different from who you were before you met Gloria. You'll probably throw yourself into work and that's OK so long as you don't lose yourself in it. Give yourself some new goals, some new dreams.'

'Dreams are bad,' he slurred, lying back on the sand.

'No. Dreams are good...' She paused and smiled. 'Just don't expect them all to come true. Your biggest problem at the moment is that all you can see is what you've done wrong, but try looking at what you've done right instead. Turn the negative into the positive.'

'Positive,' he mumbled. 'That's good. Turn the negative into the positive.' A moment later, he laughed out loud and yelled, 'I'm free!' Then he said, 'I'm going to keep my emotions under control and not get so deeply involved with anyone again.' He took another big breath and yelled again, 'I'm really free!'

Natalie couldn't help but laugh and as she turned to look over the water she realised she'd missed the sunset. She sighed, knowing Marty was worth the sacrifice. They were friends and friendship, especially with him, was something she'd always held dear, more dear than romantic relationships.

The next morning, Marty came knocking at her hotel door just before eight o'clock. She'd just finished dressing and was surprised to see him. 'How did you know where I was staying?'

'This was the sixth hotel I tried. Come on, let's go.'

'But I have to pack.'

'Packing won't take long. We only have today and I'll tell you right now, we're going to throttle it.'

'Throttle the day?'

'Yes, so don't just stand there. Grab your bag, put your shoes and hat on and let's get going, Dr Fox.'

She giggled at his infectious mood. 'That sounds so strange. What about Dr Williams?'

'Horribly strange. Let's *go,* Nat.'

They headed out to a small café for breakfast, then headed to the markets, haggling and enjoying themselves and buying things they really didn't need. In the afternoon, Natalie insisted she needed to pack or she'd be in danger of missing her plane. To her utter disgust and surprise, Marty packed for her, throwing her things in willy-nilly and jamming her suitcase closed.

'Sit on it, Nat. Then I can zip it up properly.'

'If you'd let me fold my clothes, I wouldn't need to sit on it,' she grumbled. 'I'm going to have extra washing to do when I get home.'

'And you can think of me and grumble while you're doing it,' he said good-naturedly. 'We still have more throttling to do before you get on that plane. Let's go, let's go.'

After handing in her room key and thanking the desk staff for a wonderful stay, Marty took her out for an early dinner before taking her to the airport. There, he waited with her until her flight was called.

'Give me your address,' he said, putting a piece of paper into her hands. 'That's mine. I'm in Queensland at the moment. Gloria's in Darwin and I needed to move when we separated.'

Natalie quickly wrote down her address. 'I didn't think you were the letter-writing type of guy.'

'I'm not, but you might be lucky enough to get a Christmas card.'

'Excuse me, miss,' the flight attendant said. 'You really need to get on the plane now.'

Natalie turned to face Marty. 'It's been fun. I wish we'd had more time.'

'Me, too.'

Natalie hadn't been looking forward to this moment ever since she'd realised Marty intended taking her to the airport. She hated goodbyes but she'd already lived through one goodbye with Marty so she guessed she could do it again.

To her surprise, he bent his head and pressed a tender kiss to her cheek. She breathed in deeply, her eyelids fluttering closed as his scent washed over her. His roughened jaw brushed against hers, causing tingles to spread throughout her entire body. This was Marty, she kept telling herself. You're friends. Just friends. You have a boyfriend back home.

The action had only lasted a fraction of a second and the flight attendant was once more urging her to get on the plane.

'This time it's you leaving,' he murmured as he stepped back. 'Take care, Dr Fox.'

'You, too, Dr Williams.'

The sound of Natalie's ringing cellphone woke her up just before one o'clock. She checked the display—it was the hospital.

'Alysha's vomited for the second time and is complaining of stomach cramps,' the night sister reported.

'I'll be right there.' Glad of the excuse to stop feigning sleep, Natalie quickly dressed and pulled her hair back into a ponytail before heading out to her car.

As she walked onto the ward a little later, she left her mixed thoughts about Richard and Marty at the door and concentrated on Alysha. She checked in with Andrew to let him know she'd taken over Alysha's care for the rest of the night and went to see her patient.

The child was crying in pain and Natalie's heart turned over with compassion. 'White blood cell count, check her electrolyte levels again and call the paediatric surgeon,' Natalie instructed the nurse as she washed her hands and pulled on a pair of gloves. 'Hello, darling,' she soothed. 'I need to feel your tummy and you tell me where it hurts.'

Alysha's screams of pain told Natalie exactly where it hurt and she could feel for herself the increase in abdominal distension. A moment later the poor child vomited again and Natalie ordered some pain relief.

'What about the fish oil?' Alysha's mother asked frantically.

'We were going to start it in the morning but I'm afraid we're past that for the moment. Alysha will probably need surgery within the next hour as there's got to be an obstruction in her small intestine,' Natalie explained. 'The paediatric surgeon will be here shortly and we'll explain the operation to you. At the moment we need to keep Alysha as comfortable as possible. She'll also need a new set of X-rays so once the analgesics have taken effect, we'll get her down to Radiology.'

Alysha had just returned from Radiology when the paediatric surgeon arrived. He agreed with Natalie's diagnosis and booked an emergency theatre. 'Once she's anaesthetised I'll do a colonoscopy so we can find the obstruction as well as perform a biopsy. Are the results from the white blood cell count back yet?'

'Yes. Elevated.'

'Which confirms the obstruction or possible perforation.' When everything had been explained to Alysha's mother and the consent form had been signed, Natalie accompanied the child to Theatre. She stayed through the anaesthetic consultation, giving the information required, and bent to give the little girl a kiss on her forehead before the trolley was wheeled into Theatre.

She returned to the ward and picked up the phone to arrange Alysha's transfer to ICU once the child was out of Recovery.

'Sorry, Natalie. No room at the inn,' the ICU sister reported.

'Fully booked?'

'Every bed taken.'

Natalie sighed and closed her eyes. 'All right. I'll organise for her to come back here after surgery.'

'If the situation changes, I'll let you know.'

'Thanks.' Natalie made a few more calls, requesting an extra nurse to provide one-on-one care for Alysha through the rest of the night. Four hours later, Natalie was sitting by Alysha's beside, watching her patient.

'I knew I'd find you here.'

Startled because she hadn't heard anyone come in, Natalie jumped and rose quickly from her chair. 'Marty!' She stared at him as though he was simply a figment of her imagination.

'At least you remember me.'

She frowned. 'Why wouldn't I?' she whispered, confusion filling her fuzzy mind. Something wasn't quite right.

'No reason. How's Alysha?'

'Holding her own.'

'That's good news.'

'Yes.' Natalie paused. 'What are you doing here?'

He shrugged. 'Couldn't sleep.' He edged towards the bed, making the dimly lit room seem smaller than it was.

'Why not?'

'Because I kept thinking about you.' He was close now. Closer than he'd been before. He reached up and touched her cheek. 'Can't you feel it, Nat?'

'Mmm.' Her eyelids fluttered closed at his sweet caress. Longing and need ripped through her and she wanted, so badly, for him to press his mouth to hers. As though he could read her mind, the next thing she felt was the brush of his lips against hers. She gasped, amazed to discover she'd just been given the most tantalising and precious kiss of her whole life.

CHAPTER THREE

'NAT?'

The sound of her name on Marty's lips was heaven and she slowly opened her eyes. His hand fell to her shoulder and gave her a little shake as he smiled down into her face.

'Hey. Wake up, sleepyhead.'

Natalie stayed where she was for a moment before realisation dawned on her. She was sitting in a chair at the nurses' station, her head on the desk. She'd fallen asleep. Natalie closed her eyes as embarrassment swarmed over her and she swallowed the lump in her throat, realising she'd been dreaming...dreaming about *Marty*. She risked a glance at him. He was grinning from ear to ear. Oh, no. Had she spoken out loud?

'Did I say anything?'

Marty just continued to grin and she realised he was trying to unnerve her. 'Why? Were you having hot dreams?'

Natalie's eyes widened for a moment before she realised if she rose to the bait, he'd just continue to tease her. 'Not particularly,' she lied, but couldn't meet his gaze as she spoke.

'No. You didn't say anything but my, oh, my, did you look cute.'

'Cut it out,' she said.

'I heard about Alysha. How's she doing?'

'Uh...' Natalie opened her mouth to tell him but a yawn escaped. 'Excuse me,' she said, covering her mouth. 'Uh...let's go check on her.' She stood and headed to Alysha's room. The nurse was sitting beside the little girl and smiled as they both came in. 'How is she?'

'Doing much better since you checked a few hours ago,' the nurse said. 'Did you manage to get some sleep?'

Natalie nodded as she picked up the chart. The drains were working well and the level of analgesics had decreased since she'd last checked. 'Has she woken?'

'A few times, but she settled very quickly.'

'Good.' Natalie handed the chart to Marty.

'Go have some breakfast and then some more sleep,' the nurse suggested.

'Sounds like a good idea,' Marty replied, and returned the chart to the basket at the end of the bed. 'Let's go, Dr Nat.' He linked his arm with hers and led her out of the room just as she smothered another yawn.

'What are you doing here?'

He shrugged. 'Wanted to make a good impression, you know, being the new boy and all.'

Natalie unlinked her arm from his when they reached the nurses' station and wrote in Alysha's notes while she stood at the desk. If she sat down again, she wasn't sure she'd get up. Fatigue was setting in.

She closed the file and her eyes, trying to stretch out the uncomfortable pain in her neck, back and shoulders. When she finished, she opened her eyes and was surprised to find Marty staring at her. A warmth spread over her as though he'd just caressed every part of her body. 'P-problem?' She wanted to sink into the floor at her stutter. Now he would know just how much his close proximity as well as his visual appraisal were affecting her.

He held her gaze for a moment before shaking his head, although the action was barely noticeable. 'No.' The word came out deep and husky and the warmth ignited through her again. He swallowed and she watched the action of his Adam's apple as it slid up and down, a tingling awareness enveloping them. 'No. No problem at all.' He held her gaze for a fraction of a second longer before he glanced away momentarily, his body relaxing. 'Well,' he relented, and cleared his throat, a cheeky grin spreading across his face. 'Only that your body is far more developed than it ever was in high school.'

'Marty!' she whispered, and raised her hands to her cheeks, positive he'd just made her blush. 'Don't say things like that.'

'Why not?' He shrugged. 'It's the truth. You're a beautiful woman. Why can't I appreciate that? Besides, you checked me out last night so it was only fair I take advantage of an opportunity to check you out.'

Natalie couldn't have answered even if she'd wanted to as the ward sister bustled into the room and she quickly looked away from Marty's hypnotising gaze.

'Good morning, Doctors,' Sister Dorset said briskly. She was a no-nonsense woman in her late fifties who was as starched as her uniform. 'Are you both officially on duty?'

'Er...' Natalie began, still trying to get herself under control. Thankfully, Marty came to her rescue.

'Not for another few hours, Sister.'

'Off you go, then. Out of my ward.'

Marty opened his mouth to say something but Natalie quickly came back to earth and took his arm, dragging him out the room. 'Thank you, Sister.' She collected her bag and walked through the ward to the doors at the end.

'What's going—?'

'Shh,' was all she said. 'Keep walking, Williams.' She tugged at his arm again.

'All right. I'm coming.'

Once they were out of the ward, Natalie dropped his arm and turned to face him, a wide grin on her face. 'You can thank me for saving you later.'

'Who *is* that?'

Natalie headed towards the stairs, yawning again. 'That, my dear friend, is Sister Dorset. First name is Agnes and you will not call her that under any circumstances. Not the surgeons, not the director, not even the chief executive officer of the hospital gets away with calling her by her first name.'

Marty followed her as she led him out the hospital. 'You can explain everything to me over breakfast.'

Natalie turned and stopped and he crashed into her, his arms coming about her waist momentarily to steady not only himself but her as well. She glanced up at him and the earlier awareness returned. It was as though time stood still as her senses all came on alert. The scent of him wound itself around her and the warmth emanating from his touch caused a current to course through her body before exploding. She gasped, realising just how close their mouths were as she continued to stare into his eyes.

Marty seemed to come to his senses first and quickly dropped his hands and stepped away. 'Stuie's?' he asked, but his voice wasn't so steady. He cleared his throat and shifted his feet before offering a crooked grin.

The moment passed. 'Sounds good.' They walked the short block to Stuie's and Natalie was glad the place was almost devoid of hospital staff. She was tired and hungry and not in the mood to socialise with other people. She had Marty all to herself and she was going to enjoy it.

The instant the thought entered her head, she pushed it away. They were just friends and that's the way it was going to stay. She had no right to be thinking of him in a romantic way. She was dating Richard and, besides, Marty wasn't her type. She liked men who were stable, mature and grown-up.

'What'll you have?' he asked as they sat down.

'Pancakes and maple syrup, coffee and a bowl of fruit.'

'Sounds good. I'll have the same.' The waitress came over and he gave their order. 'You've obviously had breakfast here before.'

'I like it here in the mornings. Quieter.'

'I'll say. Last night was a madhouse. I met Beth, by the way.'

'Yes. She mentioned it.'

'Very pretty woman. I'm looking forward to tonight.'

A knot in Natalie's stomach twisted at the thought of Beth and Marty together. Was she going to be an unwanted third tonight? 'Blondes your type, eh?'

Marty leaned across the table and once more his delicious fresh aftershave wound its way about her. 'All women are my type,' he said softly, his gaze melding with hers. In the next instant he'd leaned back into his chair and gave a nonchalant shrug. 'Except for women who are already taken, of course.'

'Of course,' she murmured, still slightly hypnotised by his gaze. She shook her head and re-focused. 'Well, I'm glad you and Beth hit it off. She is your type.'

'And what type is that?' His smile was broad, one eyebrow raised as though he was extremely interested in her reply.

'You know. Not serious about relationships. Likes to have fun, not interested in settling down.'

'Ah. That type. Hmm.' And that was all he said on the subject, leaving Natalie to mull over exactly what that meant. 'Now, about Sister Dorset.'

'Oh, yes. Sister Dorset apparently started nursing in the Dark Ages and still abides by all the codes and ethics of that time. She is an excellent nurse and, although very strict with our little patients, is very good with them. I think, initially, some of the children are a little frightened of her but they soon realise she's an old softy at heart. She once said to me, after a critical patient had turned the corner, that you really got to know a person when you saw them at their most vulnerable.'

'So if she's a softy with the children, why can't the staff break through?'

Natalie eyed him warily. 'Taking this as a personal challenge?'

Marty grinned. 'Why not? I've always liked a challenge. Reckon she'll let me call her Aggie?'

Natalie choked on a laugh of incredulity. 'Yeah, right, Marty.'

'What? Don't think I can do it?'

'Sister Dorset, as I've said, is the name everyone calls her, from the lowly intern to the highest-paid consultant. In turn, she calls the staff either Nurse or Doctor, regardless of their qualifications. It usually bothers those newly qualified consultants but Sister Dorset doesn't care. A doctor is a doctor. A nurse is a nurse. If she must refer to you by name it will always be Dr Williams or Dr Fox but only if she needs to make the distinction for some reason.'

Marty rubbed his hands together. 'This is just the challenge I've been looking for.'

'And seducing the female staff isn't?'

He frowned. 'Hardly challenging, my darling Nat. Besides, would you care to make a little wager?'

'That you'll one day be able to call her Agnes?' Natalie shook her head. 'You're insane.'

'Thank you. So? Bet?'

'I can't lose this one. All right. What are the terms?'

'By Christmas—that's four weeks away—I'll be allowed to call Sister Dorset, Aggie.'

Natalie choked on a laugh. 'Aggie?'

'If I succeed, you have to agree to whatever I propose.'

'And if I win?'

'I have to agree to whatever you propose.'

The waitress brought their breakfast over and Natalie was thankful for the interruption. Just the word 'propose' coming out of Marty's mouth was frightening enough. She had no problem being in a long-term relationship so long as she called the shots, which was why she chose men she thought of as safe. Marty certainly wasn't her type at all. Besides, with his dark hair and blue eyes, he reminded her—in physical appearance only—of her father and she didn't date men who reminded her of her father. Personality-wise, though, Marty and her father were poles apart, thank goodness.

She took a sip of her coffee. 'What do you mean by "propose"?'

'If I want to go...paint-balling, for instance, you have to come. If I want to go skydiving, you have to come.' He grinned at her.

'And if I win, you have to do what I propose?'

'Yes.'

'Leg waxing?'

'Ouch.' He grimaced at the thought but nodded.

'Body piercing? Head shaved?'

'Are those fetishes of yours?'

Natalie laughed, her earlier tension disappearing. She sipped at her coffee again but didn't answer his question. 'OK. You've got yourself a bet, Dr Williams.'

He held out his hand and she confidently slid her fingers into his, ignoring the tingles that shot up her arm. 'It's a bet.' The warmth he radiated as he clasped her hand to his was amazing and once more their gazes met and held.

These little moments between them were starting to become a habit, one she needed to break right now. Natalie quickly pulled back as though burnt. 'Christmas isn't that far away, Marty. You'll need to get started immediately.'

'I've already formulated my plan of action.' He cut up his pancakes and forked in a mouthful. 'Mmm. These are delicious. Is this what you were dreaming about when I woke you?'

Natalie had her fork halfway to her mouth but dropped it at his words, the metal cutlery clanging to the plate. The few people around them stopped to look. She quickly collected the fork and put the food in her mouth, once more feeling highly self-conscious. 'Mmm,' she echoed, trying to cover up her embarrassment. It was better he thought she'd been dreaming about pancakes, rather than trying to guess exactly where her thoughts had been!

Later that morning, Natalie walked into the ward to see Marty standing on a ladder, hanging tinsel from the ceiling.

'What are you doing?' she asked.

'What does it look like?'

'Have the decorations been properly aired and dusted?'

'How should I know?' he grumbled, glancing down at her. 'All I know is, this ward needs some decorations.'

'Agreed, but Sister will have a fit if they haven't been properly aired and de-dusted.' Natalie headed over to the nurses' station.

'De-dusted?' Marty quizzed. 'Is that an actual word, Dr Fox?'

'Ha. Very funny.' She picked up a set of case notes, then looked up at him. 'Then again, if Sister gets cross with you for jumping the gun, I'll have a better chance of winning the bet.' She waved a hand at him, dismissing his actions. 'Go ahead and deck those halls, my friend.'

Marty started to climb off the ladder. 'De-dusting,' he muttered, bringing the tinsel down with him. 'How on earth do you de-dust something?'

Natalie smiled sweetly at him before looking down at the case notes. 'Check with Cassie.'

Marty looked around but there was no sign of the ward clerk. 'Where is she?'

'Early lunch?' Natalie shrugged her shoulders, scribbled something in the notes and then closed them again. She took in his defeated posture before taking pity on him. 'Come on.'

'What?'

She took the tinsel from his hand and draped it around his shoulders. 'Come with me. I know just how to cheer you up.' She walked off towards the other end of the ward, knowing he would follow. When she got there, she paused for effect and indicated the room in front of her. Marty came and stood by her side, a slow smile crossing his lips.

The room was known as the playroom in the ward. There were toys for all ages, tables for drawing and craftwork and at the moment there were several children sitting at the tables with a few parents, making Christmas decorations.

'Go and have fun,' Natalie said softly. 'The ward Christmas tree is due to go up tomorrow so go and get busy. I'll see to the de-dusting.'

Marty gave her a quick hug and again she had to ignore the way his touch made her feel. 'You're a good friend, Nat. Thanks.' In the next instant he'd disappeared into the room, several of the children calling out greetings to him.

It took Natalie a moment before she could move. First, she had to recover from the tingles, which were slowly beginning to fade, and then she had to contend with the picture before her...Marty smiling, crouching down in a small chair with two of the children instantly involving him in what they were doing. He'd been at the hospital almost one whole day yet the children adored him.

'The Marty Williams charm strikes again,' she muttered to herself as she headed back to the nurses' station to see to the 'de-dusting'.

'Hi, there.' Natalie opened the door to Marty. She was wearing a red shirt and denim skirt, her legs and feet bare. Marty was dressed in a white polo shirt and khaki shorts, old, tatty sandshoes on his feet.

They appraised each other for a brief moment. Marty reached out and sifted her long, loose hair between his fingers. 'Such a beautiful colour,' he murmured, before giving the ends a little tug and letting go.

Natalie tried her best to recover from his impromptu touch, and met his gaze. 'You look exhausted.'

'I can return that compliment and say you don't look too good yourself, honey.'

Natalie smiled as she closed the door behind him. He held out a bottle of wine. 'Thank you. That was sweet.'

'Never come empty-handed.'

'Then drop around any time,' Natalie joked as she headed for the kitchen.

'Hi, Marty,' Beth called, looking up from the salad she was making. 'How's your day been?'

Marty perched himself on one of the stools at the kitchen bench and watched the two women working seamlessly around each other. Natalie finished marinating the meat for their barbecue and Beth started on the vegetable shazlicks. 'Here, let me help,' he offered, and came around to wash his hands.

Two in the kitchen was bad enough, but with Marty in there—six feet four and broad-shouldered—the small space suddenly became very crowded. 'I could say I've had worse days, but at the moment I just can't remember them.'

'Was today really that bad?' Natalie looked at him sympathetically. 'Too much for the new kid on the block?'

'Give me a drink, feed me and then perhaps I'll regale you with the day's events. Oh, and thanks for organising the de-dusting,' he said to Natalie. 'Sister Dorset has declared the decorations fit for display in the ward tomorrow.'

'Glad to be of service,' she replied.

The three of them continued to talk on various topics while they finished preparing the food, and Natalie marvelled at how easily

Marty slid right into her life. Never would Richard be seen sitting at their kitchen bench, preparing food and chatting while sipping wine—even in the old days before he'd graduated.

'Nat?'

'Hmm?' She looked up and met his gaze. 'Sorry. I was else-where.'

'Anything wrong?'

'She's feeling a little guilty,' Beth said in a stage whisper. 'Friday night's her night to see Richard but tonight she's effectively stand-ing him up.'

'I'm not standing him up,' Natalie retorted. 'That implies I've left him in the lurch.'

'But you invited me over.' Marty frowned.

'Richard cancelled on her, she invited you and then Richard un-cancelled.' Beth shrugged. 'Simple.'

'So now you've cancelled on Richard?'

'Yes.'

'Did you tell him I was coming over?'

'I said I'd invited the new registrar in our unit around.'

'But you didn't tell him I was male.' Marty gave her a thoughtful look. 'Now, I wonder why?'

'What does it matter? You're my colleague.'

'*And* your friend.'

Beth laughed and Natalie glared at them both for a moment be-fore throwing her arms in the air.

'I give up. Can we, please, just forget Richard and have a nice, friendly dinner? Please?'

'By all means,' Marty said as he carried a platter outside to the terraced garden, 'Let's forget Richard.'

In true male fashion, Marty insisted on taking the helm at the barbecue and did the cooking. Natalie lit a few citronella candles to keep the bugs and mosquitoes away while Beth set the table before disappearing back inside. 'Spray?' Natalie held out the insect repellent to Marty.

'Thanks. I've missed balmy December nights swatting mozzies.'

'Where have you come from?'

He gave her a thoughtful look as he turned the meat. 'I do believe it was one evening such as this that my parents felt rather loving towards each other and—'

Natalie gave his arm a playful push. 'Stop it. You know what I mean.'

'Where was I working last?'

'Yes.'

'I've come here from gay Paris.'

'Ah.' She held the wine bottle out to him. '*Voulez-vous coucher avec moi?*'

As she spoke, Marty was taking a sip of his wine and almost choked. He coughed a few times.

'Are you all right?'

'Sure. I just hadn't expected that.'

'What?'

He looked at her and grinned. 'You just asked me to go to bed with you.'

'*What?* I thought that meant, "Do you want to have another drink with me?"'

'Who taught you French?'

'My brother.' She groaned.

'Little Davey?'

'Little Davey is not so little any more. He was only two years behind us in school and is now about your height and a pilot.'

He nodded, impressed. 'Well, little or not, he was having a laugh at his sister's expense. How many people have you said that to?'

'Oh, no!' She was still mortified. 'None. I think. Oh, look, can we forget it, please?' Natalie was trying not to dwell on what would have happened if Marty had said yes. 'Would you like a top-up?' Again, she held out the wine bottle to him.

'Yes, please.' He checked the food while she refilled his glass. 'At least this tastes better than that moonshine we drank in Fiji.'

'*You* drank. I think I ended up having one or two mouthfuls.'

'That was potent stuff but I needed it.' He took another sip of his wine. 'Mmm. Definitely better.'

'All done?' Beth asked as she came out with the salad.

'All ready to go.'

They sat down and savoured the meat while it was hot, the citronella candles doing their job and keeping the insects at bay.

'So do tell.' Beth leaned forward on the table. 'What happened at work today?'

'Has Nat told you about our bet?'

Natalie smiled. 'Haven't had time.'

'Well...' Marty finished his last mouthful of food, took a sip of his wine and settled back in his chair. 'I've made a bet with my darling Nat that I can call Sister Dorset Aggie and get away with it.'

'By Christmas,' Natalie added.

Beth's jaw dropped open. 'Are you insane?' she asked Marty. In the next instant she turned to Natalie. 'How can I get in on this bet? You'll win it for sure.'

'I think she will, too,' Marty added. 'I'm starting to think I've bitten off more than I can chew and I'm not talking about the excellent meal we've just shared.' He put his elbows on the table and rubbed his fingers in little circles at his temple.

'What happened?' Natalie was almost on the edge of her seat with anticipation.

'This afternoon I was in the ward, innocently writing up some notes, when in bustles Sister Dorset, declaring it's time for afternoon ward round and she'd appreciate it if I would pay attention to the ward schedule and get on with the job. All of this, of course, was said in her no-nonsense brisk manner without a ''please'' or ''thank you'' anywhere.

'I'm happy to overlook this as I'm desperate to make a good impression. Naturally, I stop in mid-sentence and do her bidding.' He leaned back in his chair, his eyes twinkling with a mixture of exhaustion, disbelief and humour.

'The first few patients go fine until we get to a new patient, little Troy. He's only two, admitted with gastroenteritis. Anyway, his mother had gone to the cafeteria to eat while Troy was settled and sleeping. Not so by the time we arrive for ward round. He's wide awake, a little bit upset that his mother's not around, sitting up in his cot with a foul-smelling nappy.'

'Oh, no.' Natalie smiled, guessing what was coming.

'Oh, yes. ''Right,'' says Sister Dorset.' Natalie and Beth laughed at the high-pitched tone Marty used to imitate Sister Dorset's voice. '''Off you go, Doctor.'' Well, I look blankly at her, wondering why she's dismissing me when she dragged me away from my work to do the round in the first place. She waggles her finger at me and then at Troy and I realise with *horror* that she expects me to change the child's nappy.'

Natalie and Beth started laughing.

'I quickly glance towards the door, wishing as hard as I can that

Troy's mother is about to walk in. No such luck. Sister glares at me. "Oh, for heaven's sake, Doctor. Don't tell me you can't change a small child's nappy." She tut-tuts some more and by this time little Troy—who has thankfully quietened down because he's so enthralled by Sister tearing me to shreds—is not only sitting happily in his cot but is bouncing up and down *on his bottom*.'

Natalie and Beth continued to laugh.

'Did I mention the poor child was admitted with gastroenteritis? The stuff was *everywhere* now. I glance at the door again, hoping desperately for the mother to come in or for someone to page me or call me away. Nothing. Sister Dorset, still tut-tutting, slowly pulls the curtains around Troy's cot and I start to feel as though I'm caught in a Venus fly-trap. Still, I've not only made a bet with Nat that I can make Sister like me, but I am also a doctor who has vowed to care for his patients. I start rolling up my sleeves.' Marty mimed the action as he spoke.

'Sister, thankfully, has pulled out the tools I'll need—'

At the word 'tools', Natalie lost it and threw back her head and laughed harder than she could remember having laughed before. 'You're not fixing a bookshelf, Marty,' she choked out between chuckles.

'I have my *tools* and have not only pulled on a pair of gloves but a gown to cover my clothes—just in case.'

'I'm surprised you stopped there. Why not a mask?' Beth asked as she wiped the tears from her face.

'As I was saying...' He glared at them both. 'I begin my appointed task, telling myself I've been in far worse predicaments before, and begin changing the nappy with Sister looking over my shoulder the entire time, directing me as though I were performing the most intricate of surgical procedures. I must add here my most sincere thanks to little Troy who seemed to be so stunned by a strange doctor changing his nappy that he actually stayed still the entire time. Finally, everything is clean—the patient, the cot. Dirty sheets have been dealt with and I'm at the sink, having taken off my protective gear, frantically scrubbing at my hands. Sister pulls back the curtain and everything is as it should be when Troy's mother comes back in and thanks *Sister* for changing Troy's nappy.

'I think surely Sister will tell her I did it—after all, it was quite an ordeal for a young, single doctor such as myself, but no. Sister calmly accepts all the thanks and moves on to the next patient, leaving me standing mouth wide open, gaping at her back and desperate to tell Troy's mother that it was I and I alone who cleaned up the disgusting mess and restored her son to rights.'

'Oh, stop. Stop!' Natalie gasped, holding her sides.

'But is that all for the dashing doctor? No. We continue with the round and when we get to Elizabeth, Sister glares at me again and I start panicking in case I need to change Elizabeth's nappy. I quickly remember that Elizabeth is nine and doesn't wear nappies, but what's this? Her notes are missing. It's then I remember it was Elizabeth's notes I was writing on when Sister first dragged me away to do the ward round. I tell her I'll fix everything and quickly head to the nurses' station, when Cassie tells me there's a call for me. Why the call didn't come fifteen minutes earlier to get me out of changing Troy's nappy, I don't know. I deal expeditiously with the call, write the last few words in Elizabeth's notes and quickly return to the child's bedside. ''They're not signed, Doctor.'' That's all I get from Sister. I sign the notes and we continue, thankfully without further hiccup, with the rest of the round.'

Marty sat grinning at the two of them as they continued to laugh and wipe tears from their eyes. 'Although my first instinct was to run and hide once she'd released me from my obligation, I also remembered that animals...and sisters who have been nursing since the Dark Ages...can smell fear. So I stay in the ward, finish up my work and don't leave until Sister herself has left for the day. Then I collapse in a heap, with Cassie and the rest of the staff teasing and laughing at me.'

'I wish I'd been there. I was stuck in a meeting with Andrew.' Natalie slowly stood.

'Would you have rescued me, Nat?'

'Hardly. I plan on winning this bet.' She laughed then groaned. 'I need to go. If not, I'm going to wet my pants. Oh, Marty.' She kissed his cheek. 'You're still as funny as ever.' When she came back, Beth and Marty had cleared the table and were stacking the dishes in the dishwasher.

'Well, you're certainly handy to have around,' she murmured as she joined them.

'It's the least I can do to thank you for a wonderful evening.'

'You're not about to rush off, are you?' Beth asked urgently, and Natalie frowned. Was her housemate really interested in Marty? 'We have strawberries and ice cream for dessert.'

Marty rubbed his stomach. 'I think it may have to wait a while.' He straightened from putting the last plate in the dishwasher.

'Coffee?' Natalie asked, reaching around him to grab the kettle, making sure she didn't touch him.

'Perfect.'

They sat and chatted a while, sipping coffee and reminiscing, a Christmassy CD playing quietly in the background.

'Do you remember the last day of school?' Marty asked, his eyes half-closed in relaxation.

'The last day I saw you? Of course I remember.'

'We didn't have to do schoolwork and were able to play games all day.'

'Yes, of course.'

'Twister,' they said in unison, and Beth laughed.

'What happened?' she asked.

Natalie and Marty shared a smile.

'I won.' Again the words were said in unison and this time all three of them laughed.

'Well, which was it?' Beth asked, looking from one to the other.

'*I* won,' Marty said.

'You did not! You cheated on the last spin and fell, but because Ms Schofield didn't see you, you stayed in the game.' She turned to Beth. 'He blatantly lied, telling her he hadn't fallen, and she took one look at that innocent face he can pull and believed him. I was so cross with him and all he could do was poke his cheeky tongue out at me the instant her back was turned.'

'So who won?' Beth asked again.

'Nat did,' Marty acknowledged. 'What's the statute of limitations on apologies?'

Natalie smiled. 'Offering one?'

'Absolutely.'

'Accepted.'

'Good.'

'How about a rematch?' Beth asked, and stood up.

'Rematch?' Natalie frowned at her but her friend didn't answer. Instead, she disappeared into her room and came out a moment later, carrying a box.

'Anyone up for it?' She held out the game and Natalie gaped.

'Where did you get that from?'

'I bought it for Tristan's kids for Christmas but I think I'll keep this one and buy them another one. Tristan's a colleague of mine,' she quickly explained to Marty. 'Come on. Up, up, up, girl.' Beth tapped Natalie on the legs. 'You, too, Marty. Let's go. I'll be the spinner.'

'All right!' Marty was up and doing arm and leg flexes before Natalie had moved.

'I'm not crawling around on the floor, contorting myself into all sorts of ridiculous positions.'

'Then I will declare Marty the champion of all time—by default.'

'Hey. Why the champion of all time? Besides, if you really want to play, I'll be the spinner.'

'Stop rabbiting on, Nat, and get up,' Marty teased. 'Or haven't you got the guts?' His gaze met hers and the challenge there was real...very real.

'All right. Let me put on a pair of shorts and I'll be ready to whip your butt.'

He wiggled his eyebrows up and down. 'I'm looking forward to it.' His smile was slow and sexy and Natalie quickly raced from the room, trying to control her breathing. When she returned, she'd not only changed but tied her hair back in a ponytail.

'Ready,' she declared, and Marty nodded to Beth.

Beth spun the wheel and called out the instructions. 'Left hand—red.'

Marty laced his fingers and then flexed them before starting the game. Natalie merely rolled her eyes at his attempted intimidation.

'I won then and I'll win now.'

'Are you sure? You're much older now. Perhaps not as flexible as when you were a teenager.'

He had a point. 'Same goes for you, old man. If I recall correctly, you're a whole seven months older than me.'

Marty merely grinned and listened to Beth's next instruction. Ten minutes later they were well and truly tied up in knots when the doorbell rang. 'Coming,' Beth called as she gave the dial another spin. 'Right foot—green.'

'No!' Natalie called. 'That's impossible. My body doesn't bend that way.' But Beth wasn't listening as she'd gone to answer the door.

'Chicken, Nat?' Marty chided as he tried to contort his own body. 'If I just twist this way...' He tried shifting a little to his left.

'Marty! Marty!' Natalie called through her laughter as he bumped her. She tried to steady herself as well as put her foot on the green circle. 'Stop moving. You're making it worse.'

'Got...to...win,' he muttered with concentration, but it was too late. He overbalanced and came down...on top of Natalie. Arms and legs were sprawled everywhere and they were both laughing hard.

'Get off me, you big oaf,' she spluttered between giggles.

'My sentiments exactly,' came the deep, well modulated tones of another man.

Both Marty and Natalie froze and looked over towards the door.

'Richard!'

CHAPTER FOUR

NATALIE tried to quickly scramble out from beneath Marty but he was taking his time getting off her, shifting this way and that and making her highly conscious of just exactly how incredible their bodies felt pressed together.

Finally she was free and scrambled to her feet, pulling her top down and adjusting herself. 'Richard. What are you doing here? I thought you were going to catch up on your paperwork after surgery.'

'Amazingly, it's all finished so I thought I'd pop by for coffee.' His smile was tight.

Natalie frowned at him. Pop by? Richard wasn't the popping-by type of guy, so why tonight? 'Uh…well, we haven't had dessert yet and, of course, I can put the coffee on again.' She noticed Richard was glancing over her shoulder towards Marty. 'Oh. Sorry. Richard, this is Marty Williams. He's the newest member of the paediatric staff. Marty, this is Richard Everley.' She forced a smile but there was a highly charged moment of uncomfortable tension before Marty, being his usual cheerful self, moved and held out his hand to Richard.

'Nice to meet you. Orthopaedics, right?'

'Yes.' Richard shook hands with him but didn't seem inclined to engage in conversation.

'My cousin's in Orthopaedics.'

'Really?' Richard didn't sound at all interested.

'Yes. Overseas in London at the moment. Brilliant doctor, if I do say so myself. You may have heard of him.'

'I'm not at all familiar with orthopods in London.'

'Then I guess the name Sir Ryan Cooper doesn't ring any bells.'

Natalie's and Beth's eyes widened. Even *they* had heard of Ryan Cooper, the brilliant orthopod who'd recently been knighted. His work around the world, in war zones and with landmine victims, was legendary. He had also developed new surgical techniques for

56

dealing with those types of injuries, which had been recently added
to the training of all orthopaedic registrars around the globe.

Natalie glanced at Richard, who seemed to be staring at Marty
in astonishment. The entire moment was quite surreal but Marty
went on as though he didn't notice. 'Of course, he's just "Cuz" to
me.'

'Ryan is Sir Ryan Cooper?' Natalie was astounded.

'One and the same. He was a few years ahead of us in school.'
She smiled. 'He was always getting you out of trouble.'

'That's the one.' Marty grinned at her, then winked and she realised he knew exactly what he was doing. He could feel the tension,
he'd read Richard's pompous attitude and had promptly put the
orthopaedic surgeon in his place. She should be furious at him but
instead she found it hard to smother a smile.

'I'll get the coffee organised, shall I?' He headed to the kitchen
as though he was the one who lived there and not Natalie and Beth.
'How do you take it, Everley?' he called a moment later.

'Er...black, thank you.' Richard answered automatically, before
coming over to stand next to Natalie. 'Who *is* that man?'

'I told you. He's the new paediatric registrar.'

'When you told me you'd invited your colleague around, I'd
presumed the new registrar was female.' He'd lowered his voice
and Natalie was glad Beth had gone to help Marty. 'Imagine my
surprise when I find out from one of my secretaries that the new
registrar is male. Not only that but hospital gossip says you were
at school with him.'

'For once, gossip is at least accurate.'

'Why did you cancel out on me tonight?'

'We've been over this. When you said you couldn't make it, I
made other plans.'

'You've never done that before. You've always waited in case I
could make it.'

'And you never do, Richard. Besides, I have the right to have an
old friend around for dinner even if he is also a new colleague,'
she argued, totally annoyed with Richard and his high-handed attitude.

'But we're dating,' he snarled.

'That doesn't mean I can't have friends, Richard.'

He shook his head. 'We won't discuss this now.'

'No. We won't.' She'd been having such a wonderful time and

now he'd spoilt everything. She was just about to suggest he go when Marty carried in a coffee-mug and handed it to him.

'Beth has dessert all organised so let's eat.' Marty was still his usual happy self but Natalie knew he could feel the tension in the room. The town house wasn't that big and although both she and Richard had lowered their voices, the tone of their conversation would have carried through to the kitchen.

'Here you are, Nat. Two with moo.'

'Thanks.'

'Natalie,' Richard said.

'Yes?' she responded.

'No.' He had been directing his comment at Marty. 'Her name is Natalie.'

'I know.' Marty sat down and grinned. 'I've known her since she was twelve. First day of high school, remember that, Nat?'

'I meant, her name is not *Nat.*'

'It's not?' He glanced at Natalie. 'Doesn't bother you, does it, my darling Nat?'

Natalie closed her eyes and shook her head, unable to believe the male power play that seemed to be going on.

'Didn't think so,' Marty continued, purposely mistaking her movements as an answer to his question. Thankfully, Beth came in carrying the dessert and sat very close to Marty. After dessert he slipped his arm about Beth's shoulders and gave her a hug. 'Thank you. That was delicious.'

Beth smiled up at him and Natalie wondered if her friend had just chosen the next man to date. She refused to acknowledge the gnawing in the pit of her stomach that they were completely wrong for each other, even though she'd previously told Marty they'd be perfect together.

'Now, how about another game?' Marty stood and pulled Beth to her feet. 'You can play this time, Beth, and Everley can be the spinner.'

'Excuse me? The what?' Richard looked from one to the other.

'The spinner,' Marty repeated, and handed Richard what he needed. 'Come on, Nat. There was no decisive winner last time.'

'Marty, I don't—' But her protests were cut short as he hauled her to her feet. He caught her in his arms and danced her over to the brightly coloured mat with large colourful circles painted on it.

'Right, Everley. Spin the arrow and read out what it lands on.'

Again, Marty winked at her. 'I think it's my turn to whip some butts.'

'I'd say you've already done a good job of that,' Beth mumbled, and glanced at Richard.

'I don't believe this,' Natalie replied, her tone soft.

'Come on, Everley,' Marty said encouragingly. 'It's not that difficult.'

Reluctantly, Richard spun the arrow. 'Left foot—yellow,' he called hesitantly. All three put their left feet on a yellow circle and looked expectantly at him. He spun again. 'Left hand—green.' Again, they all obeyed his instructions. They continued on with the game and amazingly Richard actually looked as though he was enjoying himself, adjudicating where necessary.

They were all bent and twisted around each other when Beth couldn't hold her position any longer and toppled over.

'You're out, Beth,' Richard declared.

'This game is so much harder than it looks,' Beth muttered. Richard spun again.

'Right foot—red.'

'Why does it get harder as time goes on?' Natalie grumbled as she shifted around, finding it a bit easier now that Beth was out of the way. In the beginning she'd been highly conscious of whenever her body touched Marty's, especially with Richard looking on. After a few more twists her inhibitions had disappeared and her previous competitive spirit returned.

Richard went to spin again but accidentally dropped the spinner. As he did, Marty wobbled, still trying to get his right foot onto a red circle, and fell.

'Hey!' Natalie called as Marty quickly righted himself. 'Didn't you see that?' She appealed to both Richard and Beth.

'See what?' Beth asked.

'What? No one saw him fall?'

Marty started laughing.

'This is so unfair. This is Ms Schofield's class all over again. Marty, admit it.'

'Admit what?' he asked between chuckles.

'*Martin.*' Her voice was a low growl.

'Ooh. I'm in trouble now.' He collapsed, chuckling. 'All right. I admit it. I fell. Nat is the winner.'

She stayed where she was for a moment, unable to believe a victory was finally hers.

'You can move now, Nat,' he said, still lying on the mat. 'I've conceded defeat.'

'Honestly? You're not trying to trick me?'

Marty laughed again and reached out to pull her down. She landed with her head on his chest, the end of her ponytail flicking into his face. He brushed it aside and she turned to smile at him. 'Am I champion of all time?'

'Yes, my darling Nat. You are the champion of all time.' He reached down and pressed a kiss to her nose. 'But any time you want a rematch just let me know because next time I'll be taking that title back.'

'Hey, it was never rightfully yours in the—' It was then she realised he was razzing her up. 'You dolt.' She pushed herself away from him and stood, realising both Richard and Beth had been watching them. Knowing she needed to say something quickly to cover over her growing awareness of the moment she'd shared with Marty, she looked at Richard and smiled. 'Sure you don't want to have a go?'

'Thank you, Natalie, no. In fact, I must be going. Goodnight, Beth.' Richard then held out his hand to Marty, who was still lying on the floor. 'Good game, Williams.'

'Thanks.'

Richard looked meaningfully at Natalie. 'Walk me to the car?'

'Of course.' In the few times he'd been there, he much preferred to kiss her goodnight outside so she was puzzled as to why he'd specifically mentioned it now. She followed him out, closing the front door behind them.

'I think they want to be alone,' Richard said as he took her hand in his.

'Pardon?'

'Beth and Williams.'

'Oh. Uh...yes.' She frowned. 'I guess they do.' Richard pressed the button to open his car and the lights flashed. He leaned against the driver's door and tugged Natalie closer.

'I think they make a good couple. Williams seems to have his head screwed on and the fact that Sir Ryan is his cousin...well, that will stand him in good stead.' Richard shook his head slightly. 'It's such a small world. I was only thinking the other day that it would be wonderful to work with Sir Ryan and here his cousin is an old schoolfriend of yours.'

'You're thinking of going to London?' Natalie was surprised.

'Do you have any idea how a year working with Sir Ryan would look on my résumé? Say, I wonder if I could get Williams to fix up an interview.' He paused as he adjusted his arms around Natalie's back. 'Then again, how well did you know him?'

'Who? Ryan? Not that well.'

'*Sir* Ryan.'

'He'll always just be Ryan to me. I'm not into fancy titles much.'

'Well, you should be. If Sir Ryan can make it to the top of the orthopaedic profession before he turns forty, so can I.'

Natalie eased back, stepping out of his embrace. This was all wrong. She'd initially chosen to date Richard because he was safe but now...tonight...she realised he was not only safe but boring as well. She shook her head. Perhaps it wasn't Richard who had changed. Even though Marty had only been back in her life for a short time, his presence had made her realise she'd outgrown Richard.

'Something wrong, Natalie?'

'Yes. Actually, there is.' She paused, hoping Richard would understand. 'I think we need to spend more time apart.'

He didn't seem at all put out by her request. 'Let me set up this London interview first and we can take it from there.'

'No. You're not listening to me, Richard. I don't want to date you any more.'

Again, he brushed her words aside. 'I know it's been hectic and we haven't spent as much time together as we did previously, but it will settle down soon.'

'It won't, Richard.'

He merely smiled and she stared at him, unable to believe his audacity and arrogance. She opened her mouth to try again but realised it didn't matter what she said, Richard wasn't in the mood to hear it. He opened the door and slid behind the wheel. 'See you at the hospital, Natalie.' He shut the door and started the engine. A moment later he'd driven off down the street, leaving her standing in the middle of the road, staring after his car.

'Trouble in paradise?'

Natalie swivelled and saw Marty coming out of the shadows. She watched his natural movements as he came closer. 'How much did you overhear?'

'Enough.' He stopped just in front of her. 'You OK?'

'Sure. Annoyed that he's not listening to me, but he'll get the message eventually.'

Marty looked at her in the glow of the streetlamp. 'You don't seem too upset at breaking up with him. How long have you been dating?'

'About six months.'

'Another longish relationship.' He nodded. 'Nat, you've got to start letting go.'

'Letting go of what?'

'Of the barrier you erected back in ninth grade.'

'What?'

'I was there. I saw it go up. The day your parents told you they were divorcing—do you remember what happened?'

'I was grumpy in class and you cajoled the news out of me.'

'It was worse than pulling eye-teeth. I watched, right there, as you put the first brick in place. You started building this imaginary barrier around yourself and you rarely let anyone through. You're mostly fine with women and that is evident by the relationship you have with your mother and friends like Beth.'

'Is this your turn to delve into my psyche?' He gave her a maddening grin and she tossed her head and glared at him. 'And what else, Dr Freud?'

'And your relationships with men took a different turn. You didn't notice it but you started dating a different sort of guy.'

'Nev O'Grady?'

'Exactly. Nev was blond, Richard is blond and I'd be willing to bet the guy you were dating when we met up in Fiji was also blond.'

'So? Maybe I have a thing for blonds. They are supposed to have more fun, you know.'

'Your father wasn't blond.'

'So? That doesn't prove anything.'

'Maybe it does.'

'Hey.' Natalie wasn't sure where this was leading but they'd been having such a wonderful evening and she hadn't expected it to end this way. 'There's nothing wrong with me. I date guys that I like, that I find attractive and who have similar interests to my own.'

'You date guys who are *safe*.'

'So?'

'You've got to put yourself out there. For real. You were the one in Fiji who kept nagging me not to cut myself off from the female gender. "Your marriage failed," you told me. "That doesn't mean *you're* a failure," you said. "The right woman is out there, just waiting for you." You can dish out the advice, Nat, but you don't take it on board in your own personal life.'

'We weren't talking about me back then, we were talking about you, and I was quite happy in the relationship I was in.'

'Well, we're talking about you now, Nat. You've broken it off with Everley. Now what? Look around for another blond man who *doesn't* have blue eyes, like your father, and date him for about six to eight months and then decide that isn't working either?'

Natalie eyed him for a moment, unable to believe what he was saying, his words cutting like a knife. Pain and hurt and a desperate need to protect herself welled from deep within. 'No,' she replied, and even she could detect the hurt in her tone.

Marty's gaze instantly mellowed and he gathered her into his arms. 'I'm sorry. I'm sorry,' he mumbled into her hair. 'I didn't mean to push so hard.' He stroked the end of her ponytail. 'I just get frustrated seeing you going around in circles.' He pulled back and looked down at her. 'I want you to be happy, to finally get over your parents' divorce—just as I had to get over my own divorce. It's not easy when you feel as though you've been betrayed by one of the few people you trust. I know you probably felt your father left you, that he was to blame for everything that happened to you afterwards, but it's not true. You weren't the reason they got divorced.'

'I know,' she said softly. 'I've realised that but still…it's hard to trust.' She sighed and shifted away from his embrace. The fact that her body had wanted to melt into him, that her breathing had increased, that she wanted to place little butterfly kisses all the way up his neck—all these things meant Marty was becoming more dangerous to her with every passing second. She was even having trouble with her thought process, and *that* was not good. Not good at all.

'Of course it is.' He groaned and shook his head. 'Trusting is the pits but we've got to take a chance sooner or later or we'll be left on the shelf.'

'At least I'll have you for company,' she muttered, as the reality of his words started to sink in. 'It's late, Marty. I'd better get inside or Beth will send out a search party.'

'What are you going to do about Everley?'

'I don't know. At the moment, I'm still mad at him.'

'Ooh.' He gave the chuckle of a mad scientist and rubbed his hands together with glee. 'Want to get even?'

She laughed. 'Now you sound like we're back in school.'

'Hey, at least it made you laugh,' he said, reverting back to himself.

'True.' She placed her hand on his arm. 'You're a good friend, Marty.'

'Why, thank you.' She dropped her hand and he pulled a set of car keys from his pocket. 'And now that my work here is done, I'll leave you in peace. You can go inside and have a juicy post-mortem with Beth about tonight's events. It'll do you the world of good.'

'All right, then.' She smiled and when he opened his arms she instantly went into them. He kissed the top of her head and after a brief moment put her from him.

'Get some sleep and I'll see you tomorrow.'

'Yes, you will.' Natalie smiled at him. 'Thanks, Marty.'

'No. I should be the one thanking you for a terrific evening.'

'You're welcome. It was fun.'

'It was.' He started walking towards his car. 'I'll have aches and pains tomorrow from twisting my body in all sorts of strange ways but it was worth it.'

'You poor old man.' Natalie smiled and watched him climb behind the wheel of his four-wheel-drive. He waved as he drove off and she returned the wave, feeling a lot more cheerier than she had when Richard had left. She waited until Marty's car turned the corner before she went inside.

Beth was sitting on the couch, packing away the game. Natalie surveyed the kitchen. It was spotless and the dishwasher was on. 'Thanks for clearing everything away.'

'I didn't. Marty did. Said it was the least he could do to repay us for such a great evening.'

'It *was* good.' Natalie sat on the couch next to her friend.

'Even with Richard showing up?'

Natalie sighed, then frowned. 'Yes.' She quickly told her friend about her decision to avoid Richard until he came to the realisation she honestly didn't want to see him any more.

'I can't say I'm surprised.'

'And glad?'

Beth smiled at her. 'You deserve better.' She paused. 'Someone like Marty, for instance.'

Natalie shook her head. 'Marty's just a friend.'

'But there's chemistry between you.'

'What? No. He treats everyone like that.'

'I don't think so. You're his "darling Nat".'

'But that's only because he's known me for so long.' She paused for a moment and knew she had to ask the question. 'Do you want to go out with him?' Natalie held her breath as she waited for her friend's answer, wondering why the thought of Beth and Marty together bothered her so much. She didn't begrudge them happiness, and if they found it with each other, then so much the better.

'No. No chemistry.'

Natalie slowly exhaled and nodded, trying to ignore the relief she felt.

'What's your shift tomorrow?' Beth asked.

'Morning ward round then I'm on until three.'

'With Marty?'

'I'm not sure. He said he'd see me tomorrow, so possibly.'

'I still think you should give him a go. See where this friendship might lead you.'

'And what if I do? What if it wrecks the friendship we have? He's footloose and fancy-free and even if I hadn't known him for years, I would have picked that up in the last few days. No. Just friends for the two of us.'

'But you can feel it? Can't you?' Beth watched her closely and Natalie felt as trapped as a kangaroo in a spotlight.

'He's very attractive,' she finally conceded.

'I knew it.'

'But he's not my type.' As she said the words to Beth, Marty's diagnosis of her past relationships popped back into her mind. She brushed it aside.

'No. He's not your usual type but you know what they say…a change is as good as a holiday.' Beth giggled. Natalie rolled her eyes and smiled before standing and heading towards the stairs. 'Night, Beth.'

'Sweet dreams,' her friend cooed in a sing-song voice.

Natalie shook her head. 'See you in the morning, *if* you haven't been called to the hospital in the middle of the night,' she added, and Beth groaned before laughing.

As Natalie lay in bed, she thought over the evening and how easily she related to Marty. It was true what she'd said to Beth. She didn't want to ruin their friendship because right now she needed her friends. Making the decision to break up with Richard had been coming on for quite a while now, but it still wouldn't be easy and she'd have days filled with frustration.

There had also been a difference in Marty when he'd hugged her goodbye. Where she'd previously felt such a strong awareness between them, that time she hadn't. It was as though he had been holding himself aloof, which was ridiculous. Aloof wasn't a word she'd associate with Marty. Funny, kind-hearted, generous, thoughtful and gorgeous. Those were more his type of adjective. Aloof? With her?

'You're imagining things,' she told herself as she turned over and punched the pillow. Closing her eyes, she listened to the whirring of the ceiling fan and gradually fell asleep.

CHAPTER FIVE

WHEN Marty returned home, he threw the keys on the bench and checked the messages on his answering-machine. There was one from Cassie, one from her friend Lisa and one from Ryan. He checked the clock and decided now was a good time to have a chat with his cousin.

'What are you doing home this early in the afternoon?' he chided Ryan. 'It must be about four o'clock in the afternoon there. Get back to work.'

Ryan chuckled. 'How's it going, Cuz?'

'Not bad.'

'Enjoying being back in the land down under?'

'Very much, although I am missing my daily fresh croissant. Mind sending me a couple?'

'Won't be fresh by the time they reach you. How's the new job?'

Marty found himself smiling. 'Not bad.'

'Ah. I take it there's a plethora of female talent?'

'Actually, yes. You should head on back yourself.'

'I have six more months on my current contract and I might just think about it. Will someone at your new hospital give me a job?'

Both men chuckled. 'Actually, I did a bit of name dropping today so it will soon be common knowledge you're my cousin.'

'Yeah? Trying to impress the girls?'

'Well...kind of, but she already knew about you.'

'Yeah? Who?'

'Remember Natalie Fox?'

'From high school? Brunette with the long hair, right?'

Marty slowly exhaled. 'That's the one.'

'You saw her a few years back, didn't you?'

'Nine years ago and right after my divorce.'

'Man, time flies...' Ryan trailed off. 'Were there any sparks back then?'

'Oh, yeah. Plenty of sparks between us but bad timing.'

'Always the way. So she's at your hospital eh?'

'She's a colleague, same ward.'

'This is such a small world. She still pretty?'

Marty closed his eyes and thought for a moment. The word pretty didn't seem to accurately describe how incredibly beautiful Natalie was. 'Very,' he finally said.

'Interested in her, are you?'

Marty opened his eyes at the question and shrugged even though his cousin couldn't see him. 'She kind of has a boyfriend.'

'Kind of? Sounds like there's room to manoeuvre. You should have made your move on her in high school.'

'Nah. We were friends and, besides, she was going through a rough time. Her parents got divorced that year and she needed her friends. We were too young, too immature.'

'But you've always liked her.'

'She was about the only girl who really understood my sense of humour, you know, on my wavelength.'

'You thought Gloria was on your wavelength, too.'

'Are you going to throw my failed marriage in my face for the rest of my life?'

'Only when I think it's warranted.' Ryan chuckled, his humour contradicting his words. He sobered and said seriously, 'Listen, Marty, I'm only trying to say be careful because it sounds as though you want to be more than friends with Natalie now.'

Marty shook his head and raked a hand through his hair. 'I'm attracted to her, there's no denying that, but what if we get together and our friendship is ruined? I don't want to risk that, Ryan.'

'She that special to you?'

'It's hard to explain. It's as though we've just picked up where we left off since the last time we saw each other. There's this bond between us.'

'What happened when you met up in Fiji?'

'We only had about thirty-two hours together. I'd just arrived and she was just leaving.'

'Yet nothing romantic happened?'

'The day I landed in Fiji was right after I'd signed the divorce papers. I was in no state of mind to start anything up with anyone, especially someone like Nat who I hold in such high regard. No, she was as good a friend to me then as she'd been in high school. She said I'd helped her tremendously through the tough time of her parents' divorce and now she was there to help me through mine.

She listened to me moan and groan, held my hand, gave me comfort, told me the things I needed to hear.'

'She was a friend.'

'Exactly, and even though I was attracted to her, back then I needed her friendship.'

'And now? Do you need her friendship more than the chance of a relationship?'

'That's a good question,' Marty mumbled. 'And I don't think I can answer that. She also has this chip on her shoulder about relationships.'

'What's the deal? She doesn't date? Dates too much?'

'She's happy enough to be in a relationship but only if she's in control. The guy she's with now is completely wrong for her. I met him tonight and he's so stiff and...and just wrong for her. Also, he's the opposite of her father.'

'Meaning?'

'Meaning she doesn't date men who physically resemble her father. I don't even think she realises she does it, and when I pointed that out tonight, she got a bit annoyed.'

'It's never easy, hearing a home truth. So I guess you and Natalie are destined to remain friends, eh?'

Marty weighed up his cousin's words. 'Maybe. There are a few obstacles we'd need to work through first. Add to that fact I *do* have the same colouring and build as her father.'

'Strike one against you.'

'Sort of. At least she knows the *real* me and knows I'm nothing like her father—in personality.'

'That's a good sign.'

'Yeah, I guess. Anyway, enough about me. Tell me about frosty London. How's the freeze going? Any snow yet?'

'It's trying hard to snow but all we have is slush at the moment. ''Jingle Bells'' playing, Santas in every store, people being cheerful and happy. It's enough to make anyone say, ''Bah humbug.'''

Marty laughed. 'Are the wards full?'

'To the brim.'

'Well, at least that's something for you to concentrate on, Dr Scrooge.' They talked for a bit longer before Marty rang off, yawning. It was after midnight yet his mind refused to wind down. He went to the spare room and looked at the packing boxes awaiting his attention. He walked over to one marked MEMORABILIA and within a few minutes, had his old school year book out.

As he flicked through the pages, looking for her, he spotted a photograph he'd never noticed before. It was on a page filled with a collage of different people, and on the left-hand border was a picture of himself and Nat. Two of their other friends were in the photo as well, but he and Nat were in the middle, their arms around each other's shoulders as they pulled faces for the camera.

He laughed at the sight of them and tried to reconcile the face-pulling teenager with the woman he'd spent time with tonight. She was still there, a little more repressed but still there. Then he thought about the way their bodies had been pressed together during their games of Twister.

Whenever she'd touched him, he'd felt an overwhelming aware-ness, as though his body knew she belonged to him. It was such a strange and alien sensation that for a moment he hadn't been at all sure how to react. This was Nat! His friend. Although he'd been aware of her when they'd been teenagers and then later in Fiji, he'd preferred to honour their friendship.

Ever since his divorce, he'd preferred to keep any women in his life on the surface or around the edges. The wall was up and no one was getting through it...except people he trusted.

He trusted Nat.

Nat was a woman in his life.

He swallowed as he realised the truth of that thought. She was definitely someone he could confide in because she knew him. They may have both changed on the surface but deep down, he believed they were still the same. If not, their friendship wouldn't have just picked up where it had left off. You couldn't do that kind of thing with someone who didn't really know you.

He returned the book to the box and shut the door on the spare room. At the same time he shut the door on his thoughts. He and Nat were going to be friends. It was what they both needed right now and that was all there was to it.

On Wednesday evening, Natalie thankfully sank into a bath and closed her eyes. After a hectic clinic that morning and paperwork, as well as helping make more decorations for the Christmas tree which now stood proudly in the ward, she was bushed.

In fact, the last few days since Marty had come back into her life had brought a whole new set of problems and emotions and she wasn't quite sure she was ready to deal with them. Escaping into a bathtub full of bubbles, with candles around her, seemed the answer to all her prayers. 'A Christmas wish come true,' she whispered as she felt her body begin to relax.

Richard had called her a few times but she hadn't returned his calls, hoping he'd get the message. She was ready to move on, although she was a little sad that things hadn't worked out between the orthopaedic surgeon and herself.

'And another one's gone.' Natalie tried to focus on washing all thoughts of Richard and their failed relationship from her mind. It went quite easily but hard on its heels came thoughts of Marty. She opened her eyes and pushed those away faster. Marty was her friend and that's all there was to it.

She'd tried hard not to think about what he'd said the other night, that she only dated men who were the opposite of her father, and realised on that score that there actually may have been some truth in his words. When she'd learned of her parents' divorce, she'd done everything she could to try and make things better. She'd worked harder at school, she'd been polite on every occasion, she even helped clean her father's shed out, but nothing had worked. Her father had left.

Davey, being two years younger, hadn't been as affected as she had, and if it hadn't been for Marty she wouldn't have made it through. She closed her eyes again and mentally ticked off the men she'd dated since medical school and realised, with a slow and increasing sense of alarm, that Marty was correct. All of the men she'd chosen had been the opposite of her father, not necessarily in personality but definitely in looks.

'And Marty?' she whispered. Marty was gorgeous, she couldn't deny that, and he *did* have the same colouring as her father, as well being of height and build, but she also knew he was different. He was trustworthy and he genuinely cared about her. In Fiji she'd had to work hard at controlling her attraction towards him—they had been friends. 'And nothing has changed,' she told herself, knowing she was already fighting hard against this attraction that seemed to exist between them.

She thought back to his words. Had she also chosen men who weren't a threat to her? She'd told herself she was looking for a nice, steady man to settle down and have a life with...a life where she was in control. Surely it didn't matter if they fell short of some of her expectations because no marriage was perfect—she'd had daily proof with her parents' marriage.

The doorbell buzzed and she groaned. 'Go away,' she whispered, wishing Beth were home, but she knew her friend was still in Theatre. She waited, not moving, almost holding her breath and willing whoever it was to go away and leave her alone.

The doorbell went again and then again.

'I know you're home,' she heard a faint male voice say.

'Marty!' She quickly climbed from the bath, towelled herself dry and pulled on her bathrobe, before heading downstairs to answer the door. 'All right, all right,' she called as he continued to ring the bell. She threw open the door. 'What is it?'

Marty was stunned. He stood there and stared at her for ten seconds, trying to figure out how on earth he was supposed to control himself when faced with his darling Nat wearing only a bathrobe.

'Marty?' She waited another beat. 'If you're not going to speak, I'll shut the door.'

'Uh...sorry. You just surprised me, which is kind of ironic as I thought I'd surprise you instead, and, uh, you've turned the tables on me and...well...' He seemed to realise he was babbling and took a step aside and motioned to the Christmas tree behind him. 'I bought you a tree.'

'Oh.' Natalie looked at the lush, green tree and instantly melted. 'You bought me a tree?'

'Yes.' He looked at the tree. Much safer than looking at Nat. 'Well, for you and Beth. A tree for your place...town house.' He was babbling again. 'Er...why don't you go on up and put some clothes on and I'll haul it inside?' He didn't look at her as he spoke and went to grab hold of the tree, which was lying on the ground.

'OK.' Natalie clapped her hands with glee, unable to believe how in just a short time Marty had rejuvenated her spirits and revitalised her mind. She held the door open for him. When he realised she was still there, trying to help him, he turned and glared at her.

'Go—now—or I won't be held responsible for my actions.'

She returned his stare, frowning a little. 'What do you mean?'

Their gazes met and she saw the desire behind his blue eyes. Her own eyes widened in surprise and her breathing intensified. She parted her lips, about to say something, but instead she watched him take a deep breath, his chest expanding beneath his cotton polo shirt, before he slowly exhaled. It was as though he was trying to keep himself under control. 'Just put some clothes on—please? I have the greatest respect for you and our friendship but that doesn't mean I'm a saint, Nat. Get dressed and then come and help me decorate this tree.' His smile was a little lopsided and she felt her heart rate quicken. Finally, the message got through to her brain and she turned, heading for the stairs.

Without looking back, she went directly to her room where she shut the door and leant against it for a moment for support. When she was sure her legs would support her, she quickly pulled on underwear, jeans and a top, before heading back downstairs, her hair still pinned to the top of her head.

'Right,' he muttered, as he heard her on the stairs. 'Where do you want it?'

'Uh...you choose. We can shift the furniture around if we need to.'

'Beth won't mind?'

Natalie smiled. 'Not when she finds out about the Christmas tree. We were only saying last night that we needed to get one but neither of us has had the time recently.' She noticed two shopping bags on the floor and peeked inside. 'Decorations, too? You are a regular Santa Claus.'

'And I'll continue being one.'

It took Natalie a moment to comprehend his words and then she chuckled. 'You've been roped into being Santa for the children, haven't you?'

'Yes. You could have warned me.'

'What fun would that have been?' She crossed to his side. 'Besides, I think you'll make a very jolly Santa.' She patted his flat stomach, then frowned. 'Although I think you'll need some extra padding.'

'Cassie said she has it all under control.'

'That's our Cass. She's the glue that keeps the ward together.' She paused. 'Hang on a minute. You only agreed to do it to get on Sister Dorset's good side, didn't you?'

'So?'

Natalie shook her head. 'I don't know why I'm amazed.'

'Hey, we've got a bet going here...a bet I plan to win.'

'That remains to be seen, Williams.'

'You'd better believe it, Fox, and *see* it you will.'

She laughed and motioned to the tree. 'So, Santa, where are we going to put this tree?'

They chose a spot and shifted the tree over, stabilising it. 'Now, to decorate.'

'You know, as Santa, you have to read all the letters the kids in the ward write?'

'What? No one told me that bit.'

'Oh, yeah. It's part of the deal. There's a little posting box in the ward. The kids will get busy all writing letters to Santa and you're required to read each and every one.'

Marty thought about it for a moment before grinning at her. 'Then I'll need to recruit myself some elves.'

'Elves?'

'Yes.' He paused and gave her a cursory glance. 'I think you'll do very well as one of Santa's little helpers.'

'Whoa, there, Dasher. You're going a little too fast.'

'It's only fair that you help me out.' When she didn't look convinced, he grinned and said softly, 'Don't do it for me, Nat, do it for the children.'

'Ooh, you rat fink. You know I can't resist that.'

'Aha. The good, upstanding morals win again. You're such an easy target, Nat. You're going to have to work hard to protect yourself from all those other people who are just waiting take advantage of you.'

'Then why are *you* taking advantage of me?'

'Because we're friends, and that's what friends do.'

'Oh. Really?'

'Yes. Really.'

They continued to decorate the tree and received a bit of help from Beth when she finally came home. Just before nine-thirty, Marty stood and excused himself.

'Oops. Didn't realise the time. I have to go.'

'Bedtime for Santa?' Natalie asked.

Marty waggled his eyebrows up and down. 'Santa has a hot date.'

'Now?' Natalie and Beth said in unison.

'Hey, that's the life of people who work shifts.' He pulled his car keys from his pocket. 'I'll see you both tomorrow.'

Beth stood and walked him to the door. Natalie just glared at him. She murmured a grumpy goodbye and when he was gone Beth came back and sat next to her, both of them admiring the Christmas tree.

'What's the problem?'

'Problem? There's no problem.'

'Spit it out, Natalie. You don't like the idea of Marty going out on dates.'

'What? That's ridiculous. He can go out with whoever he chooses. He's a big boy.' She paused, both of them quiet for a moment before she continued. 'He just drifts from one woman to the next. It's not healthy. He's been doing that for the past nine years.' She shook her head. 'I guess I shouldn't be surprised. He told me he was going to keep his emotions in control and not get deeply involved with anyone again.'

'When did he say that?'

'After his divorce was final.'

'Marty's divorced? Well, that explains it.'

'Explains his need to shift from one woman to the next? He can't go on doing that for ever, Beth.'

'You're one to talk.'

'Me?' Natalie stood and glared down at her friend. 'I only broke up with Richard a few days ago, which I still don't think he's comprehended.'

'He hasn't,' Beth said.

'Still, am I expected to already have the next guy lined up?'

Beth sighed and crossed to Natalie's side. 'I'm sorry. I didn't mean to upset you. I guess we're all protecting ourselves from something.'

Natalie looked at her friend, knowing she spoke the truth. Beth had been terribly hurt in the past as well, which was why she continued on her dating frenzy.

'You know Marty doesn't take any of these dates seriously,' Beth said abruptly. 'Just like me. I do it because it's kind of a hobby.'

'A hobby? You're afraid of commitment.'

'Not commitment. I'm afraid to trust a man with who I really am.'

Natalie frowned. Was that what she was like? She had trusted Richard...but only to a certain extent. 'Oh, this is all too much for this time of night. I know it's still classified as early in the world according to Marty Williams, but I'm exhausted.' She gave her friend a hug. 'I think I'll go to bed.'

Beth said goodnight and Natalie headed upstairs, giving the Christmas tree with colourful flashing lights one last look before she left. Marty's generosity and caring attitude was something he should share with a woman...a woman who understood and appreciated him. He'd tried it before and had got hurt. She understood that but she hated to think he was wasting himself on one date after the next when he had so much more to give.

'Give?' she murmured into the darkness as she stared at the ceiling. 'Like giving you a look that makes you breathless and your knees go weak?'

She turned over and buried her head beneath her pillow, trying to block out the memory of Marty's blue eyes filled with desire. The attraction she felt for him was growing every day, and every day she continued to fight it with all her might.

They were friends and that was all there was to it.

By Friday, Marty felt as though he'd accomplished a worthy goal. He'd had six dates and had found time to drop in on Beth and Nat several times during the week.

'I'm...astonished,' Natalie said on Friday morning when Marty turned up for an early breakfast. 'Why aren't these women at each other's throats, fighting over you?' Beth was still asleep and Natalie was enjoying having him all to herself for a while.

'Because I'm charming, gorgeous and extremely funny. They don't take me seriously and that's the way I like it.' He started pulling out the ingredients he'd need to make pancakes. Natalie shook her head in bemusement, watching him, amazed he knew where everything was.

'You know, you haven't changed, Marty. After nine years you're still holding yourself back, not putting yourself out there.'

'I put myself out there,' he said defensively.

'Not seriously. You need to take the time to get to know someone, to find out their favourite colour, their favourite food. You know, what they like and dislike.'

He shook his head. 'I tried that once before, remember.'

'But you're still repressing all your emotions. It's not healthy. You can't bottle up your pain, your hurt about what you still see as a failure. Surely you're over the divorce by now?'

'I'm over Gloria and the fact that it didn't work out—see, *time* did help—but when it comes to the pain and hurt part, well, I can do without it. And, besides, at least I have a bottle to put things in.' He began to measure out the pancake ingredients as he spoke.

'Meaning?'

'Meaning you don't even *have* a bottle, Nat. You keep yourself so rigid, so tightly in control that you never let the real Nat out. Sure, you can ask a guy his favourite colour and all that stuff, but what importance does that play when it comes to how you feel about him?'

'We're not talking about me,' she countered, a little hurt at his words.

'Why not? What is it that makes you so scared? Scared of letting yourself get hurt? I don't mean annoyed or mad but *really* hurt. The hurt where you get chest pains, breathing is difficult and just when you think you can't cry any more, from somewhere deep down inside the gut-wrenching anguish starts to build again and overflows. It overflows so forcefully that you can't stop it even if you want to. Your whole body shakes, then trembles. You can't stand, you can't even sit. All you can do is curl yourself up, forcing yourself to remember to breathe in and out.'

He spoke the words softly but with such personal expression that Natalie knew he'd felt every single word he'd just said and her heart went out to him, sorry for the pain he'd experienced. She shrugged, then grimaced. 'Well, when you make it sound so appealing, how could I refuse!'

Marty laughed, breaking the sombre mood, and began to mix the batter. 'Good point. All I meant was, you've never felt that sort of intense pain. Sure, when your dad left you felt rejected but I don't know how many times I've said this—and I know other people have as well—it wasn't your fault, honey.'

'I know, just as you know your marriage break-up wasn't solely your fault. I know all that but, still, it doesn't necessarily filter into the rest of my life. I also have to admit, by the way, that you were right about the men I date. They do look different from my father. Very different. And I also confess that my goal is usually self-preservation. I think if I put myself out there, if I got hurt like you described, I don't know if I'd have the strength to go on.'

'Of course you would,' he countered reassuringly. 'You're one of the strongest people I know. Sure, if you feel like a failure you should rely on your friends to pick you up and help you to get back on with your life. That's what friends do.'

'And do your friends tell you to just slide right back into the dating scene, going from one woman to the next? No.' She answered her own question. 'Real friends listen to you whinge and moan and then help you to get control of your life again.'

'Control. There's that word again.'

'We're both hanging onto control. So's Beth, for that matter.'

'What do I do?' Beth mumbled sleepily from the doorway.

'Hold firmly onto your control. It's called self-preservation and we all have it, even if we express it in different ways.'

'Is she giving you a hard time about your dating habits again?' Beth asked Marty. His answer was just to smile.

'Nat, you think there's something serious going on between me and all these women, but there isn't,' Marty confessed.

'But you could be breaking their hearts. Doesn't that bother your conscience? Oh, wait a minute, do you *have* a conscience where women are concerned?'

'My darling Nat, you're taking this much too seriously. I'm just meeting new people, colleagues. We have a drink, a laugh and that's it.' He stopped whipping the pancake batter, stuck his finger in and smeared a bit on her cheek. She hadn't yet put her hair up and as his hand brushed it, the softness almost made him gasp. She was dressed in her usual straight skirt, which came to just above the knee, and a colourful cotton shirt.

'Hey.' She rubbed at her face. 'If you're not going to play nicely, you can leave.'

'No, he can't.' Beth stumbled to the bench and sat on a stool. 'As I said earlier in the week, he can drop by as many times as he likes if he's going to cook for us.'

'Pancakes, my darling Beth?'

'Mmm. Yes, please.' Beth slumped forward onto the bench.

'Hard night?' Marty went back to work while Natalie finished making coffee.

'Hard date is more like it.' Natalie couldn't resist teasing her friend, and at Marty's grin knew Beth wasn't going to get out of things easily.

'Who was it?'

'No one from the hospital. I've given up dating colleagues.'

'That'll narrow the field. Since when does a registrar have time to socialise with people outside the hospital?' Natalie quipped.

'Good question,' Beth muttered.

'Where'd you meet him?' Marty asked.

'Stuie's.'

'Interesting. I take it everything went well?'

'Uh…not really, and I don't want a post-mortem.'

'OK. So…no more dates with the bartender from Stuie's?' Natalie asked as she pulled out the frying pan for Marty.

'I guess not.'

'Well, cheer up,' he said. 'Watch me flip some pancakes while I tell you about my…interesting date last night.'

Beth lifted her head. 'Who was it with?'

'Katrina, who works in the rheumatoid arthritis clinic.'

'I know her,' Beth chimed in.

Natalie squirmed a little, not sure she wanted to hear the details. 'Be back in a moment,' she said, and walked out the room. She went straight to the bathroom and locked herself in. She leaned against the door for a moment before crossing to the sink to splash some water on her face.

She glanced at her reflection. 'It's all right. You can do this. You're just friends. Despite the fact that he makes you feel all mushy inside, you're just friends.' She dried her hands and repeated again. 'Just friends.'

When she returned to the kitchen, Beth and Marty were both laughing.

'That's too funny.'

'Laughing at Katrina?' Natalie snapped, a little too quickly.

'No.' Marty frowned at her. 'Laughing at me.'

'You didn't call her by the wrong name?' Natalie asked.

'I'd like to remind you that I have an excellent memory. What happened was we went to a Kazakhstani restaurant and I totally mangled my order.'

'There's a Kazakhstani restaurant in Sydney?' She raised her eyebrows in surprise.

'That's not the point. The point is, if you'll just keep quiet so I can tell you, I ended up ordering something that was still squirming a little when it arrived.'

'Eww. Did you eat it?'

'No. I apologised profusely, sent it back and wished I could order a Vegemite sandwich.'

'You're so lame.' Beth laughed.

'He's not.' Natalie found herself defending Marty. 'He's

just…''cuisinely'' challenged.' She came and sat by Beth as Marty started flipping pancakes.

'Thank you, Nat.' While he waited for them to cook, he found plates and cutlery and maple syrup.

'How do you remember all these women's names? I mean, what have you had? Five different dates in six nights?'

'Six,' he corrected her, and slid a pancake onto the plate for Beth before pouring another one.

'My, my. Your little black book will be getting mighty full.'

He smiled sweetly. 'I don't use a black book. As I said, I have an excellent memory. One pancake or two?'

'And what about Sister Dorset? Have you managed to charm her?'

'No, but I am seriously working on it. I think she almost smiled at me the other day.'

'Yeah, right.'

'No. I'm serious.'

'Why? Did you manage to change a two-year-old's nappy without the proper *tools*?'

'No, Miss Hospital Corners, I did not. I merely teased her…in a totally charming way, of course. She loved it. At least, she didn't scold me for it so that's a positive sign. And, as I said, she almost smiled. I know it. I was thinking about asking her to the departmental Christmas party tonight but was too scared of her.'

'I am *so* going to win this bet.' Natalie grinned.

'Are you going with anyone to the party tonight?' Marty asked her as he flipped another pancake.

'No.'

'Not even Everley?'

'No. He couldn't make it—even if I *did* want to go with him.'

'But you don't, right?' Marty needed clarification before he asked his next question.

'Correct.'

'So…' He checked the pancake. 'Shall we go together?' He slid the pancake onto her plate, hoping the question had come out as nonchalantly as he'd planned.

'Sure, but you can't chalk me up as date number seven. I don't count.' Natalie took the plate and drowned the pancake with maple syrup. She got some on her finger and licked it off, her eyelids fluttering closed in ecstasy as the sweet syrup made contact with her tongue. 'Mmm.'

Marty watched, mesmerised by her beauty. She didn't need to have her hair coloured or wear pounds of make-up to make herself look incredible. It was all there, God given, and she looked… radiant. He forced himself to swallow and look away before she caught him staring.

This was ridiculous. Why did she affect him so much? He poured more pancake batter into the pan, desperate to find coherent thoughts again. 'I hope that's real maple syrup,' he said and could have hit himself for sounding so lame. Real maple syrup? Where had that come from?

'You bet,' she replied as she opened her eyes and began cutting up her pancake. He waited, almost expectantly, while she took her first mouthful. 'Mmm. This is delicious,' she mumbled as she began to chew. 'You are a brilliant cook, Marty. Isn't he, Beth?' she demanded.

'Absolutely.' Beth raised her eyebrows at him, then winked. Marty grinned and, basking in the sunshine of feminine praise, returned his attention to the next pancake.

'Did you hear about the case that came in last night?' he asked conversationally.

'When were you at the hospital? Before or after your date?'

'After.'

Natalie filed this information away for later. Surely if he'd had fun on his date with Katrina, he wouldn't have stopped off at the hospital afterwards. Very interesting.

'A three-year-old boy presented at A and E. His mother said he fell down and hit his head. As I was around, I had his head X-rayed and everything came back fine. Then I noticed some bruises on his arms, collar-bone and legs.'

'He'd been hit?'

'That's the presumption. Social workers will be seeing him today and speaking to both parents, but I managed to keep him in overnight for observation.'

'What's his name?'

'Glen.'

'Any previous admissions?'

'No.'

'What about siblings?'

'Two older brothers.'

'Old enough to hit or torture their little brother?'

'To be decided,' Marty said as he expertly flipped a pancake in the air.

'I guess that's a big factor of working in Paediatrics,' Beth chimed in. 'Do you often see child abuse?'

'More often than not,' Natalie said as she scraped her plate. 'Pass me a spoon, Marty. I can't let this syrup go to waste.'

He chuckled. 'Now that you've had your sugar hit for the morning, are you planning on going to work any time soon? It's almost eight o'clock.'

'What?' Beth gasped. 'I've got ward round in half an hour. Richard will be spare if I'm late again.' Beth raced off and a moment later they heard the shower running.

'You all set to go?' Marty asked.

'Just have to brush my pearly whites and tie my hair back.'

'Do you have to?'

'What? Tie my hair back? Of course. Could you imagine all those sticky fingers tugging on it all day long? No, thank you.'

Marty leaned over and tugged the end. 'Aw. Go on, Dr Nat. It'll be good fun.'

She laughed and licked the spoon free of syrup. 'Sorry.' She stood. 'If you want them to play with long hair, grow yours.' She stacked the plates and carried them to the dishwasher as Marty slid another pancake out of the pan.

'I'll put the rest of the batter in the fridge and you can have pancakes later.'

'You're very well house-trained, Marty. Your mother must be proud.'

He grinned as he sat on the stool she'd just vacated and poured syrup over his pancake. 'She is. Go and do your hair. I'll eat and then we can go to the hospital together.'

'That means you'll have to bring me back here after work.'

'So? We've got the departmental thing tonight anyway.'

'Oh, yeah. OK.' Natalie headed off.

Marty sat and ate in peace, amazed at the discovery he'd made while he'd been watching Natalie devour her maple syrup. He was in love with her!

How could he have fallen in love so quickly? Or had it been quick? Had this been building for the past fifteen years or so? Was it possible? He shook his head. They knew each other so well and he never let any woman through his barriers, yet Natalie had been there before the barriers had been put in place. It wasn't supposed to have happened. He was supposed to have been keeping his distance, dating other women and not getting deeply involved with anyone. Besides, they were friends…and he'd been stupid enough to fall for her.

He groaned and closed his eyes, unable to believe it.

'Enjoying the pancake as much as Natalie?'

Beth's voice snapped him out of his thoughts, and as she was dressed for work he wondered how long he'd been sitting there, thinking about Nat. 'What? What do you mean? Enjoying Nat?'

Beth laughed. 'You misunderstood. I didn't mean— Oh, forget it. It's written all over your face, Marty.'

'What is?' He tried feigning ignorance.

'You're hooked on her.'

'What?' Why had his voice come out as an uncontrollable squeak? He cleared his throat and tried again. 'What?' Deeper, more masculine. Much better.

'I've been watching you both all week long and even though you've been going out with one girl after another, it's Natalie you want.'

Marty decided he may as well give up. 'Do you think she knows?'

'No. She's too busy trying to regain control over her life, but you've definitely thrown her a curve ball and in my opinion it was exactly what she needed.'

'Really?'

'Hey.' Beth kissed him on the cheek. 'I'm on your side, mate.' She picked up her keys. 'I gotta run.'

Marty was just about to offer her a lift when he turned and saw Natalie at the base of the stairs, staring at him.

'Bye,' Beth called, and in the next instant she was gone, leaving the two of them alone. Natalie was the first to recover.

'She's like a whirlwind, isn't she?' She walked over to the table where her bag was and began rummaging through it.

'Ready?' was all he said as he stacked the dishwasher and wiped the bench.

'I'll just check everything's locked.'

Marty waited, feeling the change in atmosphere. Natalie appeared to be a little frosty towards him but he wasn't sure why. She'd been fine when she'd gone to do her hair. Could she see straight through him, just like Beth? Did she like what she saw or not? Why was he feeling so insecure all of a sudden? He stopped watching her and tried to concentrate on getting himself together.

When she'd checked and locked the doors, they headed out to his four-wheel-drive. Natalie climbed up, trying to do it gracefully in her skirt.

'That was fun,' she murmured, and Marty laughed, the previous tension easing.

'I guess this isn't a "skirt" type of car.'

'Definitely not. Next time, we'll take my car.'

'Deal.' He turned the radio on and a song they remembered listening to at school was playing. They both sang along, laughing when they both got the words wrong.

'I haven't heard that song in years.' Natalie grinned as he pulled into the hospital car park.

'Stay there. I'll come and help you get down.'

She turned to protest but he was already striding around to her side. He opened the door and held out his hands. 'Put your hands on my shoulders.'

Natalie did as he asked and in the next instant he'd slid his hands under her arms and physically lifted her from the car. 'It's not that high up,' she told him.

'Don't want you making an undignified exit in that skirt.' His voice was deeper than usual and a little bit husky. Natalie's insides instantly responded to it and she could quite see why he had so many women chasing after him. Her hands still rested on his shoulders and that same stimulating scent was still driving her wild every time she breathed in. He hadn't removed his hands and it felt as though he was gathering her closer to him.

Their gazes locked and she wasn't sure she could have moved even if a freak hailstorm had hit in the middle of summer. She swallowed, her mouth suddenly dry as she saw his desire.

His warm fingers were now splayed across her back, thumbs around the curve of her ribs, almost brushing the sides of her breasts. Slowly he exhaled as he urged their bodies closer. 'I'm sorry, Nat,' he murmured, his breath fanning her cheek. 'I have to.'

His head started making its descent and she found it amazing that he honestly desired her. Of course he did, she realised as logic hit. She was female and she was currently unattached.

'No. Wait.' She placed three fingers across his lips. 'I'm sorry, Marty,' she whispered urgently. 'I'm sorry. I can't.' The touch of her fingers on his lips was doing more to her insides than she'd realised as tremor after tremor of zingers spread through her. She quickly removed her fingers.

'Too soon?'

'No...well...yes. I'm just... I don't want to be number seven on the list.'

'You won't be.' Even as he said the words, he slowly pulled away. 'But you're right. Now's not the time. We have a ward round and all sorts of doctor stuff to get through today, and feeling uncomfortable with each other isn't going to help.'

'So, do we pretend it didn't happen?'

'We could, or we could just accept the fact that one day we'll see what it's like.'

At his words, the zingers started all over again and she gulped, then started coughing.

He chuckled at her reaction. 'Is the prospect so daunting?'

'No,' she said on a cough, before turning to collect her bag. He shut the door and locked the car as Natalie cleared her throat. 'No. I am curious but right now I need a *friend* rather than another relationship.'

He linked their arms together and grinned, the uncomfortable and embarrassing situation almost forgotten. 'Friends it is, then. Let's go do ward round.'

A few people looked at them as they entered the hospital, some calling greetings, others watching eagerly as they continued, arm in arm, through to the paediatrics ward. At the nurses' desk Natalie tried to disengage her arm but Marty held it tightly. She glared at him but he merely smiled back. She tugged away but he simply moved closer to her.

'Marty.' There was a warning in her tone.

'We're stuck together. We'll just have to do ward round like this.'

'Oh, that'll go down a treat.'

'Morning,' Cassie said as she walked in. 'What's going on?' She glanced at the two of them.

'We're stuck together,' Marty explained.

'Excellent.' Cassie linked her arm through his other one. 'I love games. Wasn't there a nursery story about people stuck together?'

'Marty, cut it out.' Natalie tried tugging her arm out again but to no avail.

'Why? The kids will love it.'

'No doubt, but Sister won't. Then again,' she amended, 'I don't mind getting into trouble if it's going to sink you further in Sister's opinion. Oh, yes. This bet is going to be easy to win.'

'What bet?' Cassie asked, looking around Marty at Natalie.

Natalie was about to explain when Sister Dorset spoke from behind them.

'I beg your pardon, staff, but I believe this is a hospital ward, not a playground. Doctor...' she glared at Marty '...please, unhand my staff so we can get the round under way.'

Cassie, lucky thing, was released and headed to the desk to answer the phone. Natalie, on the other hand, still wasn't being released from Marty's vice-like grip. She half expected Marty to turn a bright shade of red and meekly pull away, but all he did was smile sweetly at the fuming Sister Dorset.

'Aw, come on, Sister. It'll be fun. We can all link arms and do ward round like that. The children will love it and it'll make them laugh. You know what they say—laughter is the best medicine.'

Natalie stared opened-mouthed, stunned at his audacity. To her total surprise, she actually saw Sister's lips twitch a little and behind her dull brown eyes humour began to twinkle. Had he done it? In one simple move? Surely not. In the next instant Sister seemed to pull herself together and cleared her throat.

'I have no objection to laughter, Dr Williams, but I'm sure you'll agree, it has its time and its place.'

Having now been firmly chastised, Natalie expected him to concede but no. Not Marty. He merely pulled a sad, little-boy pout. 'No fun during ward round?'

'Not today, Dr Williams, and I will ask you in future to confine your more...jovial antics to my days off. Too much humour is certainly not good for a woman of my age and experience.'

'Ah, now, Sister, that's where we will have to agree to disagree.' He turned to face Natalie, releasing her arm but taking her hand in his, bringing it to his lips so he could kiss her knuckles. 'Alas, my darling Nat, we will not be joined for ward round today. Will you be able to bear the deprivation?'

'I will endure it as best I can,' Natalie answered, her voice wavering slightly at the feel of his lips on her skin. Why did he have to do something like this in public? Couldn't he see she was having difficulty trying to hide her involuntary response to him?

'If you've quite finished, Doctors?' Sister gave them both a quick stare before whisking away to the first patient's bedside.

Natalie was pleased to see her patients. After Alysha's surgery, she'd come along in leaps and bounds, the fish oil Marty had recommended they try was working a treat.

'I think you might even be able to go home tomorrow,' Natalie told the little girl, who now looked bright and cheerful.

'Really?'

'If you have another good night, I don't see why not. You've done such a wonderful job of getting better, I think we can let you keep getting better at home.'

'Yay!' Alysha clapped her hands and grinned at her mother.

'But you have to promise to follow your special diet closely.'

'I will, Dr Natalie. I promise I'll be good.'

'Good girl.'

'And remember,' Marty said as he clicked his fingers at Alysha, 'you keep practising your clicking and when you come to see Dr Nat in her clinic, you come and show me.'

'I will,' Alysha said, her eyes sparkling brightly as she looked up at Marty. Natalie sighed and shook her head. Was every single female, regardless of age, susceptible to his charms?

'All right, Dr Charming. Let's move on to the next patient,' Natalie said, after smiling at Alysha.

Troy, the toddler who'd been suffering from gastroenteritis, had been discharged two days previously and Laura, the twelve-year-old girl Richard had operated on, had also made a good recovery and been discharged. Sometimes they had patients for weeks and months and at other times either overnight or for a few days, but at all times, seeing her patients slowly getting better was what she loved most about her job. Children often healed a lot faster than adults and their heartfelt thanks, their drawings, their cuddles were all so special to her she sometimes didn't want them to go.

When they came to three-year-old Glen, Natalie's heart twisted in pain when she saw the bruises on his body. He was very small for his age and was still wearing a nappy. He also looked a little undernourished and for a moment she found it hard to put on a brave face.

'Hey, buddy,' Marty said, lowering the side of the cot and sitting down on the mattress. 'How are you doing this morning? Feeling better?'

Glen sat up and looked solemnly at Marty. 'Better.' He was gripping one of the soft toys the ward kept to help children through the scary ordeal of being away from their homes. The toys were all bought new and donated to the ward so if a child became attached to the toy, he or she could take it home. It appeared Glen was now very attached to the blue teddy bear he held close to his body.

Marty glanced over his shoulder. 'Do we know where his mother is?'

'She and her husband are with the social worker now,' Sister informed him.

Marty nodded his thanks and turned his attention back to Glen. 'How's Mr Bear today?'

'Not good. He got a sore back.'

'Does he? Dear me. Let me see.' Marty held out his hands for the bear and, in an act of total trust, Glen handed the toy over. Marty looked thoughtfully at the bear. 'I think you're right, Dr Glen.' At the name, the little boy smiled.

'I not doctor. I Glen.'

'Oh. Silly me. Well, Glen, what should we do about teddy's back?'

Glen tapped one finger on his chin as though thinking and Natalie's heart filled with joy, watching the action. 'I tink we put bandage on it.'

'Excellent suggestion. Sister?'

'One bandage, Doctor,' Sister replied, and placed one in his hand. Marty had Glen hold the teddy very still while he bandaged the blue, furry back.

'How's that?'

'Not all better yet.'

'Oh? Why not?'

'Gotta have a *kiss*.'

'A kiss? You're absolutely right. Who needs to kiss teddy better?'

Glen pointed a finger at Natalie. 'Dat lady.'

'That lady? Yes, I think you're right. This is Dr Natalie.'

Natalie smiled at the boy. 'Hello, Glen. I get to kiss teddy?' At the boy's enthusiastic nod, more warmth filled her heart. 'I would love to.' She held out her hand and Glen gave the bear tenderly to her. 'Thank you.' She turned the toy to face her. 'Hello, Mr Bear. I hear you've got a sore back. That's no good, but I see Dr Marty and Glen have put a bandage on you. That will help, but I've got something that will help even more. I'm going to give you a kiss.' She carefully turned the bear over and tenderly kissed its back. 'There.' She looked at Mr Bear again. 'How's that?'

'All better,' Glen declared, and the smile that lit his face was as bright as the morning sunshine coming through the windows.

'Where is he?' A booming voice demanded, and Sister Dorset swept away to give whoever was making the commotion a piece of her mind. 'No one's taking my son away from me.'

Everyone was looking in the direction from which the voice had come except Marty. He watched as Glen's eyes widened in complete horror and the joy slipped from his face.

'Nat, pull the curtain,' he said briskly, and Natalie quickly returned her attention to their patient. 'Everyone out,' Marty demanded as Natalie swung the curtain around Glen's cot. 'It's all right, Glen. No one's going to hurt you.'

Natalie was astounded at the difference in the child before her. To say he was scared was an understatement. Petrified beyond belief would better fit the description of the pale and shaking child. 'Hold tight to Mr Bear,' she soothed him, reaching her hand out to comfort him. He shied away, backing to the corner of his cot.

When the commotion didn't stop, Marty stood. 'Stay with him, Nat. Sister may need a bit of help.' Marty tried to leave but Glen cried out for him.

'I'll go,' Natalie said. 'You stay with him. He trusts you.'

Marty caught her hand and squeezed it. She met his gaze. 'Be careful.'

She nodded and headed out to find a man who looked to be in his early twenties standing there, yelling at Sister Dorset. Sister, to her absolute credit, hadn't even raised her voice but was a wall of steel against the man's demands.

'Please, Mr Hailstock. Calm down.'

'No. You people are not taking my kid from me. He belongs to me.'

'He needs medical treatment, Mr Hailstock. Surely you don't want your son to be sick.'

'There's nothing wrong with him. Never was. The woman just panicked and brought him in. Stupid idiot.'

'If you're referring to your wife, she did the right thing. Glen requires medical attention.'

Mr Hailstock hitched up his pants, snorted and glared at Sister. 'And you're hardly a match for me. I could snap you like a twig.'

Sister's answer was merely to raise a disbelieving eyebrow. 'You don't want to do anything silly, Mr Hailstock.'

'Stop calling me that and get out of my way.' With one large arm he shoved Sister Dorset out of his way and barrelled on through. Sister landed on the floor with a thud, wincing in pain. Natalie had noticed Cassie on the phone and knew the ward clerk had called Security. Help wouldn't be far away. Many parents and nursing staff had ushered their children back to their rooms, making sure they were safe.

Natalie took all this in at a glance and realised with a start that Mr Hailstock, with Sister now out of his way, was now headed in her direction. 'Are you next?' he growled.

Natalie had dealt with bullies before and, like Sister, there was no way she was going to let this man get to his son. 'Who are you looking for?' she asked, as though she was disinterested in the whole affair.

'My kid.'

'Which one in particular?'

'His name is Glen, and don't play games with me, girlie. I'm not in the mood. I'm not going to have any social worker *freak* telling me I can't see my kid. He's *my* kid. I can do what I want.'

'Actually, that's where you're wrong and, besides, Glen's not here.'

That stopped him for a moment before he shook his head. 'Nah. I saw his name written up there on that big white board. He's in *that* room.' Mr Hailstock pointed to the ward that housed four beds.

'He's not there. He's been taken down to X-Ray.' At her words, she saw the briefest flicker of hesitation in the man's eyes.

'Nah.' The man pointed to the only bed in the room that had a curtain around it. 'He's in there. I know it. If he's not, why is the curtain around it?'

'Because I was just about to pull it back when you came in, making a fuss.' On legs that felt like jelly, she forced herself to

walk to the curtain, praying that Marty had performed some sort
of miracle and made both himself and Glen disappear.

She found the edge of the curtain and opened it a little, peering
inside in an inconspicuous fashion. Marty was standing right
around at the other edge of the curtain, holding Glen and Mr Bear
securely in his arms. Their gazes locked and she realised they were
both on the same wavelength. He nodded to her and she realised
he was ready.

'Come and see for yourself,' she said to Mr Hailstock, and the
instant the man moved closer to the curtain, Marty slipped out.
'See,' she said as she slowly drew the shorter part of the curtain
back. 'He's not here.'

Mr Hailstock put his hands to his face and growled with frustration. It was just the diversion they needed and while the angry
man's back was turned, Marty whisked the frightened child from
the room. The other children in the room were crying in fright.

'Now that you've seen for yourself, would you like to come
and wait in the parents' room until Glen returns from X-Ray?'

Mr Hailstock shook his head. 'But I—'

'You're scaring the other children,' she said in her best no-
nonsense doctor voice. 'Now, either accompany me to the parents'
room or I'll have to call Security. You've caused enough of a
disruption in my ward for one morning, and I won't have any
more children frightened.'

He snarled at her and stalked out. Natalie wanted to collapse in
a puddle on the floor but she once more forced her body to comply
with the signals her brain was sending out and followed Mr
Hailstock from the room.

'Which way to X-Ray?'

'I'm sorry, Mr Hailstock. You won't be allowed into the radiology department, but if you'd like to—'

As she spoke, Mr Hailstock stopped walking and stared at the
two security officers who had come into the ward.

'Excuse me, sir, but we need to ask you to come with us.'

'I'm not going anywhere without my kid.' Then, to the horror
of everyone around, Mr Hailstock withdrew a switchblade from
his jeans and held it towards Natalie.

CHAPTER SIX

'SOMEONE find my kid. *Now!* Or else something bad's gonna happen to the lady doctor.'

'You don't want to do that, mate,' the security officer said, and Natalie watched as the man came slowly into the direct vision of Mr Hailstock. 'No one needs to get hurt.'

'That's right. So get my kid and keep your hands where I can see them.'

'All right. All right.' He put his hands in the air. 'No one needs to get hurt,' he said again. The security officer looked over at Natalie. 'Dr Fox. Where's Mr Hailstock's son?'

'In Radiology,' Natalie blatantly lied, unsure exactly what was going to happen next. How could she possibly signal to the security guard that little Glen was really in the next room with Marty and not in X-Ray at all? Oh, dear. What had she done? She'd thought she'd been protecting Glen by saying he wasn't there and now if the security guard called down to X-Ray and they said he wasn't there...

Natalie shut her eyes for a moment, trying to get control over her thoughts. She was behaving like a bumbling fool, and she wasn't a fool. It was her job to protect her patient and that's what she'd done.

'Hey!' At Mr Hailstock's shout, her eyes snapped open. He was now pointing his knife at the second security officer. 'Why don't you come around here and keep your buddy company? Right where I can see you. No sneaking up behind me, understand? Come on. Round you come.'

'I was just making sure Sister here was all right,' the security officer said, pointing to where Sister Dorset was sitting on a chair at the nurses' station.

'Don't play the wise guy. Now, get over there.' The security guard did as he was told. As he moved around, Natalie saw Marty come out of a room and slip behind Mr Hailstock. Her eyes widened in disbelief but she quickly schooled her expression lest she gave anything away. What was he doing? Where was Glen? He certainly wasn't holding the boy now and although there were quite a few children crying, she couldn't see whether one of them was Glen. She knew the three-year-old was all right otherwise Marty would still be with him.

She glanced down at her hands and realised she was starting to tremble. She clamped her hands together, willing herself to remain calm and focused. She dared a surreptitious look at where Marty now was and realised at the look in his eyes that he was definitely up to something, and that something was removing the threat to the paediatric ward.

'You!' Mr Hailstock pointed his finger at Cassie. 'Get on the phone and get my kid here now.'

Cassie looked at Natalie for confirmation and Natalie nodded. She picked up the phone and dialled. 'Lise? It's Cassie. Listen.' Cassie's voice was wavering slightly and she cleared her throat. 'Um, we have a patient down there. Glen Hailstock. Would you mind checking if he's finished?' Cassie paused a moment, then said clearly, 'That's OK. I'll wait while you find out.' She turned her attention to Mr Hailstock. 'They're going to find him.'

Mr Hailstock seemed to calm a little at this news and the instant he heaved a sigh of relief Natalie saw Marty move. Where she'd thought he might charge across the room and knock the other man to the floor, he did no such thing. He just waltzed in, as though he'd just entered the ward.

'Hey, what's going on?' he asked when he was just behind the boy's father. Mr Hailstock swung around again, pointing the knife at Marty. Natalie sucked in a breath, terror and fear in her eyes. The knife was only a few centimetres away from Marty's chest. With a quick lunge, Mr Hailstock could easily stab him through the heart.

'Sorry, mate,' Marty said jovially, and in one deft motion removed the knife from the man's hand. He continued walking and placed the knife on the nurses' desk. 'We don't allow weapons in Paediatrics. Not safe with so many children around. Now, if you want to wield a knife, I suggest you head on down to Theatres. Knives are allowed there.' He glanced across at Natalie. 'Aren't they, Nat? Or have I got Theatres mixed up with another department?'

He was so cool, calm and collected that for a moment everyone simply stared at him in stunned amazement, especially Mr Hailstock.

The security guards sprang into action and wrestled the stunned father to the floor, but not without a fight. Everyone moved out of the way as arms and legs seemed to be writhing in all directions.

In the next instant one security guard was thrown back and Mr Hailstock jumped up and headed towards the window. 'That's enough. Now, someone get my kid here or I'll jump.'

Marty frowned. 'Jump? But we're on the eighth floor, mate. That's not safe.'

Natalie smothered a nervous chuckle and quickly turned away in case the distraught man saw her.

'That's the idea.' He pointed to Cassie. 'Have they found him?' Mr Hailstock was now quite agitated as he edged towards the window. They all watched him in stunned disbelief. The man was really serious. He honestly thought he could jump through the window. Surely he realised it was double-glazed, shatterproof glass? There was no way he could get out. '*Have they found him?*' he yelled at Cassie.

'He's still being X-rayed.'

'No. Get him here, *now*. I'm sick of this and I mean it. I want my kid.'

The security guards were back on their feet and slowly walking towards him, one on either side.

'Stop! I'll jump. I swear. I've been through windows before. I know what to do. I'm not joking here.'

'You don't want to do that, Mr Hailstock,' the security officer said. 'Just come with us and we'll arrange for you to see your son. No one needs to get—'

'*No!*' Mr Hailstock yelled, and ran for the window, crashing into it with his shoulder and head. The noise was deafening and Natalie jumped in fright. The glass bowed but didn't break. In the next instant Mr Hailstock grunted in pain and fell to the floor. He didn't move.

Marty frowned and Natalie could have sworn she heard him say, 'Huh!' They both moved at the same time, edging over towards the man.

'Just a second,' the security guard said. 'Let me check him.'

They waited.

'He's out.' The security guard chuckled with incredulity. 'He's knocked himself unconscious.'

'Right,' said Sister Dorset in her best commanding voice. 'The drama is over. Everyone, see to your patients. Doctors, assess the damage to Mr Hailstock and arrange his transfer to a ward that accepts patients over the age of eighteen.' With that, she bustled off to settle her brood.

'Where's Glen?' Natalie asked.

'With Jim, the orderly. He was in one of the other rooms and I managed to peel poor Glen off me and hand him over.'

'Good. Mr Hailstock?' Natalie crouched down. 'Can you hear me?'

Marty had his fingers on the man's carotid pulse. 'Pulse feels fast, Nat. Let's check him. Cassie,' he called. 'Get an orthopod up here, stat.'

'He's really out,' she said as one of the nurses brought over a trolley containing the equipment they'd need to monitor their patient properly. 'Do his obs, please.' Natalie accepted the gloves handed to her by the nurse and pulled them on before checking the bleeding wound to Mr Hailstock's right temple. She pressed her fingers to the bleeding area. 'Can I have some gauze and a bandage, please?' Natalie said, and a moment later they were put into her free hand. She used the gauze pad to apply pressure to stem the bleeding before wrapping the bandage around Mr Hailstock's head, keeping the gauze pad in place.

'BP is 90 over 40, pulse is rapid, pupils equal and reacting to light, respiratory rate is rapid. Skin is quite pale, cold and clammy.'

'The body's having a delayed reaction to his mental anxiety,' Marty said. 'Get an IV line in to boost his fluids. Neuro obs every five minutes.' He took the stethoscope from around his neck and listened to Mr Hailstock's heart. 'No arrhythmias. Now that he's unconscious, his vitals should settle down.' Marty put the stethoscope on the floor. 'Let's see what damage he's done to his bones. The way he landed, that shoulder has got to be dislocated. I need a neck brace, a blanket and we'll need a pat-slide from another ward to shift him onto the barouche,' he said as he continued to feel along the man's arm. 'No sign of open fractures but I want his arm X-rayed.'

'Mr Hailstock?' Natalie called again, but there was still no response. 'Skull X-rays as well just to check he doesn't have a hairline fracture, although he'll definitely need stitches for that gash just above his temple.'

'What size needles do we need for the IV? Have we got needles big enough?' Marty asked the nurse before shaking his head. 'I'm not used to patients this big any more.'

Natalie smiled and agreed. 'Check what we've got and if necessary go to the next ward and get supplies from there,' she told the nurse. Sister Dorset came over to check their progress.

'We're doing fine here, Sister,' Marty reported. 'How's Glen?'

'Sitting in his cot, clutching his teddy bear. I'll be filing a report on Mr Hailstock and will need your input and signatures.'

'Of course,' Natalie replied.

'Ortho's on their way,' Cassie reported.

Thankfully, Mr Hailstock's vital signs had settled down by the time Richard and Beth walked into the ward. 'Drumming up business for us?' Beth asked Marty.

'Why should Paediatrics have all the fun? We thought we'd share.'

'How sweet,' Beth said, bending down as she pulled on a pair of gloves.

'What have we got?' Richard asked briskly.

'Male approximately twenty years old, right shoulder dislocation, suspected fractures to the right arm, scapula and a possible hairline fracture to the skull,' Marty reported.

'Laceration to the head just above the temple—will need sutures. Patient is stable but hasn't regained consciousness.'

'Good.' Richard went to the desk. 'I need an admission form.'

'What on earth happened?' Beth asked as she felt Mr Hailstock's arm. 'I need to see what damage is done to that shoulder before we relocate it,' she mumbled, more to herself than anyone in particular.

'What happened?' Marty repeated Beth's question. 'My darling Beth, you wouldn't believe me if I told you.'

'Try me.'

So Marty explained what had transpired to an astounded Beth.

'He pulled a knife on Natalie?' Richard was amazed and for a moment forgot the forms he was filling in. Beth looked at her friend, stunned.

'Are you all right?'

Richard crossed to Natalie's side. 'Of course she's not all right.' He met her gaze and held it and she saw genuine concern which, for some reason, surprised her. 'Beth, organise X-rays for Mr Hailstock, then organise for him to be added to the end of my operating list this afternoon.'

'I'm on it.' Beth smiled at Natalie. 'Glad to see you're OK.'

'Mr Hailstock finally gets to go to X-Ray,' Cassie said, chuckling.

Richard took Natalie's hand in his, surprising her further. 'You must have received an awful fright.'

She looked down at their hands and then back to him, amazed at his concern and open display of affection. She opened her mouth to talk but he went on.

'Just as well Security were here to deal with things. They know how to get through to people like that.'

Natalie frowned at his words, her throat now beginning to work. 'But it wasn't Security, it was—'

'Never mind. It's over now.' He gave her hand a little squeeze and edged closer. 'I think I can even shuffle my schedule and make your department Christmas party tonight. That should help you get over your shock. Not a nice thing to happen but, then, this is a nasty world. Anyway, I'd better go. We'll talk later.' He dropped her hand and walked out, not looking back.

Natalie just stood there and stared at him, totally confused. Hadn't he got the message? Didn't he realise she'd called their relationship off? Why was he coming to the Christmas party tonight? She didn't need any help getting over her shock and if she did, it wouldn't be from him.

'Nat?'

She didn't move.

'Nat?' Marty's voice finally broke through and he placed his arm about her shoulders. 'Hey.' He came to stand in front of her, placing his hands on her shoulders. 'You all right?'

Natalie finally focused on his gorgeous blue eyes, bringing her back to reality. 'Yeah. I'm OK.'

'You sure?'

'Yes.' She smiled at him. 'Except for being mad at you for putting yourself in danger.'

'I knew what I was doing.' He waved away her concern.

'Are *you* all right, Dr Hero?'

He grinned and slung an arm around her shoulders. 'Absolutely. After all, I am Dr Hero!'

'Oh, no. Now it's going to go to your head,' she groaned as they walked to the nurses' station. 'Seriously, Marty.' She turned to face him and he dropped his arm. 'You are all right, aren't you?'

'Yes.' He met her gaze and she could see for herself that he was indeed fine about the whole thing. 'Of course,' he said as he straightened his shoulders and placed his hands on his hips in a superhero pose, 'I am Dr Hero. Here to save the ward from un-wanted visitors.' He was thinking more about Everley as he spoke, rather than Mr Hailstock. 'Taking them by surprise is my speciality. I am courageous and fearless.'

'Dr Williams,' Sister Dorset said from behind him, and Natalie laughed when Marty jumped. When he turned to grin at Sister, Natalie realised he'd been playacting. 'Will you kindly get back to work? The orthopods are taking care of Mr Hailstock and we have a ward round to finish.'

Again, Marty's cool, calm and collected demeanour came to the fore. 'Not just yet, Sister.'

'I beg your pardon?' She glared at him.

'Not until I've had a closer look at your wrist.'

'My wrist is fine.'

'No, it's not,' he said softly, as though he were dealing with one of his young patients. Once more, Marty was completely baffling Natalie in the way he was handling things. 'If you'll please come with me to the treatment room, I'll have a quick look. Dr Fox, would you care to assist me? After all, it's been a while since I've seen a wrist this...' He hesitated and smiled sweetly at Sister. 'This mature for quite a while, and a second opinion would be appreciated.'

'Of course,' Natalie replied. Sister Dorset glared at them both before walking stiffly to the treatment room. Marty followed her, grinning confidently at Natalie as if to say, Winning this bet is going to be a cinch.

'That man is way too perfect.' Cassie sighed romantically once Marty had disappeared from view. 'Everyone likes him, the staff, the patients, and now even Sister Dorset seems to be taking a shine to him.'

'Yes.' Natalie frowned as she headed to the treatment room. She wasn't quite sure what she could do to sabotage Marty's chances of winning their bet and at that moment she wasn't sure she wanted to. If he did win, what would he propose? All she knew was with Marty anything was possible.

'Now, Sister Dorset,' Marty said as he washed and dried his

hands before pulling on a pair of gloves, 'how's the range of motion?' He tenderly took Sister's hand in his and gently checked it, watching her eyes in case she grimaced.

Natalie, too, was watching carefully as she washed and dried her hands. 'Please, tell us if it's tender, Sister.'

'It's fine,' Sister maintained briskly.

'I don't think it needs an X-ray,' Marty declared. 'Nat? What do you think?'

Natalie pulled on a pair of gloves and gave Sister's wrist a brief examination. 'I don't think it's fine, Sister is putting on a brave front. But neither do I think it needs X-raying. Nothing feels broken, although resting it for the next few days wouldn't go amiss.'

'I'm well aware of first-aid procedures,' Sister Dorset retorted.

'Then I can rely on you to adhere to them,' Marty said firmly as he took an elastic bandage from the cupboard, then hunted around for an ice-pack. 'Where are the ice-packs, Nat?'

'I'll get one,' she said, and disappeared out the room.

'So, is all this to get into my good books, Dr Williams?' Sister asked as Marty started to wind the bandage around her arm.

'Meaning?'

'Meaning I believe you have a bet going with Dr Fox.'

Marty was taken aback and concentrated on his bandaging before smiling at Sister. 'No pulling the wool over your eyes, is there? Although I'd just like to add that even if there wasn't a bet, I'd still have rendered first aid.'

Sister nodded, acknowledging his words.

'Besides, I didn't think you listened to hospital gossip,' Marty continued as he secured the bandage. 'Do you think you'll need a sling or will you honestly try not to use it too much for the remainder of the day?'

'I do not need a sling, Doctor, and neither do I actively listen to gossip, but sometimes it is rather hard not to overhear. I'd just like to warn you that I'm no pushover and although you may have been born with a barrel of natural charm, you will only get to call me by my first name when you have earned that right. Bet or no bet. Do I make myself clear?'

Sister glared at him and Marty couldn't help but smile, genuinely liking Sister Dorset more and more. 'Perfectly, Sister.'

Natalie came back into the room with the ice-pack. 'Here you are, Sister.'

'Thank you, Doctor.' She put the ice-pack on her wrist and then glanced at them both. 'May we return to the ward round now or must I sit in the treatment room for the next fifteen minutes?'

'Will you be good?' Marty asked. 'Do as the doctors have told you?'

'I will.'

'What do you think, Nat?'

'I think we can trust Sister.'

Marty looked at the sister. 'Yes, I think we *can* trust Sister,' Marty said pointedly, and watched as Sister Dorset's lips twitched with humour before she quickly regained her composure.

'Thank you. Let's get on then, staff.' She stood and headed out of the treatment room.

'You do like living dangerously,' Natalie said with a laugh as they took off their gloves and quickly tidied the treatment room before following Sister out.

'Just trying to win that bet.'

'Is it working? I'm only asking so I know whether or not I need to resort to underhand tactics.'

'I'm not at liberty to say.' They finished ward round without further complication then Marty looked towards Glen's room. 'I'm going to go check on Glen.'

Natalie nodded. 'Do you think he might need a sedative?'

'He may do. It depends how distraught the poor kid is.'

'I'm going to head to the playroom and spend a bit of time there. After all the drama we've had here, I need a bit of downtime.'

'Good idea.'

They headed off in different directions and Natalie was pleased to find several children enjoying themselves in the playroom. Some were drawing, some were making more Christmas decorations for the already crowded Christmas tree at the entrance to the ward. Others were playing with little plastic building bricks that snapped together. Georgina, who was eight and a half and had been admitted with a fractured tibia three days previously, had built a Christmas tree with the bricks and was starting on some square boxes for presents.

'Well done,' Natalie praised her. 'You're very clever with them.'

Georgina was trying to get two red bricks apart, without much success. She held them out to Natalie. 'Can you get these apart for me, please?'

'Sure.' Natalie had to use her fingernails to get them apart. 'Wow. They're tough.'

'Yeah. Sometimes I use my teeth to separate them.'

'Try not to,' Natalie warned her. 'But I know what you mean. I remember playing with those sorts of bricks when I was your age and they're just as tough now as they were back then.'

Georgina continued making her presents, her leg in its cast propped up on some pillows and her crutches to one side. Natalie sat down at one of the tables and picked up a piece of paper. While she talked to the children, she folded the paper a couple of times into a rectangle and then started to cut. When she'd finished, she carefully pulled and opened it, making a line of paper dolls.

'Wow, Dr Nat. That's so cool.'

'You can decorate that and we'll put it up around the ward,' she said, handing it to one of the girls to colour in.

'Dr Nat is very talented,' Marty said as he walked through the door and took up a chair opposite Natalie. He, too, folded some paper and began to cut, but his paper dolls came out looking a little different from Natalie's smooth-shaped ones. 'Hmm. You're going to have to give me another lesson. It's been years since I've done this.'

Natalie showed him and the other children what to do and soon they were all cutting out paper dolls. She even cut one lot with Santa hats.

'They're so cool,' one boy said.

'Cool Santa.' Marty nodded his head. 'And he'll need to be cool, coming to Australia. It's way too hot here for his red velvet suit, but he does insist upon wearing it.'

Georgina laughed and in the next instant started choking. Natalie and Marty were out of their chairs in an instant. Georgina kept trying to suck air in.

'Try and cough,' Marty said, his voice calm and controlled. Natalie took Georgina's hand in hers.

'It's all right, Georgina. We're here to help you.' Natalie looked at the rest of the children in the playroom. 'She'll be fine. Can one of you get a nurse for me, please?' No sooner had she voiced the request than most of the kids left the room. Georgina was still gasping for air.

'I'm going to pick you up,' Marty told her. 'Then I'm going to firmly hit you between the shoulder blades and hopefully we'll remove the obstruction.'

Natalie helped him get her up and quickly stacked a few chairs together, giving the usually small chairs extra height so Georgina could lean over them.

'All right. Try and cough if you can.'

Natalie shifted Georgina's torso so she was leaning well over the back of the chairs, her head down, before Marty gave four sharp blows with the flat of his hand between the girl's shoulder blades. On the fourth blow Georgina coughed again and out came a small red building brick.

'There we go,' Marty said triumphantly. 'Dr Hero strikes again.'

'We're lucky Dr Hero was around,' Natalie said to Georgina as she helped the girl upright. The child looked at her before bursting into tears. 'Oh, darling.' The little girl buried her face into Natalie who immediately put her arms around her. 'It's all right. It was frightening and it's over. You're fine now.'

One of the nurses came into the room as Marty scooped the offending brick off the floor. 'It's smaller than my thumbnail,' he said as he held it out to the nurse. 'Wash this, will you, please?' He grinned as he handed it over, then turned his attention back to Georgina. 'Don't worry about it, Georgie. Let's get you back to bed and perhaps order some ice cream to soothe your sore throat.'

Georgina lifted her head momentarily from Natalie and looked at Marty.

'Ah, I thought the mention of ice cream might do the trick. Think you can walk on your crutches or do you want me to get a wheelchair to take you back to bed?'

'Wheelch—' She stopped and swallowed, grimacing at the pain in her throat.

'Wheelchair it is,' Marty replied. 'Be back in a moment.'

Natalie looked down at Georgina. 'We'll give your mum a call and let her know what's happened, then we'll see about ordering you some ice cream. Let me see if I can guess your favourite flavour. Don't talk, just nod or shake your head.' She sat the girl down on one of the chairs and started guessing different flavours. Georgina shook and nodded her head as appropriate.

'Um...' Natalie thought of a different flavour just as Marty came back in with a wheelchair. 'What other flavours of ice cream can you think of?' she asked him. 'I've done vanilla, chocolate and strawberry. Pineapple and butterscotch.'

'Banana?' Marty asked, and Georgina nodded enthusiastically.

'Oh, yeah! Dr Hero is on a roll,' he said, puffing out his chest.

'Dr Hero might need help keeping his ego in check,' Natalie suggested with a smile. Once Georgina was in the wheelchair, Marty pushed her back to her bed while Natalie carried her crutches. When Georgina was settled, Natalie performed an examination of her throat and declared that everything was fine. 'A bit of banana-flavoured ice cream, if we can possibly find it, and you'll be back to your usual self in no time.'

'And I'm never going to put one of those bricks in my mouth again,' Georgina whispered emphatically.

'Glad to hear it.'

Natalie and Marty headed to the nurses' station to update Georgina's notes. 'Have you called her mother?' Natalie asked Cassie.

'Just got off the phone with her. Do we need an ENT registrar up here?'

Marty shook his head. 'I don't think so. Nat's checked her out and, apart from being frightened, she'll be fine.'

'OK. I'd better call down to the kitchen to see if it's too late to get some ice cream sent up with the lunch orders.'

Natalie looked at her watch. 'Is that the time?'

'Lunchtime already, is it?' Marty asked. 'If we're quiet, how about we go have lunch together and then tackle the afternoon with gusto?'

'OK.'

'Just let me check on Glen again and I'll be all yours.'

Natalie forced a smile, glancing quickly at Cassie who, although she was on the phone, raised her eyebrows and grinned. Marty headed off and a moment later Cassie put down the phone.

'Ice cream has been ordered for Georgina.'

'Thanks.'

Cassie motioned to Marty. 'Is he always this jovial?'

Natalie thought for a moment. He certainly hadn't been jovial in Fiji and there had been many times at school where, after she'd begged him to be serious, he'd oblige. 'There is a serious side to him,' she eventually replied. 'He's good to have around in an emergency and always keeps his head.'

'As any good doctor should,' Cassie remarked with a smirk. 'I'm glad there's more to him than just laughter, although I think it would take a woman years to unlock it.'

Natalie thought about Cassie's words as she walked to the cafeteria with Marty. It was true that Marty held himself back when he dated, but he certainly didn't do that with her. With the kiss they'd almost shared in the car park, did that mean he saw her as something more than a friend? She knew he trusted her but was he willing to trust her with his heart?

Was that what she wanted?

CHAPTER SEVEN

THANKFULLY, the afternoon passed without further drama and finally Marty drove Natalie home so she'd have time to bathe and change before he picked her up for the Christmas party.

Once she was in her dress, she changed her earrings, putting on a pair of dangling Christmas trees that had little flashing lights in them. They didn't match her dress but it was Christmas after all. She paused, her gaze dropping to a very special box which held a piece of very special jewellery. Slowly she reached out and picked it up. Opening it slowly, she ran her finger over the bracelet inside, thrilling at the touch. This was the Christmas present Marty had given her on their last day of school. Should she wear it tonight? She usually only wore it on special occasions and this was certainly a special occasion.

Natalie took it out of the box and put it on. It was pretty and quite inexpensive compared to some of the jewellery she'd bought or been given as an adult, but it was her absolute favourite. Her new emotions towards Marty made her feel highly self-conscious about wearing it. Would he think she'd worn it just to get his attention?

She took the bracelet off and placed it back in the box, which she then put back in her drawer. She heard his car engine in the driveway, which snapped her back to reality. Quickly she finished brushing her hair and slipped on her shoes before collecting her bag and heading downstairs.

When she opened the door, he stood before her, looking incredible in a dark suit. Natalie's jaw hung open as she appraised him. It was the first time since...well...ever, she realised, that she'd seen him formally dressed. 'You're wearing a tie,' she declared, and instantly realised what a stupid thing that had been to say.

'Yes.' He pulled at it, obviously uncomfortable. 'Why do we have to swelter in this get-up and you girls get to dress in skimpy things?' He gestured to her dress, his gaze travelling the length of her. 'Which will keep you cool,' he finished, his voice a little thicker.

'Why do you get to wear comfortable shoes and I have to wear these potential ankle-twisters?' she argued right back.

They paused, neither of them speaking, but their bodies were certainly talking to each other.

Marty broke the moment, clearing his throat. 'Ready to go?'

'Uh...yes.' She picked up her bag and keys before checking the town house was locked. She was a little disappointed that he hadn't said anything about her dress. It was burgundy in colour and ended at mid-thigh, with a scooped neckline and shoestring straps. Then again, she hadn't said that he'd looked nice so perhaps he was equally as annoyed with her for not paying him a compliment.

She glanced at him as they walked to the car but he appeared in quite good spirits. He unlocked her door and then to her utter astonishment he scooped her up into his arms. She squealed but he merely smiled.

'Let's get you into the car in a dignified manner.'

'Oh, yeah. Real dignified,' she countered as he placed her gently on the seat. 'You could at least have warned me,' she snapped, still feeling the warmth of where his arms had been around her and the scent of his aftershave had instantly electrified her entire body.

'My apologies.' He took her hand in his and kissed it in a gentlemanly fashion, making her body quiver even more.

'Just get in and drive,' she said, trying desperately to pull herself together.

They didn't talk much on the journey and once they arrived at the party venue, Marty again came around to help her out. This time, though, as she slid from the seat with his help, he kept his distance and she was a little disappointed that he hadn't tried a repeat of that morning's attempted kiss.

And if he had? she asked herself.

You'd have kissed him, came the answer. Natalie swallowed, her breathing increasing at the thought. She wanted to kiss Marty. In fact, if she admitted it to herself, she'd been wanting to kiss him ever since he'd waltzed back into her life.

She forced a smile when he looked down at her, not wanting him to guess her thoughts. They made their way inside, Marty linking arms with her. 'Let's make sure you don't twist your ankle,' he said softly.

They were greeted warmly by their friends and colleagues, no one seeming surprised they'd come together. It wasn't just members of the paediatric staff but the hospital staff in general who had bought tickets to support the fundraising aspect of the evening. Christmas was the season of giving and with the money they raised they would be able to purchase a vital piece of equipment for their unit.

The function room was decked out in different-coloured tinsel, which made Natalie feel as though she was leaving all her cares and worries behind her and just concentrating on the spirit of Christmas. They were shown to their table and, from what she could see, everyone enjoyed their scrumptious dinner, complete with turkey, ham and chicken. Natalie loved every single bite but was unable to finish her Christmas plum pudding with brandy sauce, much to her chagrin. When she pushed it aside, declaring herself full, she was astonished when Marty picked up the bowl and finished it off.

She blinked at him in shock as tingles flooded her body. Watching him wolf down her half-eaten dessert shouldn't have given her a feeling of intimacy, but it did. No one else at their table saw anything wrong with it so Natalie took a deep breath and tried to ignore her body's reaction to the man who sat beside her.

'Want to dance?' Marty asked as the lights dimmed, the coloured lights flickered on the dance floor and the volume level of the song the DJ had been playing increased. He shed his jacket and took off his tie, undoing the top two buttons of his shirt. Natalie stared at him for a moment, unable to believe how incredibly handsome he looked. The clean-cut image didn't suit him, but ruffle him up a bit and he was irresistible.

Marty took her hand in his and immediately zingers shot up her arm. Her reactions to him were becoming more intense the more time they spent together…and the more he touched her. Just his hand resting on her shoulder or linking arms with her or taking her hand as he'd just done. It didn't stop there, she realised. His smile or even just their gazes meeting was enough to send her body into overdrive. How on earth was she supposed to stand up on the dance floor when he would be almost squashed up against her? It would be impossible.

'I'm not much of a dancer.' She cleared her throat, surprised to find her throat so dry.

'Oh, yeah? What about the school play? You know, when you wore your streaker suit.'

She took a sip of water. 'That was choreographed, Marty.

Besides, I'm a little full. If I went out there, I'd just roll around the floor.'

He considered that for a moment. 'That might be fun to watch.'

She gave his hand a squeeze and pulled away. 'You go. Have fun. I'll let my dinner settle and then maybe I'll dance.'

He looked as though he was going to dispute her words but shrugged and stood up. 'Anyone care to join me on the dance floor?' he asked the table in general, and received overwhelming responses from almost everyone…most of whom were female.

They all trooped onto the dance floor and for a moment Natalie regretted her decision. She wanted to be there with him, to be having fun with him, but at the moment she simply couldn't rely on her body not to give away the extent of her growing feelings for her friend.

She waved to Marty, who was dancing like a maniac out of control but making everyone around him laugh. He was surrounded by a gaggle of women shaking their assets at him to the latest pop version of a Christmas carol and Natalie couldn't help the pang of jealousy that coursed through her.

Marty beckoned her to join him, but she simply smiled and shook her head. She was not about to join the long line of women trying to impress him. Instead, she checked her watch and glanced around the room, pleasantly surprised when she saw Beth heading in her direction.

'Hey, you made it.'

Beth sank thankfully into the vacant chair beside her friend. 'I didn't think I'd ever finish in Theatre.'

'How's Mr Hailstock?'

'All patched up and back together. He was in Recovery when I left, a security guard posted at the end of his bed.'

Natalie smiled. 'I hardly think he's in any position to cause more trouble. Sedated and bandaged.'

Beth agreed. 'Still, it's protocol and although he didn't hurt anyone besides himself, he's still being charged.'

Natalie nodded. 'I called the ward before coming here to find out how Glen was. Apparently his mother realised she had to speak out about what was happening at home so there are more charges coming Mr Hailstock's way.'

'Anyway, we're here to have fun and be jolly. Isn't this supposed to be a Christmas party?' As she spoke, she glanced around the room, waving to Marty on the dance floor. 'I am so hungry. Is there any food left?'

'There might be. Want me to go check with the kitchen staff?' As she spoke, a gorgeous waiter walked by and Beth instantly grabbed him.

'Hi.' She smiled sweetly at the man. 'I've just come out of a gruelling operating session and I'm starving. Is there any possibility of leftovers in the kitchen?'

'Sure.' He held out his hand to her. 'Come with me and we'll see what we can do.'

Beth's smile increased as she accepted his hand, giving Natalie a look that said, What do you think about that, then? She disappeared with the waiter through a swinging white door.

'Hey!' Marty was beside her a minute later. 'You have got to come and dance with me.'

'I'm good. Thanks.'

He looked around at the tables as he sat down. 'Where did Beth go?'

'She found a nice handsome waiter to satisfy her hunger—for food,' Natalie added, but they both grinned.

'Typical Beth.' He took her hand in his again. 'Come on, Nat. Time to dance.'

'You have enough partners.' She gestured to the dance floor where a few of the women were glancing their way, impatiently waiting for Marty to return.

'Don't mind them. *I* want to dance with *you*. Come on, Nat. It's Christmas.'

'It's the first week in December, Marty.'

'Close enough.' She glanced over his shoulder at the doorway and he followed her gaze. 'Waiting for Everley? He's not going to show.'

'I know.'

'Then what are you waiting for?'

'My dinner to go down. I don't fancy being sick on the dance floor.'

'You won't be sick. You didn't even finish your dessert.'

'No. *You* did.' She felt that warm tingle return at the mention of that shared intimacy.

'I'm not going to give up.'

'I believe you. Just give me a few more minutes.'

'OK.' He leaned back in the chair.

'You can go.'

'I'm fine here. I'll wait with you.' He watched her for a moment before saying, 'Are you disappointed Everley didn't show?'

'No.'

'Don't lie to me, Nat. I've seen you checking your watch, looking at the door. Now that Beth's here, you must know that even if Everley had been held up in Theatre, it's now well and truly finished.'

'Just like Richard and myself. We're through, Marty. You know that.'

'Really? You know, the guy was never really into you in the first place.'

'I think the same could be said of me.' She shrugged. 'I just want to make sure he accepts I don't want to see him any more.' She sighed and shook her head. 'Who knows when he'll eventually get the message that it's over?'

Marty leaned even closer, his mouth near her ear. 'Have you?' His breath fanned down her neck, causing goose-bumps to break out. Natalie caught her breath and tried not to be affected by the mesmerising scent whirling around him. All rational thought deserted her and all she could concentrate on was the minute distance between them.

She wet her lips and nodded. 'I know it's over.' She leaned back, trying to put some distance between them. 'I need some air.' Natalie pushed her chair back and stood, her feet wobbling a bit in the high-heeled shoes until she got her balance.

Marty was on his feet, one hand coming around her waist to steady her, the other reaching for her hand. 'Those shoes are lethal. Let me help you.'

'I'll be fine,' she protested, but he didn't answer. Instead, he led her out to the balcony, the warm December air hitting them. 'It's a little muggy out here.'

'When isn't it muggy in Sydney in December?' he asked rhetorically. 'I think we're supposed to hit the forty-degree mark for the next few days.'

Natalie groaned as she ran a hand down the skirt of her burgundy dress. Her motive when buying it had been to keep as cool as possible but it also made her feel special and beautiful.

'Wherever did you get that dress?' Marty dropped his arm from her waist and she was extremely grateful. The warmth his touch had evoked had set her entire body on fire—no wonder she'd had a bit of trouble walking. He quickly rolled up his shirtsleeves before gripping the balcony railing with both hands and looking out at the city lights beyond them.

'Why?' She glanced down at her dress. 'Don't you like it?'

He snorted with derision. 'Hate it.'

'Why?' She frowned, a little hurt at his reply. 'I thought it was pretty.' She'd hoped he'd think the same thing.

'I hate it because it makes you look irresistible.'

'Oh.' Her heart rate immediately intensified.

'I'm having trouble keeping my hands off you, Nat.'

His words ignited her body and she immediately felt breathless and light-headed. 'Marty!' She closed her eyes and shook her head. 'Don't say things like that.'

'Why not?'

She swallowed, her tongue coming out to wet her lips again, and Marty groaned. Her eyes snapped open and she found him watching her intently.

'Why not, Nat?'

'Because...'

'Because why?'

'Because we're friends.'

'*Curious* friends. You even admitted as much this morning.'

Natalie sighed. 'It seems so long ago.'

'You *are* attracted to me, aren't you?' He brushed her hair back from her face, thrilled she'd left it loose. 'You do feel this...this *thing* between us?' His hand brushed her neck and she gasped, unable to break eye contact. 'See? Your body tells me you're attracted. What about your mind? Has it accepted the fact yet?'

'Marty.' His name was a tortured whisper and she was desperately losing control. 'I do want to but—'

'But you're over-thinking this.'

'You're under-thinking it.'

'No.' He shook his head, his fingers sifting through her hair ensuring her every sense stayed alert and tuned to his touch. 'I've thought about this for years.'

'Years?' That stunned her.

'Don't you remember the last day of school?'

'Yes.'

'I wanted to kiss you then.' He gave her a wry smile. 'I know we were friends and very young, but I was curious. I wanted to know but at the same time I didn't.' He shrugged. 'If I liked it a lot, there was nothing I could do about it because I was leaving Sydney.'

'And if you didn't like it?'

'Then it would have helped me to leave with no regrets. So I put your present into your hands, said something silly to make you smile and left.'

'You said I'd finally have peace in my chemistry class.' She smiled at the memory but he didn't return it.

'And *did* you?' His gaze was intent on holding hers and it was impossible for her to look away.

'No. It was boring.'

'Glad to hear it.'

Neither of them spoke for a moment as their minds absorbed everything that had been said. Their bodies were having a completely different conversation. His touch, the way he was tenderly caressing her hair, her neck, her cheek...it was enough to drive her to distraction.

'So...you were curious back then. What about Fiji?'

'Fiji was mildly different.'

'You weren't curious?'

'Oh, I was curious all right. I wanted to drown myself in you, lose myself in you. Forget about everything that had happened to me and find comfort in your arms.'

She opened her mouth to say something but nothing came out.

'I also needed you as my friend, to listen to my tale of woe and tell me everything would be all right. In fact, I needed that more, which was why my curiosity was pushed aside.'

Natalie swallowed. 'What about now?' The words came out as a breathless but pleading whisper. Right now she wanted his mouth on hers and she knew that need was reflected in her gaze.

'Now? Well, for a start, I'm not leaving the city. I'm stuck at this hospital for the next few years at least, and as I'm not recovering from a relationship, I can give way to the curiosity.' His gaze was flicking between her eyes and her lips, his visual caress increasing the tension in both of them.

'What if we give in to this...this thing between us and you don't like it?' she asked with nervous anticipation.

'I doubt that.'

'How do you know?'

'I *don't*. That's the point.' Feeling exasperated with her, he dropped his hand and moved away, raking his fingers through his hair. 'Are you sure you want to do this? Because you're giving me mixed signals, Nat.' He paused before asking, 'Are you sure this isn't about Everley?'

'No. I've already told you it's over. I know Richard is definitely not the man for me. I used to watch him and admire his dedication and wish I could be like that.'

'You are dedicated.' He jumped to her defence.

'I know, and I've realised I have a completely different focus.'

'Yeah, one that doesn't require your head to be stuck up your butt.'

Natalie chuckled at his words.

'Everley's a jerk, Nat, and a fool because he didn't realise exactly who the woman was right in front of him. Well, I *do* realise who you are and I *like* who you are. I always have.'

They were silent for a moment. 'What if it's not good?' she asked quietly, knowing they were both still thinking about the kiss they so desperately wanted to share.

'What if it is?'

'Exactly. What if it is? What then?'

Marty shook his head impatiently and within an instant had covered the distance between them, pulling her into his arms and pressing his mouth to hers in one swift motion. In that first taste, while she adjusted to his actions, he knew…knew she was everything he'd ever dreamed of. If she was this incredible after the first moment, his dreams were about to explode.

After the initial shock she relaxed and wound her arms about his neck, sighing into the kiss. Her mouth was smooth and warm and, oh, so ready for him. It was as though her lips had been made specifically for *him* to kiss, and he was relishing every second.

He slowly slid his hands up her back and beneath the silkiness of her hair his fingers made contact with her skin. Tenderly he touched her shoulder blades, loving the feel of his skin on hers in such an intimate way. When she groaned, he took that as an invitation to increase the intensity of the kiss.

Her mouth opened beneath his and they went on a mutual journey of discovery, going deeper into their relationship than they'd ever dared before. It was exciting, enthralling and exhilarating, and she couldn't get enough. Why in the world hadn't she kissed him years ago? If she'd known it was going to be like this, they could have been doing it for the past week since his return into her life.

Never before had any other kiss made her feel like this. Richard's kisses had initially made her knees go weak. Marty's turned her entire body to mush and she leaned closer into him, not only wanting his firm body pressed against her own but to find more stability to keep her from sliding to the floor in a boneless mess.

It was Marty's turn to groan as he gathered her as close as he possibly could, still giving and receiving in equal portions, feeding his need. He'd been a fool not to take the opportunity years ago, but the years of waiting had only made it better. She was everything he'd known she would be and finally, when he thought his lungs would burst if he didn't drag oxygen into them, he reluctantly lifted his head from hers, but he didn't relinquish his hold on her delectable body.

Both of them gasping for air, she leaned her head on his chest, listening to the wild pounding rhythm of his heartbeat.

'Nat?'

'*Wow!*'

'Yeah. *Wow!*' He chuckled and continued moving his thumbs in little circles on her back.

'Marty, that was...'

'*Amazing,*' they said in unison.

'And I didn't even need to drag out the mistletoe.'

She laughed, her breathing almost back to normal, but she still wasn't sure whether she could stand without his help. There was no rush so they simply stood there, absorbed in each other, while the world around them continued to move.

As reality slowly returned, Natalie couldn't help feeling highly self-conscious. It was ridiculous really. This was Marty! Her friend. The friend she'd just kissed. Beginning to feel uncomfortable, unsure what was supposed to happen next, she gently eased from his arms, finding it difficult to look at him.

'Want to go in?' he asked, one arm still around her back. She turned so she was looking over the balcony, her body tucked into his.

'Uh...yes. No. Oh, I don't know,' she wailed. 'Now I'm even more confused.' She shifted and he dropped his arm. Finally raising her gaze to meet his, she found him watching her intently. 'What do we do now, Marty? We've satisfied our curiosity and kissed. Now what?'

He shrugged. 'We can do it again.'

She laughed without humour. 'Spoken like a man.'

'What? What do you want me to say, Nat? That kiss was spectacular and unique and I'm not going to have a post-mortem on it.'

'But what about us? Does this change our friendship or was the kiss just an experimental thing?'

'Why does anything need to change?'

It was the wrong thing to say, or at least Natalie took it the wrong way. He saw the hurt come into her beautiful brown eyes and wished he could explain himself better. Explain that he'd been a complete fool and fallen in love with her and that he wanted her in his life for ever. But he knew if he said those words right now, he'd risk losing her for ever. She wasn't ready to hear them and he wasn't quite sure he was ready to say them out loud.

All he knew was that he'd needed to taste her, to feel her mouth against his, to have his hands on her body, holding her close. The need had been too great for him to fight and now, due to his inability to explain his feelings, he was paying the price.

Natalie moved from the railing, taking a few steps away from him.

'Nat. I didn't mean it like that.' He groaned and shook his head. 'All I'm saying is, let's just take things one step at a time.'

'Why? So you can figure out how to extricate yourself from your harem? You don't need to do that on account of me, Marty. I'm just the old friend. Go! Have fun with the masses of women you like to date.'

'They're just dates, Nat.'

'Like this? In a romantic, secluded atmosphere where you can kiss them?' Her hand was reaching for the door handle.

'Nat. Wait.' He held out his hand. 'I haven't kissed any of them.'

She gave him a sceptical look.

'It's true. You can ask them if you don't believe me. Kissing is... Kissing is personal, it's intimate.' He shifted his weight. 'Let's go somewhere where we can talk this out.'

'No, Martin.' She shook her head sadly, her hair swishing from side to side. 'Right now, I need to be alone...and I'd appreciate it if you didn't drop around for a few days.'

'What if Beth wants my company?'

'Oh, that's right. You haven't conquered Beth yet, although you looked like you were well on your way this morning.'

'What are you—?'

'I saw her kiss you. The Martin Williams charm strikes again.' She shook her head. 'I can't believe I fell for it.' Her voice cracked on the last few words and she grimaced. The pain was there in her voice and she was annoyed with herself for showing it. He could probably read the vulnerability in her face and right now he had the advantage over her. He had the ability to inflict long-lasting emotional pain on her and the fact that he wasn't readily jumping in to deny anything she was saying, only made her realise what a fool she'd been to fall for his well-practised, seductive art.

Wrenching back a sob, she opened the door and stepped inside.

'Natalie!' he called, but she'd gone.

Marty wasn't sure whether to follow her or not. They'd come together so how was she going to get home?

He headed for the door but stopped with his hand over the handle. He needed to let her cool off. Anything he said to her now, even if he blurted out the truth about his feelings, would be misconstrued. He'd just succeeded in alienating her when that was the last thing he wanted to do. It was better to leave her... But he wouldn't leave her for long.

He hit himself in the head. 'How could you have been so stupid?' He paused and shook his head. 'Because you're in love,' he murmured softly into the night. Kissing Nat had been amazing and the feeling that he'd finally come home couldn't be shaken. It was right, *so* right between the two of them. He had to believe they would sort everything out or he'd go insane. He wasn't a fool like Everley. He appreciated everything about Nat and he would spend the rest of his life showing her *exactly* how much.

With that resolution firmly made, he returned inside just in time to see Natalie heading for the door, Beth behind her, pulling her car keys from her bag. He watched them and just as Beth reached the door their gazes met. Beth shrugged, a questioning look in her eyes.

Marty held up his thumb and little finger in the 'phone' signal and Beth nodded. It was all he could do as he watched both women walk out of the room.

CHAPTER EIGHT

BETH was trailing behind and Natalie could feel herself becoming impatient. All she wanted to do was to get out of there as fast as possible.

'Can you slow down a second?' Beth grumbled, but it did no good. 'What happened? What's wrong?'

'Can we just get out of here, please?' Her voice quivered as she spoke and she knew if she didn't get to the privacy of Beth's car as soon as possible, she'd be in tears before the lift arrived. She punched the button repeatedly and found she couldn't look at her friend when she finally caught up.

'Natalie...' Beth stretched out her arm to her friend but Natalie shrank back from it.

'No. Don't touch me or I'll break down, and I don't *want* to break down.'

'OK.' The lift arrived and they rode it down, neither saying a word. It took them to the car park beneath the hotel and Beth led the way. She navigated the car through the city streets, not speaking until she'd turned off the motorway. 'Hungry?'

'No. Sorry if I took you away from your handsome waiter.'

'That's OK. I got his number anyway.'

Natalie shook her head in bewilderment. 'How do you do it? How do you stay so cut off from all emotion?'

'Walls. I put up walls. The same as everyone else.' Beth stopped at a red light. 'Because I've had my life trampled on, chewed up and spat out, I put up walls and rarely do I let people behind the walls. I need to find a man I can trust in *every* aspect of my life.'

'How do you do that?'

'You can find out a lot about people in the first hour you spend with them. I'm simply not interested in wasting my hours on a man who doesn't think along the same lines as I do, no matter how cute he might be.'

'So you keep them at arm's length, ignoring the fact your special person could be right under your nose.'

'Do you mean Marty?' Beth shook her head. 'He is *so* not my type.'

'Yes, he is.'

'No, he's not.'

'But he likes to play the field and so do you.'

Beth laughed. 'That doesn't make him my type, Natalie.' The light turned green and she headed off. There was quite a bit of traffic on the road for the late hour of the night but then, with Christmas just around the corner, stores were open all hours so people were shopping at all hours.

'Are you going to tell me what happened?' Beth asked quietly.

'I don't know if I can.'

'Come on. I'm guessing it has to do with Marty.'

'We kissed.'

'Woo-hoo!' Beth pumped the air with her fist. 'Yeah!' She settled. 'Sorry. So how was it? Good?'

Natalie rolled her eyes. '*Good?* Good doesn't even *begin* to describe it. It was...out of this world, like nothing I've ever felt before.'

'Really? Wow.'

'Yeah—wow.' Natalie's tone was despondent.

'So what's the problem?'

'How can you ask that? He's my friend, my colleague, we work together and he's dating every other woman in the hospital.'

'No, he's not.'

'Yes, he is. He's always out on dates.'

'Maybe that's just his way of getting to know people.' Beth glanced at her.

'That's what he said, but the hospital's not made up of female staff alone, Beth.' Natalie shook her head, staring out the windscreen. 'Brake. Brake!' she yelled, and Beth slammed her foot down. The screech of brakes, the instant smell of burning rubber was all around them as Beth narrowly missed hitting the stationary car in front of her.

Both of them sat there for a split second, inhaling and exhaling slowly, trying to calm themselves down. 'Let's investigate,' Natalie suggested. Checking behind her for oncoming traffic, she opened the door and climbed out.

'There's been an accident. It's just happened,' Beth said after

she'd switched off the engine, put on her hazard warning lights and
left her headlights on.

'I'll call it in. What supplies have you got?'

Natalie took her mobile phone from the small evening bag she
carried and dialled the emergency number. 'My name is Dr Natalie
Fox. I'd like to report an accident.' She gave her location. 'I'm not
sure how many people are injured.' While she spoke she climbed
from the car, looking out into the dark night. 'There are at least
three or more cars involved. Send the police and the fire brigade,
as well as a couple of ambulances.'

Beth rummaged around in the back of her car and pulled out her
first-aid kit and a blanket. 'We're just about to take a look at the
situation,' Natalie said into her phone as she shut the car door and
headed after Beth. As she walked carefully and quickly up the road,
she gasped. 'No, there's four cars...no, five involved. The street-
lights aren't providing much help but they're better than nothing. I
need to go. Get those crews here immediately.'

'The call has already gone out, Dr Fox,' the emergency operator
told her.

Natalie disconnected the call. She went to put the phone away
then remembered she was wearing a brand-new dress that didn't
have pockets. She followed Beth and put her phone in the first-aid
kit before pulling out a set of gloves and a resuscitation mask.

'I wish we had more direct light,' Beth muttered. 'I only have
one torch besides the medical torch.'

'We'll have to make do.'

'This car...' she pointed to the one at the head of the pack, even
though all five cars were strewn in the middle of the road '...seems
to be in front. I'll check it first. You check over there.' Beth pointed
to the other side of the road where the front car had swerved and
taken out a few oncoming cars. 'Then report back so we can decide
on triage, unless you find an urgent case.'

'Right.' Natalie turned and walked between the mounds of shattered glass, the smell of petrol strong in the air. 'Do you have an
extinguisher in the car?' she called to Beth.

'No. Sorry.' Beth replied, before pulling on a pair of gloves and
heading to the first car. Natalie checked the cars Beth had indicated.
It was after ten o'clock in the evening yet there were still a number
of cars going past on either side. They needed to get traffic control

under way as soon as possible. The driver of one of the cars involved in the accident was getting out.

'That's a good sign,' Natalie mumbled to herself. 'Are you all right?'

'A bit shaken up,' the man answered. He turned and motioned to the other people in his car. 'We're all fine—my wife and kids,' he said.

'I'm Dr Fox. Emergency services have already been called but if you wouldn't mind helping to control the passing traffic, that would be a great help. Probably better if your kids stay in the car at this stage.' The man went to turn off his lights. 'No. Please, leave them on so we can see a bit better. My colleague, Dr Durant, and I need as much light as we can get.'

'Pretty handy, two doctors coming by,' the man said.

'Returning from a Christmas party,' Natalie replied as she headed for the next car. This one had been hit from almost every side and was currently facing in the wrong direction on the road. Glass was everywhere and Natalie was glad of her high-heeled shoes, even though they were uncomfortable as well as impractical. The light from the car behind helped her to see a woman slumped over the steering-wheel. The front windscreen was broken, as though something—or someone—had gone through. A sickening feeling raced through her as she quickened her step.

'Hello?' she called to the woman. 'Can you hear me?' No response. Very carefully, she reached through the front windscreen and shook the woman gently. 'Can you hear me?' A murmured response. 'It's all right. Help is on the way. Stay where you are and we'll be with you as soon as we can. Was there anyone else with you in the car?' Natalie tried to see into the rear of the car but it was too dark. 'Can you hear me?' she asked again when she received no response. 'Was there someone in your car?'

'Sammy,' the woman muttered, then choked on a sob.

'Sammy?' Natalie shifted away. 'Who's Sammy? Is he your husband? Your son or daughter?' The woman merely started crying and Natalie knew she had to leave her. If someone had gone through the windscreen, she needed to find them. She went around the car, the smell of petrol increasing, but she ignored it as she looked on the ground for a dark shadow.

'Sammy?' she called, but received no reply. Another step and then she stopped and stared, her breath caught in her throat for a second. A small, dark shadow was lying on the road between the rear of the car she'd just checked and another car that had also swerved onto the wrong side of the road—the car she and Beth had parked behind. How the child hadn't been crushed was a miracle and one she was willing to take. She edged her way past the side of the last car, surprised she and Beth hadn't seen the body when they'd first arrived. But they hadn't been looking for a small boy lying on the road. She guessed he wasn't even five years old.

'Beth?' she called as she crouched down beside the small body, his arm twisted over his body, his leg out at an odd angle. 'Sammy?' She gently gave the little boy's shoulder a firm shake. Nothing. 'Sammy?' Natalie checked his breathing. Nothing. She quickly checked he hadn't swallowed his tongue before putting the protective resuscitation mask over his face so she could begin. She pinched his nose, tilted his head back and began breathing into his mouth. After two breaths, she checked Sammy's carotid pulse. Nothing. She measured the distance on his chest, realising there was bleeding around his lower abdomen before beginning cardiopulmonary resuscitation. 'Beth?' she called again, hearing her friend walking nearby. She counted the beats in her head before dipping down and doing EAR again.

'Nat?'

She began CPR again. 'Marty!' Natalie was stunned for a moment then immediately thankful he was there. 'Marty,' she called again and in the next instant he was crouching beside her. 'The child's mother is in the car just here. She's conscious but I've told her not to move,' she gestured with her head. 'What's Beth doing?'

'She's checking this last car, which contains two little girls. Parents probably have whiplash and maybe a broken bone or two. This little fellow looks like the worst.'

Natalie blew into his mouth again, then checked the pulse. 'It's there,' she gasped, her fingers willing the faint beats to become stronger. 'It's there.'

'Good work. Here.' He unfolded a blanket and placed it partially over the boy. It was then Natalie noticed he was wearing gloves and had carried over a medical kit—probably from his car.

'Check his pupils and hand me a gauze pad, please. He's bleeding.'

Marty handed her what she needed. She lifted up Sammy's shirt and saw a seat-belt bruise across his lap. 'Scissors.' Again they were put into her hand. Natalie cut away Sammy's stained T-shirt but there was no sign of a bruise across his shoulder or chest. She shook her head. 'He must have been sitting in the middle seat with just a lap-sash seat belt on.'

'If it wasn't tight enough, that would explain why he went through the windscreen. Pupils equal and reacting to light. How's the abdomen?'

Sammy moaned.

'It's all right, darling. Help is here. Check his legs, Marty, to see if he has any spinal damage.'

Marty called to Sammy. 'Hey, matey. I'm Dr Marty. Can you try and lift your leg for me?' Marty put his hand on one of Sammy's legs. The other was bent at a very odd angle. He had probably dislocated the hip. 'Sammy? Can you try for me? Think really hard, mate.'

With a whimpering groan Sammy actually managed to tense his muscles. 'Excellent. Well done,' Marty said enthusiastically. He put his fingers into Sammy's clammy hands. 'Can you squeeze my fingers?'

Again, a small, marginal movement but a movement nonetheless. 'That's the stuff we're looking for. Good boy. OK.' Marty placed his hands on Sammy's shoulders. 'Can you bring your shoulders up for me?'

There was no movement. 'Sammy?' Marty called again, and received a whimper in reply. 'I know it's difficult but if you could try really hard,' he urged. There was a very slight movement.

'Terrific. You are such an amazing boy,' Marty praised. He turned back to Natalie. 'No apparent spinal damage but I'd get him checked once he gets to hospital.'

Natalie checked Sammy's vitals again. 'Pulse and resp. rate getting stronger.'

'That's what we like to hear.'

'Do you have anything in your kit for pain relief?'

'Yes, of course.'

'Perfect. I can't see any medical alert chains so we'll presume he's not allergic to anything.'

Marty drew up the injection while Natalie rechecked the abdomen. 'He has a small gash on the lower part of his abdomen, his pants feel wet around the top of the leg so he's voided.'

'Bladder rupture?'

'Most probably, and that'll be just the beginning, I'm sure. Pass me a large bandage and we'll get this abdomen stabilised. You're doing good, Sammy. Real good. Sammy?' she called. 'Can you hear me?'

He coughed a little and she turned his head just in time. He vomited onto the road but there wasn't much. 'It's all right, darling,' she told him when he started to whimper. She checked his pulse again. It was stronger than before. 'Good boy. That's it.'

Marty administered the injection. 'Double-check his fractures, Nat.'

Natalie did as he'd said, carefully running her hands over the small bones. 'Dislocated hip, fractured tibia and fibula.' She shook her head. 'Poor baby.'

'He's lucky to be alive.'

'You're not wrong. Sammy, we're going to get you to hospital real soon.' Carefully, she turned his head in case he was sick again before pulling the blanket over him.

'Natalie?' Beth called, and Natalie smiled down at Sammy, even though the little boy still had his eyes closed.

'I'll leave you with Dr Marty for a while, but I'll be back.' She glanced at Marty. 'I'll have someone come and stay with him, which will free you up.'

'Thanks.' He looked at her and their gazes held. A lot was said in that one moment. An emergency like this put life into perspective and although they were still facing a lot of problems, she had the feeling they'd slowly work their way through them. 'Get going,' he said after a moment.

Natalie stood and picked her way carefully through to where Beth was standing by the last car.

'What have you found?' Beth asked, and together they compared notes. 'Sammy's stable?'

'For the moment. If we can get someone to sit with him, that'll free up all three of us, but he needs to be monitored until an ambulance arrives.' Natalie told Beth what she'd found and how at least one of the cars didn't appear to have any casualties.

'The first car has two elderly people—male and female. Looks as though the man had a heart attack. He's dead and his wife, although her pulse is fairly strong, is still unconscious. Second car has two people, male and female, in their late teens, early twenties at best. They're both completely trapped in the car and will need to be cut out. We could possibly get in through the back to monitor or set up a drip so there's that option but no way of seeing exactly what type of injuries they have.'

'And this car?' Natalie asked, pointing to the one they'd parked behind.

'Two adults, two children. The twin girls in the back have asthma and when I just checked them, they were both starting to wheeze heavily.'

'Right. I'll deal with the girls,' Natalie said. 'Get Marty to check on Sammy's mother.'

'Yes. I'll take another look at the woman in the top car and then check on the teenagers.' She shook her head. 'I'll send someone to relieve Marty,' Beth said, and Natalie thanked her while she changed her gloves, grabbed the stethoscope and found the asthma medication and spacer Beth kept in her kit, before heading to the car.

'Hello. I'm Natalie Fox,' she told the parents.

'Can we get out?' the father asked.

'If you can give me a minute to get the girls under control, I'll check you both. It's just better for now if you can stay where you are.'

'That's what the other doctor said,' the mother replied.

Natalie managed to get the rear passenger door open, giving her access to the girls. 'Hello,' she said to the two crying girls, who were dragging air into their lungs. They were dressed identically, their blonde curls tied up in pigtails. Apart from their screwed-up faces and the loud noise they were both making, they looked adorable. 'I'm Dr Natalie. How old are you both?' No response.

'They're almost three,' their mother answered for them.

'Right.' Natalie hooked the spacer together, showing the girls what she was doing and explaining. 'Have you ever used one of these before?

'Both of them have.' Again the information came from their mother, just as Natalie had known it would.

'Excellent. First of all, I'm just going to listen to your chests.' Thankfully, with the appearance of a stranger half in and half out of their car, their crying had dropped to a whimper along with the gasping of air into their lungs. The twin on the left seemed slightly worse so she decided to start with her. 'What's your name?' Both were still strapped into their car seats and she silently thanked their parents for properly restraining their children.

'Liesel,' the mother replied. 'The one with the pink bow is Lillian. I'm Lauren and my husband is Lawrence.'

Natalie smiled. 'Cute. All right, Liesel. I'm going to loosen your seat belt then have a listen to your chest.' Natalie did just that, closing her eyes to concentrate as she placed the bowl of the stethoscope on Liesel's chest. She listened intently, moving it around. 'Try and lean forward for me, darling,' she said soothingly, moving the child a little. She managed to get the stethoscope down the back of Liesel's top, glad it was summer and the girls weren't dressed in layers of clothes. Again she listened and this time when Liesel coughed, she shook her head. 'Good girl.'

She shook the medication they were about to have before connecting it to the spacer. 'All right, Liesel. Remember what you need to do? Nice, slow, deep breaths.' Liesel seemed to calm a little at the routine and as she'd stopped crying, Lillian followed suit. Once Liesel was a little more settled, Natalie turned her attention to Lillian, listening to her chest and administering the medication.

'All right, girls.' She shifted a little. 'I'm just going to see how Mummy and Daddy are. Just relax.' Both girls looked too tired to move yet both sets of big blue eyes followed every move she made.

Natalie extracted herself from the car and went around to the driver's door, which didn't appear to be as badly mangled as the passenger door. 'Lawrence. Where's the most pain?' she asked, crouching down beside him.

'My neck. My back. My ribs. It hurts a little to breathe.'

Natalie nodded. 'Can you move your feet? Your legs?'

'Yes.'

Natalie watched as he moved his feet and legs. She had him squeeze her hands and checked he could shrug his shoulders.

'I can wiggle my toes, too,' Lauren assured her.

'Good. Let me just listen to Lawrence's chest. I'm just going to undo your seat belt which will give me better access.' He'd no doubt hit his chest on the steering-wheel and although his skin was pale, he didn't appear to be having too much difficulty breathing. She listened to his chest and was pleased to hear no obstruction. In one place where she put the stethoscope, Lawrence winced.

'Hurts there, does it?' Natalie wished for more light but checked the area out, pressing it gently. Lawrence winced again, more strongly than before.

'You may have fractured a rib. Keep still, concentrate on relaxing and deep breathing. Once the ambulance arrives, we'll get you off to hospital for X-rays.'

'Can I move yet?' Lauren wanted to know. 'I feel so helpless, just sitting here unable to do anything.'

'I'm trying to figure out the best way to get to you, Lauren. I can't open your door and I think the best way is to come around behind you.'

Lauren undid her seat belt. 'I can climb out through the back seat and you can examine me out of the car.'

'No.' The word held urgency but was also a command. 'I will get to you but you can't move until I've checked you.' Natalie came around the car again and climbed in the back seat. She smiled at the girls and was pleased they were both breathing more normally, although they would need extra salbutamol to keep the asthma under control.

She squeezed around until she was between the twins' car seats, facing the front and kind of squatting on the floor. 'All right.' She slipped her arms around, careful not to elbow Lawrence in the head, and took Lauren's hands in hers. 'Squeeze my fingers.'

They went through all the other checks and only once Natalie was satisfied did she let Lauren move. 'If you could continue to monitor the girls and their breathing, that would be good. Lawrence, if you start coughing up blood, I need to know immediately.'

'Will that happen?'

'I doubt it, but at least you'll know what to watch for. Otherwise just stay as still as you can. We'll need to get a neck brace on you and you'll need some analgesics before you can be moved.'

'You have other people to see to,' Lauren said. 'Go. I'm used to taking care of my family.'

'All right, but call if you have the slightest doubt or worry.' Natalie met the other woman's gaze.

'I will.' Lauren promised.

Natalie headed over to check on Sammy, who was being watched by one of the teenagers from the end car. 'The other doctor just came and checked him,' the teenager said.

'Good. How are you feeling?'

'Scared. What if something happens to him and I don't know what to do?'

'Come and get one of us if you think there's anything different in his condition.'

'I get scared with all these cars going past and I want the ambulance to hurry up and get here,' the girl whimpered.

'I'm with you there but your dad is doing a great job of making them go slowly and, besides, everyone likes to slow down so they can have a look at what's happened. At least, in that respect, it makes them go slowly.'

'A few other people have stopped to help.'

'That's good, but sometimes too many helpers can make things more difficult. Still, I'm sure your dad has everything under control.'

'He's a Wing Commander in the Air Force,' the girl said.

'That explains why he has everything under control.'

'Yeah. I've never seen him like this...you know, in action before.'

Natalie smiled, realising that although the teenager didn't have any life-threatening injuries, this night would not only change her perceptions but would mould her in years to come. 'I need to go and help. You're doing a good job with Sammy. Just keep talking to him and checking that he's breathing.'

'What if he talks back?'

'Then that's a good sign.' Natalie headed over to where Marty was still dealing with Sammy's mother.

'We're almost there, Chrissy. That's good. Just breathe.' Marty had just finished bandaging Chrissy's arm where it had been cut. He glanced up at Natalie, speaking softly. 'Any word on the ambulances?'

'My phone's in Beth's medical kit.'

'They should be here soon, though?' His words were said with purpose and Natalie looked at Sammy's mother.

'Absolutely.'

'Chrissy, this is Natalie. She's a doctor as well.'

Chrissy opened her eyes and gazed unseeingly at Natalie. 'Where's my boy? I need Sammy.'

Natalie wondered why Marty wasn't letting Chrissy see her son, but there was obviously a reason.

'I've just checked on him and he's doing fine.'

'This man...' Chrissy hit out at Marty, who managed to move out of the way just in time '...won't let me see him.'

'I need you to stay still, Chrissy,' Marty tried to reassure her. He'd fashioned a neck brace from a few bandages, as well as putting a gauze pad and bandage around Chrissy's head where it had obviously been cut.

'I tried to grab him.' The anger Chrissy had just displayed towards Marty now turned into a fresh bout of tears. 'I saw Sammy go through the window and I tried to grab him but I couldn't.' She closed her eyes in shame and Natalie realised that was how her arm had been cut. Marty stood so he could talk to Natalie.

'She can't move her legs and I've even done a pinprick test. No feeling.' He looked down at the ground and shook his head. 'Her car's been hit the most, first from the initial car, then the Wing Commander's and then from the car with the twins. If I leave her, she'll try and get out of the car, and although she may not physically be able to move her legs, she may still find a way of getting to her son. She's too unstable to be left without proper supervision.'

'And we can't even bring him to her.' Natalie felt desolate. 'I'm checking on those ambulances. We need oxygen, we need bandages, we need plasma—we need more than we have.' She stalked towards where Beth was and found the medical kit. She picked up her phone and punched in the number.

'This is Dr Fox. I called in an accident.' Again, she gave the particulars. 'Where are the ambulances? We need the equipment here *now*. Please, check how far away they are.' Natalie closed her eyes as she waited, feelings of helplessness and anger coursing through her.

'Natalie!' The call came from Beth, who wasn't that far from her.

'What's wrong?'

'I need you.'

'One more minute, Dr Fox,' the emergency operator said, and Natalie disconnected and dropped the phone, quickly changing her gloves.

'Hurry,' Beth called. She was leaning over the smashed bonnet of the car through the windscreen, which was broken, and breathing into a young man's mouth, the protective face shield in place.

'See if you can get in. Try the back doors, the boot. Anything. He needs CPR.'

Natalie immediately went around the car and tried the rear doors. Jammed. She looked around for something to smash through the rear window in the hope she could get in that way, but couldn't find anything. 'I can't get in. Can I go through the front?' She came around the car again but Beth had the only position that looked safe enough. 'The doors are jammed, the rear of the car's been hit as well.'

'Crowbar?' It was the Wing Commander, walking towards her with the tool she would need.

'Brilliant.' Natalie walked around the car with him and he jimmied the crushed boot open.

'Stand back,' he said and climbed in, feet first, then kicked the rear seats down so Natalie could slide through.

'Thank you.' She went in head first just as she heard the wail of sirens getting closer. She exhaled, saying a silent prayer. The cavalry had arrived.

'Natalie!' Beth's tone was urgent and breathless.

Natalie knew what she had to do and crawled on her elbows through to where she needed to be. She carefully pulled herself as upright as she could and leaned through to the front. 'There's just no room, Beth. I can't get to his chest properly.' She felt around for a button or lever to release the seat to make it recline. 'Got it. Beth, I'm going to wind it back. You'll need to come further into the car to continue until I've got him.'

'OK. Start winding,' Beth said between breaths. 'Pulse is still absent.'

Natalie's hands started cramping as they were squashed around the side of the seat, trying to manoeuvre the dial. Beth kept going for as long as she could.

'I hope you're lying on something or that glass is going to cut into you.'

'I'm on a blanket the Wing Commander gave me.'

'Yay for the Wing Commander.' Natalie shifted around. 'All right. I've got him.' She began CPR on her almost supine patient, silently counting. Beth carefully extracted herself and Natalie continued with the EAR when it was required, checking desperately for the pulse.

Natalie continued, concentrating on what she was doing. Hopefully, this young man had the will to live because right now she needed all the help she could get. Although the first ambulance had arrived, it would be used to transport Sammy and probably his mother to the hospital. She had no idea how the elderly wife of the deceased driver was doing and knew Beth was probably seeing to her now.

'Nat?' The call came from Marty. She gave two breaths into the young man's mouth and felt for a pulse before beginning the next round of CPR.

'Here,' she called.

'Where?'

She counted in her head. 'In the car.'

'*You're in the car?*' Marty stopped short, his chest tightening in pain. She was in the car! That car was basically crushed. How on earth had she got inside? His breathing increased and he swallowed over the dryness in his throat. The woman he loved had put herself in danger and suddenly he was a mass of jelly. What if something went wrong? What if she couldn't get out? What if she got hurt?

His stomach churned and he was astonished at how sick he felt. Was this what loving her was going to be like?

CHAPTER NINE

MARTY raked his hand through his hair, desperately trying to pull himself together. Natalie needed his help right now as a colleague and he wasn't about to let her down.

'Nat.' He stuck his head through the crushed windscreen of the car. 'The cavalry has arrived.'

'I need a soft bag resuscitator, if there's one. The girl here needs to be checked out but she still hasn't regained consciousness. Is the fire brigade here yet? We need to cut these two out as soon as possible.'

'I'll check it out.'

'How's Sammy?'

'Being taken care of. I'll be right back, honey.'

Natalie breathed into her patient's mouth and checked his pulse again. It was there and she felt weak with relief. 'Marty!' She called, her fingers still on the man's carotid pulse.

'Yeah?'

'I've got it.' She smiled at him through the shattered windscreen.

He returned the smile and her insides began to turn to mush. 'Looks as though it's your night for reviving. I'll be right back.'

Natalie looked down at her still unconscious but breathing patient. 'We'll get you through this,' she promised, before trying to shift around so she could check the other passenger. 'Now, don't you go getting any ideas and stop breathing.' She pressed two fingers to the teenager's pulse. 'Good.' Although she didn't have a medical torch, she lifted the woman's eyelids. With the small amount of light that surrounded them, the pupils dilated a fraction and that was enough for Natalie. 'Can you hear me?' she called, but received no response. It was probably best if the girl stayed unconscious because if she could see where she was, trapped in a squashed car, she might start to panic.

Natalie shifted again and checked her other patient. 'Still breathing? Excellent. Keep it up,' she told him.

'OK, I'm back,' Marty said.

'Did you bring gear?'

'Did I bring gear?' he asked rhetorically. 'I most certainly did. What do you want first?'

'Cervical collars.'

'Coming right up.'

With Marty's help, she managed to stabilise both patients, although it did take a lot of shifting and twisting. Once she got a cramp and had to stretch at an odd angle to get the pain to ease, but soon she was happier with the situation.

'Pass me the sphygmomanometer,' she said. 'I need to check his blood pressure again.' Natalie waited for Marty to pass it through, then checked the man's BP again. 'He's bleeding internally somewhere, but I can't see anything.'

'They're almost ready to cut them both out.'

'Good. I am surprised neither has regained consciousness.'

'Must have been quite a hit.' Marty surveyed the damage. 'I'd say he was tailgating the car in front and that's why the front of the car is so crushed. How on earth did you manage to climb through the rear of the car? It's almost as badly smashed as the front.'

'With skill and finesse,' she said. 'Although I would have preferred to be wearing jeans rather than a brand-new dress.'

'Accidents never happen at a convenient time,' he agreed.

'What's the status on the other patients?'

'Sammy's long gone to the hospital, so has his mother. The twin girls—'

'They're both asthmatics.'

'They're about to go off in an ambulance with their parents.'

'Their father? Lawrence? How is he?'

'As far as I can tell, just fractured ribs at this stage.'

'Good.'

'The paramedics have taken care of him.'

'Good,' she said again. 'And the woman in the front car? How's she doing?'

'Not too well.'

'Has she regained consciousness?'

'Only a few minutes ago. Beth's with her but when the woman enquired about her husband and learned the truth...' Marty paused.

'She's giving up.'

'Beth will watch her carefully.' He turned and spoke to someone else. 'OK, Nat. They're ready to start cutting into the car. We need to get you out.'

'I don't know if I can get out. I'm kind of wedged in.'

Marty was silent at this news and for a moment Natalie thought he'd moved away. 'Marty?'

'I'm here, honey.' His voice was strained. 'I'll just let the fire-fighters know.' Marty closed his eyes for a second, cross with Natalie for putting herself in a potentially dangerous position and cross with himself for being so much in love with her it was affecting his ability to think straight.

Twenty minutes later Marty helped lift Natalie from the car after the roof had been peeled back, allowing the paramedics access to the patients. 'We'll take it from here, Dr Fox,' one of them said.

Marty gathered Natalie into his arms and held her close.

'Marty, I need to breathe,' she said, and he realised he was holding her too tightly. He loosened his grip and looked down at her. He wanted to tell her he was sorry about before, to let her know how he felt, but at that moment just holding her and looking at her was enough. He needed to take things slowly or he'd wind up losing her for ever and that was a risk he wasn't going to take.

He placed a kiss on her forehead before putting her from him. 'Let's see how Beth is doing.' They headed over to where Beth was leaning against a police car, sipping a drink.

'Sickly tea, anyone?'

'How's the elderly woman?'

'Distraught but alive. They've just taken her to hospital.' Beth sighed and closed her eyes for a moment. 'Happy Christmas,' she murmured, then opened her eyes and looked at her friends. 'Guess we'd better get to the hospital and see how everyone is.'

'What about the Wing Commander and his family?'

'They've been checked over by the paramedics and, apart from giving a report to the police, all of them are fine.'

'Good. The Wing Commander was brilliant,' Natalie remarked.

'Yes, he was,' Beth agreed.

'I never would have got into that car without his help.'

'So *he's* the one who got you in there.' Marty scowled darkly.

Natalie laughed. 'You think you're the only one who can play at being Dr Hero? Think again, buddy, because Beth and I were definitely Dr Heroines tonight.'

Marty conceded that with a smile. 'Let's get to the hospital. Are you all right to drive, Beth?'

'Should be. I just have to figure out how to get my car out of this mess. Traffic is banked up for miles.'

'Well, you can come with me and get someone to deliver your car to the hospital later, if that makes life any easier,' Marty volunteered. 'I at least had the good sense to park to the side of the mess, rather than in the middle of it,' he teased.

'Hey, if it wasn't for Natalie, we might have been *part* of the mess. She saw the accident first.'

Marty looked down at Natalie and grinned. 'You *have* been Dr Heroine this evening, haven't you.'

'And that's more than enough. I'm ready to hang up my costume and become boring Dr Natalie again.'

'Hardly boring,' Marty said in his usual teasing tone. He was about to make a wisecrack about not hanging up her superhero costume, especially if it was made of Spandex, but he stopped. Now that they'd kissed and realised how amazing the attraction was between them, she might take his words the wrong way and feel as though he was pressuring her. He looked away and shoved his hand into his trouser pocket, pulling out his keys. 'Let us away, friends. Duty and honour call all three super-docs back to the hospital.'

'Super-docs?' Beth giggled as she drained her drink. 'I think I prefer Dr Hero and Dr Heroine better.'

They spoke to the police officer in charge who promised to return Beth's car to her at the hospital. Then they checked on their remaining patients before heading to Marty's car.

As he drove them to the hospital, Natalie was pleased he hadn't stayed much longer at the Christmas party, although she was sure he would have had several of his harem begging him to stay. Not only had he been able to provide much-needed help at the accident site but it meant he hadn't wanted to stay on at the party once she'd left. At least, that's what she hoped had happened. She wasn't ready to analyse the reasons *why* she was glad he'd left as she was far too tired and even a little scared to face those feelings right now.

Once they arrived at the hospital, it was even more hectic. She managed to check on Sammy and found he was being prepped for Theatre. He was still drowsy but she spent a few minutes with him, tenderly brushing his hair from his forehead. 'You'll be fine,' she promised him. 'I'll see you later.'

She watched him being wheeled into Theatre before heading to the female changing rooms. She had a very quick shower, dressed in theatre scrubs and hung her dress in her locker. She always kept an extra hairbrush, bands and hairclips in her locker and pinned her hair into her usual bun. She didn't have a spare set of shoes so kept her high heels on. Now that she felt a little more human, she went to check on the other patients.

Marty had also showered and changed and was taking care of the twin girls, Liesel and Lillian. Lawrence, their father, was in Radiology.

'You were right,' Lauren said when she bumped into Natalie in the corridor. 'Lawrence has a fractured rib but thankfully nothing more.' Lauren took Natalie's hands in hers. 'Thank you so much for helping us.'

'You're welcome.'

'And I'm sorry if I came across a bit abrupt. It's just that—'

'You don't need to explain, Lauren. Your family was hurt and you needed to look after them. I understand. How are the girls?'

'Settled, but Dr Marty wants to admit them, at least overnight.'

'I agree with him.'

Lauren smiled. 'He's wonderful with the children.'

Yes, she thought.

'Does he have children of his own?'

'No.'

'Ah, he's the good-looking single doctor creating havoc among the female staff?'

Natalie's smile was strained. 'You could say that. Excuse me.'

'Of course. You must have a thousand other things to be doing. I just wanted to say thank you.'

'I appreciate it.' Natalie headed off towards the ward, pushing all thoughts of Marty and his hypnotic presence over all females from her mind. After doing a quick round and warning the night sister there would be a few more admissions, Natalie paged Beth. She wasn't surprised when the reply came that her friend was in Theatre.

For the next few hours Natalie kept busy, anxiously waiting to hear the results of Sammy's operation. Finally, Theatre paged her and gave her the news that he was in Recovery.

'He's doing very well,' the recovery sister informed her.

'I think he's a fighter,' Natalie agreed.

'I heard you resuscitated him at the scene.'

'Yes.'

'No wonder you're attached to him. Go and sit with him for a while.'

Natalie was pleased to do so and looked down at her small charge with fondness. 'I'm expecting great things from you, Sammy,' she said softly as she held his hand. 'You haven't come through this for nothing.'

Later, she went to the tearoom and finally sipped a relaxing cup of tea, kicking off her shoes and putting her feet up. She put the cup on the table before tipping her head back and closing her eyes, unable to believe just how exhausted she felt. It was a little ridiculous to feel so washed out, especially when she was used to working such long hours.

It wasn't just the hours, she realised, and groaned. Oh, no, she could cope with the long hours all right. It was the fact that she'd kissed Marty that was making her so uneasy.

She finally allowed the thoughts she'd been holding at bay since the accident to come to the fore. What had she been thinking? How could she have kissed him? He was her friend and now everything had changed. She was now just another notch on his belt, another name in his little black book. 'Oh, that's right,' she mumbled as her head flopped forward and she started massaging the base of her neck. 'He doesn't need a book. He can remember all the three billion names in his head.'

It was ridiculous. They'd been friends for a long time and back in their high school days she'd never been jealous of any of the girls he'd dated. Probably because, despite whom he'd dated, he'd always hung out with her. His girlfriends had been the ones who'd been jealous of her, and she'd never been able to figure that out.

So why was she jealous now? Her eyelids snapped open. She was jealous? Oh, gosh. She *was* jealous of all the other women Marty had dated and probably would continue to date. She closed her eyes again and shook her head. This attraction towards him was getting more out of control every day.

'Neck sore?'

The man of the moment walked into the room and before she could move or say a word he'd crossed to her side and placed his hands on her shoulders. 'I know how you feel. What a day this has been.'

She hated that he could read her mind but she allowed herself to let go and wallow in his touch. Just this once. The warmth of his hands was having a mesmerising effect on her and she allowed the tingles that always flowed through her at his simple touch to spread and invigorate her exhausted body.

'Man, you're knotted tight.'

'Mmm.'

'Good?'

'Mmm,' she murmured again. 'How are the children?'

'Liesel and Lillian are settled in the ward and Sammy's just been taken to ICU.'

'Sammy's mother?'

'She's been handed over to the spinal surgeon. It doesn't look good.'

Natalie groaned. 'That poor woman. Have they managed to contact Sammy's father? Anyone?'

'Not yet.'

'What about the two teenagers who were cut from the car? Give me some good news.'

'Beth's in Theatre with the girl—multiple fractures to her legs—and the boy's been taken to Theatre by the general surgical registrar.'

'And the elderly wife?'

His hands stilled for a moment and Natalie felt a prickle of apprehension wash over her. 'She died ten minutes ago.'

Natalie sighed. 'She couldn't live without him.'

'It appears that way.' They were both silent for a moment.

'Maybe love does conquer all,' she whispered. Immediately, she sensed a change in the atmosphere around them, as though Marty was trying to find the right words to say. Why did she know him so well? Where the familiarity between the two of them was an asset in some ways, it was definitely a drawback when it came to being able to read him like a book.

'Nat, about the kiss—'

'Stop!' She shifted out of his grasp and stood, swaying a little at the sudden movement. She put her hand on the chair closest to her. 'Not now, Marty. I've had enough for the time being. If we're not needed here, please, just take me home so I can sleep.'

They both stood still, watching each other for a minute before Marty nodded. 'Sure. Get your bag and we'll go.'

She groaned. 'It's in Beth's car.'

'OK. So we need to check where Beth's car is and where her keys are.'

'Good question. Have the police brought her car back yet?'

Marty crossed to the wall phone and picked up the receiver. He spoke to the orderlies and discovered Beth's car had been returned to the hospital car park not that long ago and they were in possession of her keys.

'Excellent.'

'Come on, Dr Fox. The sooner we can get those keys, the sooner we can get your bag and the sooner we can get you home so you can go to sleep.' He held out his hand and Natalie eyed it warily.

'I won't try anything. I promise. Just let me help you, Nat.' He looked so sweet, so adorable and so wholesome. Marty? Wholesome? Yet that was how he looked and it made her feel very safe and very special.

She held out one hand and collected her shoes with the other. 'OK, but I need to stop by my locker and pick up my dress.' He nodded and led the way to the female changing rooms.

'I'll just let you do this bit by yourself.'

'Not coming in?'

'Uh...no. I'm good.'

'I'm sure you are. I'm also sure that if there are any other women in here, you've probably already dated them so there won't be any uneasiness.' The instant the words were out of her mouth, she wished she'd kept quiet. Apart from a slight jaw clench, he showed no sign of being annoyed with her words, probably because he could see she was more annoyed with herself for saying them. They seemed to be well attuned to each other tonight. Unsure of what to do, she turned and headed into the changing rooms, punching in the number for her locker and retrieving her dress. She'd only been gone a few minutes but when she came out there was Marty, laughing and chatting with one of the A and E nurses.

Natalie tried her best not to glare at him but knew she was failing, the green-eyed monster rising to the fore.

'Sounds good. I'll see you then,' the nurse said, then turned and saw her. 'Oh, hi, Natalie. Good work tonight.'

'Thanks,' Natalie replied through clenched teeth.

'Ready? Right. Off to see the orderlies.' Again he took her hand as they walked through the hospital. Jim, the orderly, was on duty.

'How are those little kiddies?' he asked, concerned.

'Doing well, Jim,' Marty answered. 'All of them doing well.'

'That's good news, Doc. Taking young Natalie home, then? Right you are.'

'Actually, we need to get into Beth's car and retrieve Nat's bag first.'

'A break-in?' Jim's eyebrows hit his hairline.

Marty grinned. 'Only if you can't find Beth's car keys.'

'They're right here. I'll come with you so you don't have to bring them back.'

'Thanks, Jim. I'm exhausted, and Natalie would no doubt appreciate it.'

'Glad to be of service.' Jim told his colleague he'd be back soon and headed outside with them. 'Aren't they beautiful?' he said, pointing up at the stars in the clear night sky. 'They match the twinkle lights around the hospital buildings perfectly.'

'Or do the twinkling buildings match them?' Marty asked, his hand at Natalie's elbow as the warm night air enfolded them.

'I love Christmas,' Jim muttered. 'How about you, Doctor?'

'It's one of my favourite times of the year. Everyone's happier, nicer to each other. Complete strangers smile and wish you a merry Christmas and although the shops are packed with present-buying people, there's a feeling of hope in the air.'

'That there is and we need plenty of hope after that accident tonight.'

'Too true,' Marty agreed. 'Everyone needs hope.' Natalie glanced up at him and felt rather than saw the hope deep inside him...the hope that they'd sort everything out.

She stood on a small stone and winced in pain. 'Careful.' Marty's arm came around her waist, drawing her closer to him. 'You all right, my barefooted Nat?'

'I'm fine.'

'You're already half-asleep, honey.'

'Better get her home right quick, Doc.'

'Will do, Jim. Which one's Beth's car? Yellow isn't it? I've seen one in your driveway a few times.'

Natalie pointed. 'Yellow canary straight ahead.'

'Appropriate name, and such a bright shade of yellow.' He unlocked the door and opened it, allowing Natalie to retrieve her bag. 'Right. Jim.' He shut the door, locked the car and placed the keys in the orderly's hand. 'Please, make sure Beth gets these. I'm going to escort Nat over to my car and get her home.'

'Right you are, Doc. Goodnight to you both.'

Natalie murmured the appropriate response before Marty guided her the few rows to where his vehicle was parked. 'You shouldn't have given me that massage,' she said. 'It's turned me to mush.'

He ginned and raised his eyebrows. 'Maybe I like you like that. All mushy and soft, instead of hard and chewy.'

She laughed. 'I'm not a lollipop, Marty.'

He unlocked his car door and once more held it open for her. 'I don't know about that. Pretty to look at, nice to smell and delicious to taste.'

'Walked right into that one, didn't I?' She was too tired to be cross or try and pick a fight with him. Ever since she'd walked outside, it was as though the heat had turned her brain off and she was functioning on a very shaky auto pilot.

'Yes, you did. Let's get you up and into the car.'

'Was it only just this morning you drove me to work?'

'Yes, my darling.' He helped her in before closing the door and coming around to the driver's side. 'Well, yesterday morning, to be correct. It's almost three o'clock.'

She sighed. 'No wonder I'm tired.'

'You're physically and mentally exhausted, Nat. Rest your head, close your eyes and let Uncle Marty take care of everything.'

'You're hardly avuncular, Marty.'

'I have to be right now because you look too good to resist, but resist I must.'

'Hmm.' She clipped her seat belt into place and leaned her head back as he started the engine. Yawning, she closed her eyes. 'Very tired.'

The next thing she knew, she was being carried inside, her front door already open. 'I didn't need my keys after all,' she mumbled, unsure why she'd left the door open.

'I opened it,' Marty said as he made his way to her bedroom. 'Why couldn't you have the room on the ground floor, rather than the first floor?' he muttered as he carried her up the stairs.

'So you could do your Rhett Butler impersonation.'

'Gee, thanks.' He made it to the top and opened the first door he came to. 'Bathroom. Let's try the next one.'

'You've never been up here before?'

'You've never invited me.'

'Too dangerous.'

'Careful. You might give something away.' He opened the next door and carried her to the unmade bed. 'I've put your shoes, your destroyed dress and your bag by the front door, and I'll lock up after myself.' He stood by her bed, looking down at her for a moment, desperate to pull superhuman strength from somewhere—*any-where*—so he wouldn't do what he was longing to do.

'You're such a flirt,' she murmured as she snuggled into the pillow and covers. Marty switched on her ceiling fan to stir up the air and opened one of her windows. He stopped for a moment and stared out into the night.

'Yeah. Locking you inside your house with me on the outside. Definitely constitutes the ''flirt'' label.'

'You know what I mean. Playing the field. Don't you ever want to settle down?'

Marty swallowed over the sudden dryness in his throat as he walked slowly back to her bedside. 'One day. I need to find the right woman.'

'Ah. So that's what the quest is for. Well, what's wrong with me?'

He closed his eyes at her words, his gut twisting. Her inhibitions were almost gone...either that or Everley had knocked her self-esteem completely off kilter. Either way, now was not the time to go into it. She'd been furious with him after he'd kissed her and he didn't want to risk her wrath twice in such a short space of time, even though he was longing to kiss her and show her just how perfect they were together.

'Well?' She turned her head and looked at him, one eye open, one eye closed.

'Nothing, my darling Nat,' he replied, determined to keep it light, for both their sakes. She closed her eye and relaxed. 'Fatigue has definitely set in. Go to sleep, honey.' With that, he turned and stalked from the room, allowing himself a last look at her. 'Sleeping beauty.'

Doing as he'd promised, he checked the rest of the town house to ensure the rest of the windows and outside doors were locked before leaving. He drove home and the instant he was in the door, he picked up the phone and called his cousin.

'Marty. Good to hear from you. Late shift?'

'You could say that.'

There was a pause before Ryan said, 'What's wrong?'

'How do you know there's anything wrong?'

'Hey. We've been friends all our lives. We're more like brothers than cousins. What's wrong?'

Marty raked a hand through his hair. 'I'm in love.'

'Wow. That was quick.' Ryan laughed then paused. 'You're serious?'

'Dead serious.'

'That really *was* quick.'

'Ha!' Marty laughed without humour. 'I don't think I'd call sixteen years quick.'

Another pause, then Ryan gulped, 'With *Natalie?*'

'Bingo.' Marty closed his eyes and shook his head, unable to believe the predicament he was in. 'Yes, with Nat.'

Ryan whistled. 'Looks as though I might have to come home for Christmas.'

'No. No.' Marty's eyes snapped open. Having Ryan around wouldn't help the situation at all. He'd joke and tease and make matters worse, and Marty was quite capable of stuffing everything up on his own. 'That's a bad idea, Ry. Stay where you are. Enjoy the cold.'

'I'm sick of the cold. Mum's already been bugging me to come home and this has just clinched it. I'll make the arrangements today.'

'Really, Ryan. It's not necessary.'

'On the contrary, Cuz. The man who was voted bachelor of the year at the leading Paris hospital now hopelessly in love?' Ryan chuckled. 'This I've got to see for myself!'

CHAPTER TEN

ONE week after the Christmas party, Natalie walked wearily into the town house after a double shift to find Beth and Marty sitting on the lounge watching a movie, a large bowl of popcorn between them.

'You're home early,' Beth said, jumping up, a guilty expression on her face. 'Er...Marty and I were just watching a movie. That's all. Nothing fancy.'

Natalie shrugged as she dumped her bag on the table. 'I'm going to shower.'

'How was Sammy when you left?' Marty asked, not moving from his spot, remote control in hand, having paused the movie.

'Much better.' A tired smile tugged at her lips. 'He managed to eat some jelly tonight.'

'Really?' Marty's eyes lit up. 'That's terrific.'

'Yeah. It's been the highlight of my week.' Their gazes held for a moment before she forced herself to look away.

'What about Glen?' he asked, desperate to keep her there a moment longer.

'He was sleeping soundly. The social worker said he could probably go home tomorrow.'

'Really?' This wasn't anything new to him as he'd spoken to the social worker that morning, but he just wanted to talk to Natalie and if talking about their patients was the only conversation she'd have with him, he'd gladly cover old ground. 'Do you think his mother will be able to cope now?'

'I hope so,' she said earnestly. 'With the home help the social worker has set up and with the removal of Glen's father, there's hope for the whole family—even the two older children.'

'I really hope so, too.'

They stared at each other once more before Natalie looked away. 'I'm going to shower,' she said again. 'Enjoy the movie.' With that, she headed upstairs.

Beth sat back down but Marty didn't take the movie off pause. 'You OK?' she asked.

'Sure. Sammy ate jelly and Glen gets to go home to a less abusive environment. That's fantastic.'

'I meant about Natalie.'

'Oh, Nat. Yeah, I'm fine. I think she was a bit shocked at seeing me, though.'

'I take it she's still avoiding you?'

'All week long. The only conversations we have are about the patients, as you have just witnessed.' He fiddled with the remote, not meeting Beth's gaze.

'Does that hurt?'

'I want to move past this. I hate not being able to joke with her, to share little anecdotes with her.'

'Don't rush her.'

Marty turned eagerly, looking at the woman who had been his lifeline throughout the past week. 'Has she said anything? I thought she didn't want to talk about me.'

'I've known her for a long time, too, Marty, and, no, she hasn't said anything, although even if she had, I wouldn't be able to tell you.'

'I know, and I respect that.' He flicked the remote onto the lounge and stood up, the movie forgotten. He'd spoken or seen Beth every day since the Christmas party because he'd needed to know Natalie was all right. He was prepared to give her the space she seemed to need and therefore hadn't pushed, but it was getting harder and harder as time went on. Had he ruined their relationship for ever by kissing her? He'd shifted the ground, he knew that, but he'd never thought it would be a permanent shift.

'Richard called her yesterday.'

'What?' Marty glared at Beth. 'You're telling me this *now*?'

'I forgot.'

'What did he want?'

'He wants to see her on Monday.'

'What for?'

'I don't know, Marty. Gosh, I didn't expect the Spanish Inquisition.'

He frowned then grinned. 'No one expects the Spanish Inquisition!' He shook his head. 'Sorry.'

'That's all right. You've been under a lot of pressure.'

'And Ryan arrives tomorrow.'

'Your cousin? Sir Ryan Cooper! The orthopod?'

'Yes. I thought I told you he was coming.'

'No. Oh, my gosh. Does Richard know?'

'Beth, you're acting like he's royalty and, believe me, he's not.'

'He's *orthopaedic* royalty.'

'I'll remember to crown him with some surgical plates and screws when he arrives.'

'This isn't a joking matter. Does the hospital know?'

'He's here...in an unofficial capacity.'

'Oh.' She thought for a moment. 'Can't we organise a little dinner or reception for him? Do you think he'd mind?'

'I don't know. His mother might.'

'His mother? She lives in Sydney?'

'Sure. Two houses down from her sister—my mother.'

'I didn't know your mother lived here.'

'You never asked.'

'So he's coming home to see his mum?'

'Among other things.' Marty rolled his eyes, thinking of what had prompted his cousin to come home. 'Look, I'll ask him and see what I can do.'

Beth jumped up and hugged Marty. 'Thank you. You're the greatest.'

'Beth? Is there any soap?' Natalie called, as she came down the stairs. When she saw Marty with Beth's arms around him, pain seared through her heart at the sight and she quickly spun around and ran up the stairs, eager to get away. If she needed any more proof that she meant nothing to him, that was it. He'd kissed her, made her swoon with longing and delight, then moved on to the next girl. Didn't he at least care about her feelings? After all they'd been through?

And what about Beth? She was supposed to be one of her best friends and had vowed that Marty wasn't her type. How could they both do this to her?

'Nat?' He was coming up behind her. 'Nat?' She rushed, desperate to make it to the bathroom before he could catch her. Thankfully, she made it and locked the door just in time.

'Nat, it's not what you think.'

She closed her eyes and leaned against the door, tears already beginning to flow down her cheeks. 'Go away, Marty. I can't deal with this now,' she called, desperately hoping her voice didn't sound as distraught as she felt.

'We need to talk about things.'

'No.'

'Yes, Nat, and I won't wait for ever. Beth and I are friends. Nothing more. We're not dating—in fact, I'm not dating *anyone* any more—but you need to know I don't want to kiss Beth and that was a friendly hug because I'm going to try and organise for some of the orthopods to see Ryan while he's here for Christmas. That's all. I promise.'

Natalie digested the information, knowing deep down he was telling the truth but also wanting to stay mad at him for as long as she could. 'Marty, *please*. I'm exhausted.' She bit her lower lip to help control the trembling. He was so near, yet so far. There was silence and for a moment she thought he'd gone.

Then he spoke. 'All right, but we *will* talk.' She heard him take a few steps away...then he was gone.

She stayed against the door for a moment longer, the pain of seeing Beth in his arms still washing over her. She didn't like it. Not one bit. Marty's arms belonged around her—her and no one else. Her heart ached for him and she desperately wanted to open the door, run after him and throw herself into his arms. She wouldn't, of course. She couldn't in case she got hurt. Taking a few deep breaths, she waited for the pain in her chest to subside but it took some time.

Admitting she was in love with the man, would only cause more anxiety, so she pushed that irrational thought away as well, wrapping herself up in a cocoon of self-preservation.

Natalie didn't see Marty for the rest of the weekend, although she learned more from Beth about Ryan's visit home and how Marty had managed to set up a dinner for the orthopods.

'What's he like?' Beth's whole face radiated excitement as she flitted around in the kitchen, preparing dinner on Sunday evening.

'Ryan? I don't know. Why? Interested in him already? What happened to the waiter from the function centre?'

'Oh. Too clingy. So?'

Natalie forced herself to ask the question she didn't want to ask. She stared down into her wineglass. 'What about Marty?'

'Marty? What's he got to do with it?'

Natalie slammed her hand down on the bench. 'Just be honest with me, Beth. *Please?*'

'I have been honest with you.'

'Really? Well, so far, since the magnificent Martin Williams came back into my life I've seen you kissing and hugging him. It's obvious you're interested in him, even though you've told me you're not. It's not fair to him if you're going to run hot and cold.'

Beth stirred the pot on the stove thoughtfully before putting the spoon down and taking Natalie's hands in hers. 'OK. I want you to look at me and listen to me, then I want you to *truthfully* answer one simple question. All right?'

Natalie rolled her eyes and nodded.

'Good. We've been over this before but it looks as though we need to go over it again.' Beth looked Natalie in the eye. 'Marty and I are friends. That's it. Just friends. He's kind of like the big brother I never had—you know, dropping in, fixing things, making breakfast, watching movies. Nothing—*nothing*—romantic is going on between us.'

'But I saw you kissing him.'

'When?'

'The morning of the Christmas party when he dropped by for breakfast and made pancakes.'

Beth thought. 'Yes. Yes, I did kiss him but it was a very quick, *friendly* peck on the cheek because he'd just told me some good news.'

'What good news?'

'Does it matter? Do you believe me?'

Natalie looked at her friend, desperately wanting to but still very unsure.

'Friends, Natalie. I swear. Besides, if I *was* interested in him, I would have told you straight out, but the truth is, there's just no chemistry between us. No buzz. No fire.' Beth squeezed her hands and focused intently on holding her gaze. 'You know exactly what I'm talking about.'

Natalie groaned and closed her eyes, pulling her hands from her friend's.

'You feel that buzz, that fire when you're with him, don't you,' she stated firmly. 'I know you do because you're acting so loopy about all this. Natalie, look at me.'

She did.

'Do you love him?'

Natalie gasped and put her hand over her mouth, her mind whirring at a frantic pace. Was she in love with Marty? If she was, that would certainly explain the jealousy she felt every time he so much as looked at another woman. But no...she couldn't possibly be. Could she? They were friends...friends who'd shared the most passionate and earth-tilting kiss she'd ever experienced.

'I'm miserable. That's about all I can tell you.'

'Miserable without him. Admit it, Natalie. If not to me, at least to yourself.'

'I can't. Not yet. I need to work it out. It doesn't make sense.'

'Of course it does, and it's really not that difficult. The answer is either yes or no.'

'What about "I don't know"?'

'Not an option.'

'Well that's my answer.' She dropped her hands to her sides.

'Do you love Richard?'

Natalie paused, her turmoil over Marty suspended. 'No.'

'Thank goodness.'

'But that's the part that doesn't make sense. Richard and I were perfect for each other. We both had similar goals, we both love our jobs and we always had a nice time and—'

'He was wrong for you, Natalie. Face it and get over it. Stop trying to put Richard up as a barrier so you can deny what you feel for Marty. I know you're in love with him but that means a loss of control and we all know how you need to be in control of your emotions. I know you love him because I can see it in your face. You've told me he kissed you and that it was incredible. The two of you are friends and you know about each other's pasts, so what's the problem?'

'I...I...I don't know,' she wailed, and buried her face in her hands.

'He's not like your dad,' Beth said softly, and Natalie slowly lifted her head to look at her friend.

'I know that. He's nothing like my dad—personality-wise. The pain of my parents' divorce has almost vanished but there's no denying it's made me who I am today. It's affected me so deeply that I've built such strong walls around myself.'

'And Marty's breaking through them.'

'Yes.'

'And it scares you senseless.'

'Yes. I'm so miserable.'

'Well, you can make yourself happy very easily.' Beth picked up the spoon and stirred the dinner once more. 'Now, ready to eat?'

'That's it? Inquisition over?'

Beth smiled. 'Yes. Did I tell you Marty's managed to get his cousin to meet some of us from the orthopaedic department on Tuesday?'

'Yes, you did. So you get to find out what Ryan's like for yourself.'

'Yes, but I just wanted some extra info from you. Are you sure you don't remember anything about him?'

'He was tall. He has the same colouring as Marty. They kind of look like brothers.' Natalie shrugged. 'That's about all I can remember. When you're at high school, you usually only associate with the people in your grade. Ryan was three years ahead of us.'

Beth dished the food up. 'You're no help.'

'So you have the ortho dinner on Tuesday evening, eh?'

'Yes, but don't worry about your birthday.' At Natalie's raised eyebrow, Beth continued. 'I managed to wangle the day off.'

'So did I.'

'I know. Marty told me,' she added. 'Anyway, let's go to a spa, get facials and massages and mud packs and relax and enjoy ourselves. Have a real girlie day.'

Natalie smiled. 'That sounds wonderful. You're a good friend, Beth.'

'Good, because I've already booked it.'

After dinner, the phone rang and Beth snatched it up. 'Oh, hi, Marty.'

Natalie shook her head then made the 'cut' sign across her throat.

'Yes, she's right here,' Beth announced, and held out the receiver.

'Did I say you were a good friend?' Natalie snarled, covering the mouthpiece.

Beth merely laughed and continued eating.

'Hi, Marty. Problem?'

'Not unless you're booked up on Tuesday evening.'

'Uh...' She tried to ignore the way her body reacted to the sound of his voice, as well as trying to get her brain to work. She closed her eyes and concentrated. 'Why?'

'Because I'd like to take you out to dinner.'

Natalie was stunned. 'You mean...like a date?'

'Well...kind of, but more like a birthday celebration.'

'You know it's my birthday?'

'Of course I do. It's the reason your name is Natalie. It means "nativity" and that's why your mum chose it, because you were born around Christmas.'

Her eyes snapped open in surprise. 'You *remember* that?'

'Sure. I have an excellent memory. So, are you free?'

Her brain refused to function and her body was trembling because of his words. His thoughtfulness, his natural caring abilities, his gentleness. He was different. Different to every blond-haired man she'd dated. He had dark hair, he had blue eyes and he was amazing. Could she take the chance? She might get hurt, but what if she didn't? She was swamped with emotion and realised she'd been a fool. 'Yes,' she managed to whisper, and quickly cleared her throat. 'I'm free.'

'Good. I don't finish until seven that night—because someone I won't mention has the entire day off. So I'll book for eight-thirty.'

'OK.'

'You all right?'

'Mmm-hmm.' She dragged in a breath. 'I need to go.'

'OK. I'd better go see what darling Aggie wants as she's late going home.'

'Aggie?' Natalie's heart started beating even faster than before. Had he won the bet? In some ways she hoped he had managed to call Sister Dorset by her first name without being torn to shreds. If he'd succeeded, it meant she would have to do what he proposed, and right now she was looking forward to the prospect—whatever he chose.

'Ah...not yet, but she's really coming around. Anyway, sorry to interrupt your night. Sleep sweet, Nat, and I'll see you tomorrow at ward round.'

Natalie held the phone in her hand, listening to the disconnected signal, staring into space.

'Natalie?' Beth held out her hand but still Natalie didn't pass the phone over. Beth leaned over the bench and took it. 'What's up, hon?'

Her dazed gaze swung around to meet her friend's. 'I'm in love with Marty.' Even to her own ears her voice sounded incredulous and disbelieving, but the truth was in her heart and she knew it would never go away. This wasn't what her parents had shared, she realised. This was one soul blending with another…Marty's soul and hers. In fact, if she was honest with herself, their souls had joined back in the ninth grade only then their motive had been friendship and support. So, too, in Fiji, friendship and support. They knew each other inside out and still…she loved him. Faults and all. No. This was not what her parents had shared and probably not what Marty had shared with his ex-wife.

This love was for life and she had no idea what to do next. 'I've fallen in love with my friend!' She paused, letting the words sink in. 'What am I going to do?' she wailed with a heart full of love and fear.

On Monday evening, Natalie dressed for her date with Richard. She was sure he was going to tell her things weren't working out between them—at least, that's what she hoped he'd say. The sooner he realised it was over, the better.

When the phone rang, she half expected it to be Richard, cancelling as usual because something had come up at work.

'Hello?'

'Natalie.' It *was* Richard.

'Yes, Richard?'

'Listen, do you mind if we postpone our evening out?'

'Yes.'

He was silent for a moment. 'I'm sorry. Did you say you *do* mind?'

'Yes, Richard. I do mind.'

'Oh.' Another pause. 'It's just that Sir Ryan is here at the hospital and I thought I'd take the opportunity to have a chat with him.'

'But there's an orthopaedic dinner tomorrow night for you to do that.'

'Ah, yes. Of course. You know about that because of Beth.'

'Yes. She is in your unit, remember?'

'Of course I remember.' He sounded perplexed.

'Is Ryan with you now?'

'Er…yes. Yes, he is.'

'Put him on the phone.'

'What? I don't think—'

'Please, hand the receiver to him, Richard.' She could tell she'd stunned him but she wanted to get this thing with Richard sorted out before tomorrow night. Tomorrow night with Marty was going to be an important night and she didn't want any excess baggage hanging around. Tonight she would make certain Richard understood it was over between them and that it was final. She'd had enough!

She heard Richard clear his throat, mumble something and a moment later Ryan said, 'Hello?'

'Ryan, this is Natalie Fox. I'm not sure if you remember me.'

'Natalie. Good to hear your voice.'

'Er, thanks.'

'I hope we're going to have a chance to get together and catch up while I'm here.'

'Sounds good.' She swallowed, feeling a little overwhelmed at Ryan's cheery reception.

'Anyway, what can I do for you?'

'Well...this might sound rather strange and I hope you'll forgive me, but Richard and I had plans this evening and he's about to cancel simply because he wants to talk shop with you. Now, I don't want to hold his career back but it's imperative that I see him tonight.'

Ryan was silent for a moment and Natalie grimaced, wondering if she'd overstepped the mark. 'If you don't mind me asking—why?'

'Um...well...Richard and I were dating and I've tried to call it off but the message just doesn't seem to be getting through. When he arranged for us to go to dinner tonight, I was going to make sure he understood it was well and truly over.'

'Any particular reason why?' Ryan's words were soft and slightly muffled, and she realised he was trying not to let Richard hear the question.

'Um...well...' she said again. 'As a matter of fact, there's someone else I'm interested in.' She paused before continuing. 'Your cousin.'

'Right. Say no more. Consider it done. I'll pass you back to Everley.' And just like that she had her date with Richard restored, although Richard was none too happy.

'I'll meet you at the restaurant, Natalie...*if* that's all right with you?'

Sarcasm? From Richard?

'That will give me a little extra time with Sir Ryan,' he continued.

'Fine.' Natalie hung up and finished dressing, feeling as though a weight had been lifted from her shoulders. She drove to the restaurant where they often ate and was greeted by the *maître d'* like an old friend.

'Is Dr Everley joining you this evening?'

'Yes. He should be here soon.'

'Very good, Dr Fox. I've reserved your usual table.'

'Thank you.' A few minutes after she was seated Richard strode into the restaurant and he did not look at all happy. Natalie bit her lip, hoping he wouldn't make a scene. Usually Richard was highly predictable in behaviour, but with his earlier sarcasm she now wasn't quite sure what he would do.

He allowed himself to be ushered to their table and then they were left alone.

'Have you ordered?'

'No.' Natalie took a deep breath. 'I can tell by the look on your face that this won't take long.'

'How could you do that, Natalie? Sir Ryan is only in town for a short time to visit his family. His time is limited and he may be an old schoolfriend of yours but that doesn't give you the right to rearrange my schedule.'

'I agree, but I really needed to talk to you tonight.' She clenched her hands together in her lap and took a deep breath. 'I've tried to tell you several times that it's over between us, Richard, but it doesn't seem to penetrate. That's why I needed to see you tonight.'

'Why? Reconsidered?'

'No. I need you to know there is no more...*us*. I'm interested in someone else and I wanted to make sure you accept there is nothing between us any more.' To her surprise, this news seemed to stun Richard.

'Someone else?'

'Yes. It wasn't intentional. It just happened.'

'Who? Andrew?'

'Andrew?' She looked at him as though he'd grown an extra head. Andrew? Her fellow registrar? How could Richard not have a clue? Obviously he hadn't noticed the sparks flying between herself and Marty. 'No. Not Andrew,' she said. 'Who it is isn't important where you and I are concerned. I need to know you accept things are over.'

'Well, after your appalling behaviour tonight, you could hardly expect anything else. My career is important to me and I thought you had understood that. Work always comes first.'

'I know, and that's why we're no good together, Richard. I want someone who'll put *me* first. I know as doctors we have responsibilities to our patients, but I want someone who's at least *willing* to try and put me first.'

He rubbed his chin with his finger and thumb before nodding. 'It's over. I accept that.'

Natalie breathed a sigh of relief. 'Thank you.'

'So that's that, then.'

'I guess it is.'

He nodded. 'I'll let the *maître d'* know we'll be leaving.' He stood and escorted her out. 'Thank you, Natalie.' He bent and kissed her cheek, surprising her. 'I'm sorry if I overreacted before. Tonight has been very...liberating. Yes, it's helped more than you could know.'

'Meaning?'

'Sir Ryan was discussing the possibility of me joining him in London soon.'

'And I actually factored into your decision?'

Richard smiled but she had absolutely no reaction to him. Her body didn't warm, her knees didn't go weak...nothing. It was liberating. 'Sort of. I knew I needed to figure out how to break it off gently.'

Natalie frowned, wanting to point out she'd been trying to do that but he hadn't accepted it. Right now Richard needed to hear the words that would ensure they could maintain a successful working relationship. 'Thank you, Richard. I appreciate your honesty and your friendly attitude.'

'Likewise, Natalie. I'll walk you to your car.' He did and then they parted.

As she lay in bed that night, waiting for the clock to tick over to midnight so she could see the beginning of her birthday, her excitement started to grow. She would be going out with Marty and she would tell him how she felt. He deserved her honesty and if he still wanted to remain friends then that would be fine with her...well, not really but she'd take whatever he could offer. She needed to be around him, needed it like she needed air to breathe.

'I'm in love with Marty Williams,' she whispered into the night, and as the clock clicked over to midnight she smiled. It was her birthday.

Her mobile phone rang and she jumped in fright. Realising it was probably her brother, who always called her as early as he could on her birthday, she snatched up her phone. 'Hi, Slimy-breath.'

'Pardon?'

Natalie pulled the phone back from her ear and checked the caller-display screen. It only said 'private call', not her brother's name. 'Sorry. Marty?'

'Yes, Stinky-feet. Happy birthday.'

'Oh.' She melted at his thoughtfulness. 'Thank you.'

'Who's Slimy-breath?'

'Davey.'

'Ah...of course.'

'And I don't have stinky feet.'

'Hey, I was just joining in the name-calling. I didn't wake you, did I?'

'No. I like waiting for my birthday to begin.'

'I know.'

'Don't tell me I told you that, too?'

'Afraid you did.' He paused. 'Did you go out with Everley?'

'Yes.' She frowned. 'Have you been talking to Ryan?'

'Ryan? No. Haven't seen him all day. Why?'

'How did you know I was going out with—'

'Beth told me,' he interrupted.

'Oh.'

'Ryan knows you went out with Everley?'

Natalie sighed. 'It's a long story.'

'Give me the abridged version.' So she quickly told him about the phone conversation with Ryan, leaving out the part where she'd told Ryan she was interested in his cousin.

'OK. So...what happened? With Everley,' he clarified.

Warm tingles spread through Natalie at hearing the uncertainty in his voice. Perhaps Marty didn't want to remain just friends after all. Hope welled to life. 'I made sure he knew it was over.'

'And does he?'

'Yes.'

'Finally,' they both said in unison, then laughed.

'So you're footloose and fancy-free?'

'Seems that way.'

'Not confused any more?'

'No.'

There was a pause. 'Know exactly what you want?' His voice was slightly deeper, more husky, and Natalie's body instantly responded, a warmth flooding through her.

'Yes.'

'Think you're going to get it?'

Natalie's breathing started to shallow at this question. 'I hope so.'

'Can you tell me what it is?'

'Why?'

'So I can make your birthday wishes come true.'

'You can't make *all* of them come true.'

'I can try.'

'New car?'

'Hmm. I take your point. Perhaps I'll have to work on some of my own.'

'Birthday wishes?'

'Yes.'

'But your birthday's not until April.'

'You remembered?'

'You're not the only one with a good memory. April Fool's Day fits you so perfectly, Marty.'

'You're not the only one to think that.' He chuckled. 'So, what other birthday wishes do you have besides a new car?'

'Having the day off work.'

'Check.'

'Spending the day at the spa, getting pampered with Beth.'

'Check?'

'Check,' she confirmed.

'Good.'

'Buying a new dress and shoes.'

'Hmm, might need to leave that one up to Beth as well. A new dress for...?'

'For my special birthday dinner, of course. Not that I need an excuse to buy new clothes, but it's nice to have one, especially after my Christmas party dress was ruined. Justifies the expense.'

'Right. Justification of spending money—check. What else?'

'A present from you?' she asked softly.

'Check.'

Natalie breathed a sigh of happiness, then bit her lip, wanting to ask the next question but unsure of his reaction. Then she remembered this was a brand-new year for her and she wasn't going to blow it. 'Lots of birthday kisses.'

He groaned. 'From anyone in particular?' His voice was thick with repressed desire.

'Yes.'

'Who?'

'You.'

There was a pause and Natalie held her breath, waiting for his response, desperate for him to say 'check'. Had she overstepped the mark? Had she read the signals wrong? Was Marty interested in her in an exclusive way? That was what she needed to talk to him about at dinner. She shook her head and closed her eyes, wishing he'd hurry up and answer the question, then at least she'd have some indication of where she stood.

'*Big* check on that one,' he finally said, and she sighed with longing. 'It's going to be a long day.'

'I was just thinking the same thing.'

'Perhaps I can come and make pancakes again?'

'I'd really like that...but Davey's coming into town specifically to take me out to breakfast.'

'You didn't mention that.'

'Sorry. Breakfast with my brother.'

'Check,' he said, but the verve wasn't there any more. 'You've got a busy day ahead of you and no doubt little Davey's trying to get through to you right now to play his name-calling game.'

'Probably.' Natalie bit her lip before saying, 'You could always drop in for a quick cup of coffee. How's seven-thirty?'

'Seven hours too long.'

'Better than the alternative?'

'Definitely. After this conversation it would have been impossible to wait until eight-thirty tonight.'

'I agree.'

'Get some sleep, my darling Nat,' he said, then hung up. This time, when he said those words they were more of an endearment than a teasing name to call, and she hugged the knowledge close as she pulled the cotton sheet up.

Yawning, she smiled as she closed her eyes. 'Sleep? Check.'

CHAPTER ELEVEN

AT SEVEN twenty-eight in the morning, there was a pounding on the front door as well as a finger being continuously pressed on the doorbell.

'What?' Beth muttered as she came out of her room as Natalie raced down the stairs.

'Don't open it,' she called excitedly to her friend.

'What?' Beth said again.

'Nat? Open the door,' Marty yelled.

Natalie grinned. 'It's not seven-thirty yet.'

'Marty?' Beth asked, frowning at the door and then back at Natalie.

'Beth? Let me in.'

Natalie violently shook her head, laughter bubbling up. 'You have another two minutes to wait. I said seven-thirty.'

'Will someone, please, tell me what's going on?' Beth demanded.

'Your friend is mean and horrible,' Marty called through the door. 'My watch says seven thirty-one.'

'Then it's fast.'

Beth looked closely at Natalie, her frown increasing. 'Marty's here and you seem very happy about it,' she said softly.

'I am.'

'You've talked?'

Natalie nodded then shrugged. 'Sort of.'

'Why is he here?'

'Come on, Nat,' Marty moaned.

'Seven twenty-nine,' she announced.

'Why is he here?' Beth asked again.

'To give me birthday kisses.' Natalie clutched both hands to her chest in delight and giggled.

'You're like a child at Christmas,' Beth muttered.

Natalie laughed again. 'That's exactly how I feel.' Beth rolled her eyes and headed to the kitchen. 'The coffee's almost ready,'

Natalie told her. 'I'd meant to organise it sooner but I spent too long getting ready.'

Beth glanced across at her and then out to the back of the town house, then quickly back to Natalie. 'You look lovely so the extra time was worth it.' Dressed in a black skirt and pink shirt, Natalie looked down at her attire.

'Do you think so?'

'Yes.' Beth headed off towards the back of the lounge room while Natalie checked her watch.

'Ten seconds,' she called, and put her hands on the doorhandle, watching the second hand tick slowly around to the twelve. '*Now* it's seven-thirty,' she said, and opened the door—only to find he had gone. 'Marty!' The delight instantly disappeared from her face as she took a step out to look for him. 'Marty!' Fear, panic and depression started to swamp her. What had she done? She'd only been joking. Eyes wide with despair, she looked all around, then thankfully spotted his car still parked in the driveway. She forced herself to take a breath. He hadn't left.

She swallowed and turned around—jumping in fright at coming face to face with her beloved Marty. Natalie screamed and covered her face in embarrassment. 'Don't *do* that!' She gave his arm a playful hit as he laughed. 'Horrible man.' He didn't look the least bit horrible as he gathered her greedily into his arms. 'How did you get in?'

'Beth let me in the back.'

'You climbed our fence?'

'Yes, and nearly ripped my trousers, I'll have you know.' Her arms were trapped firmly against his chest as he continued to smile down at her. 'How dare you make me wait?'

Natalie merely raised an eyebrow. 'Who's making who wait now?'

'Good point.' He lowered his head, pressing his mouth eagerly to hers. Warmth flooded through her at his soft yet intimate touch and all the sensations she'd experienced the last time they'd kissed settled over her with a wave of tingles and excitement. 'Birthday kiss number one,' he murmured, before lowering his head again, this time seeking a little more of the response she was so willing to give. 'Birthday kiss number two.'

'You're not seriously going to count them all, are you?'

'All? Expecting a plethora, eh?'

'As a matter of fact, yes, I was.'

'Good. Happy birthday, my darling Nat.' He gazed down at her and Natalie saw his own happiness reflected in his eyes. Again, the way he'd said those last three words were the most perfect endearment, and she wondered whether he'd meant them that way every other time he'd said them.

'If you two are going to stand there sucking face all day long, I'll cancel the spa and go shopping,' Beth called from the kitchen. 'Coffee's ready.'

Marty kissed Natalie one more time and murmured, 'Birthday kiss number three.' Then he turned her in his arms and walked them over to the kitchen bench, his chest pressed against her back. Once there, she sat on one of the stools, and although Marty loosened his hold, he didn't stop touching her. It was as though he'd been waiting too long for the privilege and now that he had it, he was making up for lost time.

He stood with his arm about her shoulders and chatted with Beth while sipping at his coffee, stopping every now and then in mid-sentence to give Natalie another birthday kiss. It was the most perfect way to start her day.

'Marty, it's almost eight,' Beth said as she glanced at the clock. 'You'd better get going or you'll be late for ward round.'

Natalie smiled up at him. 'Stay a little longer. I'm sure dear Aggie won't mind, the two of you being so chummy and all.'

Marty groaned and kissed her again. 'I do need to go but only because I'm determined to win our bet.'

'You don't have long left.'

Marty's smile was hypnotising. 'As I've said before, I love a challenge.'

The doorbell rang. 'That'll be Davey.'

'I'll get it,' Beth said, and headed off.

'Did he call you?' Marty asked as Natalie stood. He took the opportunity to wrap himself about her again.

'Yes. At three o'clock.'

Marty smiled and lowered his head for another kiss. 'Birthday kiss number... Oh, man, I've lost count.' He shook his head. 'Guess I'll just have to start again.' He pressed his lips to hers. 'Birthday kiss number one...again.'

Natalie laughed and looked over his shoulder at her brother, who was now staring at her in utter astonishment. Marty released her momentarily so she could hug her brother. 'Hi, bro'.'

'Hi, yourself.' He didn't even look at his sister but merely glowered at Marty before recognition dawned. 'Marty? Marty Williams?'

'One and the same,' he said, and the two men shook hands.

'Wow. It's been so long.' Davey looked from his sister to Marty and back again. 'And the two of you are together?'

'As of this morning,' Beth said. 'Which is why they can't keep their lips off each other.'

Marty smiled and took Natalie's hand. 'I've got ward round so if I can borrow your sister for a few more seconds, she'll be all yours for breakfast.'

'Hey, you might like eating her, but not me,' Davey joked.

'Same sick sense of humour,' Marty added with a chuckle as he tugged Natalie towards the door. 'And stop teaching your sister incorrect French phrases.'

'Huh?' Davey was puzzled for a moment before bursting out laughing. 'She didn't?'

'She did.' Marty raised his eyebrows suggestively and Natalie gave him a playful thump. 'Anyway, thanks for the coffee, Beth, and have fun tonight at the ortho dinner.'

'Ryan is definitely coming, isn't he?' Beth asked.

'I've told him all about you and he said he wouldn't miss it for the world.'

'You did *what?*' Beth demanded.

'I'm joking. He'll be there.' They headed out the door.

'I'll have you know that *I* put the coffee on this morning, not Beth,' she said as they walked to his car.

'I stand corrected. Here.' He leaned against his car. 'Let me thank you properly.'

Natalie smiled and accepted his kisses.

'I have to go,' he said eventually. 'Have a wonderful day and I'll see you tonight.'

'Yes. Be safe.'

Marty nodded, then smiled and climbed behind the wheel. Natalie closed the door and he put the window down. 'One for the road?'

'Definitely.' This one was more thorough than all the other birthday kisses she'd received. It was as though they were back on the balcony at the Christmas party but this time she wasn't shying away from the emotions he evoked, she was embracing them. She loved this man and it seemed he was equally as interested in her. There was still a niggling doubt in the back of her mind about all the other women he'd dated, but she pushed the thought away. Right now he was kissing her and she was loving every moment of it.

He finally pulled back, their breathing erratic as he rested his forehead against hers. 'If I don't go now, dear Aggie will have my guts for garters.'

'Charming.'

He smiled. 'That's me. Marty ''Charming'' Williams. Have a wonderful day, Nat. If I can get off any earlier, I'll let you know.'

'OK.' She stepped back and watched as he started the engine and smiled at her once more before heading off down the street. Natalie, like a soppy, lovesick fool, stood in the middle of the road, watching until his car was out of sight.

'Hey, Toad-face?' Davey called from the door. 'You ready to go?'

'Nothing like coming back to earth with a thud,' she mumbled, as she headed inside.

Natalie dressed with care, wanting to look perfect not only for herself but for Marty as well. Breakfast with Davey had been a hoot and she wished she had more time to spend with her brother, but he had a flight that evening, although he'd said he'd try and get back to spend part of Christmas day with her.

Her hair was loose, brushing over her bare back due to the halterneck dress she'd chosen. It was a deep plum colour and came to mid-thigh. The instant she'd tried it on, both she and Beth had known it was *the* dress. Finding shoes had been an ordeal but they'd persevered until just the right pair had been found. The slingbacks were dressy yet casual. She wore a pair of earrings Davey had given her and the bracelet Marty had given her the year he'd left school. Even though she only wore it on special occasions, preferring to keep it safe, she would take it out every now and then, remembering the good times she'd shared with Marty. Now she was reminded of how important he was to her. All in all, she felt like Cinderella waiting for her Prince Charming...who was running exceedingly late.

Beth had left over an hour ago to attend the orthopaedic dinner in Ryan's honour and Natalie was sitting on her lounge, flicking through the television channels while listening intently for the sound of Marty's car.

Finally, she heard the sound of a car approaching and quickly switched the TV off and slipped her feet into her shoes. Her bag was by the front door and she'd already locked up the rest of the town house. She checked through the window to make sure it was him and her heart jumped in delight as she saw him barely wait for his car to come to a halt before he jumped out.

Natalie smoothed her hand down her dress and flipped her hair over her shoulder before impatiently opening the door. He stood with his finger extended to ring the doorbell and froze the instant he saw her.

He simply stared. There was nothing else for him to do because drinking in the sight of her was definitely his first priority. 'Nat.' He swallowed. 'You're...exquisite.' The smile that lit her face only enhanced her beauty. 'Ready?'

She nodded, incapable of speech. Marty wore a short-sleeved cotton shirt that matched the colour of his eyes, making them even more hypnotic than usual. His shorts were crisply ironed and the urge to run her hands up and down his gorgeous legs was almost too much for her.

'Nat?'

'Hmm?' She raised her gaze to meet his and smiled. 'I'm ready.' She picked up her bag and stepped outside into the warm December evening, closing the door behind her. They walked to the car, and as he opened her door he leaned in to kiss her.

'Sorry I'm so late.'

'I completely understand.'

'Thank you.' He helped her in and then went quickly around to the driver's side.

'Any problems?'

'At work? No. Andrew was just being Andrew.'

'Oh, no. You didn't tell him you had a hot date, did you?'

'Yes. I've now realised how stupid that was.'

'I'm not surprised he delayed you. I'll be glad when he graduates and goes into private practice.' She paused. 'Did you tell him you were going out with me?'

'No—but only because it didn't come up in conversation,' he added quickly. 'Why?'

'Nothing. It's probably better he doesn't know.'

Marty gripped the steering-wheel. 'Do you want to hide the fact that we're seeing each other?'

'Are we?'

'Hey, my eyes are open,' was all he said.

'I only meant that if he knew, he'd take great pleasure in interfering as much as possible—as far as scheduling goes. Just because he doesn't have a private life, he thinks everyone else should be the same.' Natalie frowned. This wasn't going the way she'd planned. They shouldn't be talking about Andrew or the hospital or how she'd been wondering—especially after the way Marty had kissed her that morning—how his hordes of women would take his defection. Although he'd only been at the hospital for a short time, he already had the reputation of a Casanova. She doubted many of the women would be happy to hear he was off the market—if indeed that was what was happening.

'Can we forget anything to do with the hospital and have a good evening?' she ventured.

He smiled and reached for her hand. 'Absolutely.'

Was he placating her? She shook her head, desperate to refocus her attention on just the two of them. 'Where are we going?'

Marty squeezed her hand then let go as he turned a corner. 'Somewhere very special.' He claimed her hand again and started asking about her day. Natalie talked until they arrived at their destination, which didn't look at all like a restaurant.

'We're here?'

'We certainly are.' Marty came and helped her out before locking his car and leading her into the building.

'Do you live here?'

'No.' They walked through reception, down a corridor and out to what appeared to be a courtyard. A horse-drawn carriage, complete with driver and footman, awaited them. Marty stooped and gave her another birthday kiss. 'Happy birthday, Nat.'

Natalie was overwhelmed. She carefully climbed into the open carriage with Marty's assistance, but before he joined her he disappeared for a moment and came back with a bunch of bright gerberas.

'For you.'

'Thank you.'

He nodded to the driver before settling himself next to her, his arm around her shoulders.

As the carriage moved off, she laughed. 'Marty, this is wonderful. Thank you.'

'No. Thank you. I've always wanted to ride in one of these and you've given me the excuse to do it.'

Natalie kissed him. 'I'm glad to give you the excuse.' As they drove along, she realised the carriage was decorated with fairy lights, making it all the more enchanting. She snuggled into him as they took in their surroundings. 'It's amazing how much you miss when you're driving in a car.'

'I was just thinking the same thing,' he murmured, and smiled. They passed a neighbourhood centre holding its Christmas party— lights and decorations everywhere, as well as children running around, enjoying themselves.

'I love this time of year,' she sighed. 'It's *my* time of year.'

'Birthday and Christmas all in the same week.'

'Presents galore.' She smiled lovingly down at her flowers.

'That's not your main present,' he murmured. 'Neither is this ride.'

'You're spoiling me.'

'You deserve it.' They soon came to a halt outside a quiet Italian restaurant. 'Here we are.'

Again, he helped her, drawing her close to his side when she reached ground level. She pulled away for a moment, handing him her flowers, and went to thank both the driver and the footman. Marty watched as she first asked permission, then went around and thanked the horse, allowing herself to be nuzzled. The way she laughed shot straight to his heart. Her hair fell like a rich, chestnut mane of her own down her back and she looked stunning. There was a lot riding on tonight and the last thing he wanted was to blow it. He only had a short while until Christmas, which was when he planned to win their bet and propose marriage to her.

When they entered the restaurant, the *maître d'* personally greeted them before leading the way to a secluded table, lit by romantic candlelight. Natalie looked around the room, loving everything about it.

'Where did you find this place?'

'You've never been here before?' Marty seemed surprised.

'No.'

'It has the best Italian food in all of Sydney, possibly New South Wales.'

'But not Australia?'

'No.' He grinned. 'You think I'm exaggerating, but I have to admit there are some excellent Italian restaurants in Victoria.'

'Of course.'

Marty reached across the table and took her hand in his. 'Anyway, as I remembered your fondness for Italian food, this seemed the perfect place to bring you.'

'It's fantastic.'

'Wait until you try the food.' He slowly raised her hand to his lips and pressed a kiss to her smooth skin. 'I love your bracelet.'

Natalie blushed and lowered her gaze. 'It was a Christmas gift from a very special friend.'

'No, it wasn't.' At the contradiction, she looked at him. He shook his head. 'It wasn't a Christmas present, Nat, it was a birthday present.'

'Oh.' She frowned, realising what that meant. The fact that Marty had given her a present at all had astounded her. She'd thought it had been a parting Christmas present and as she'd seen him give a few of their other friends gifts, she'd just accepted it with thanks. 'Really?'

'Yes. It wasn't wrapped in Christmas paper.'

'But that implies...' She stopped, her mind whirring, trying to come to terms with this new information.

'That I liked you more than just a friend? Nat, I've already told you I wanted to kiss you that day.'

'So you did but I thought that was just curiosity.'

He shrugged. 'Curiosity and a *lot* more, Nat.'

'Oh,' she said again as his thumb brushed over the beautiful piece of jewellery.

'Do you wear it often?'

She held his gaze and said softly, 'Only on very special occasions, and I would always think of you.'

'Really?' He puffed out his chest at this information and she laughed.

'Really,' she confirmed. Marty kissed her hand again and reluctantly let it go when the waiter brought over some menus. As the evening continued, Natalie felt herself completely unwind and knew without a doubt that Marty was definitely the man for her, but was she the woman for him? Again she pushed the thought aside. That was something for her to ponder later because right now she was going to enjoy every moment she had with him.

'How did you mastermind all this?' she asked as she finished off her last mouthful of lasagne.

'What's ''all this''?'

'Tonight. The carriage, the flowers, the restaurant...'

'The present,' he said, pulling a large box from beside him.

'What? Where were you hiding that?'

'Not hiding. It's been just beside me since we arrived.' He held it out. 'Don't you want it?'

Natalie gratefully accepted the present, frowning at the size of the box. Slowly she unwrapped it, carefully pulling the sticky tape from the paper and smiling when Marty became impatient. 'My present. My birthday. I open it the way I like.'

'Just rip it.'

'No.' She shifted it out of his grasp. 'You're not doing it this time. You ripped open the paper when you gave me my bracelet. Not this time.' Finally, she opened the paper and laughed. '*Twister?*'

'Thought you needed the practice.'

'Ha. You said I was the champion.'

His blue gaze pinned her and she felt the mood instantly change. His voice was deep and sensual as he said, 'I'm demanding a re-match.'

Natalie felt the blood pump faster around her body as her breathing increased. She held his gaze, her tongue coming out to wet her lips. Her mind was having trouble with coherent thought as the picture of the two of them playing the game in a secluded environment buzzed through her brain.

'You're on.' The words came out as a husky whisper and she swallowed, reaching for her water glass with a not-so-steady hand. She sipped at the cooling liquid, although it did nothing to help extinguish the fire deep within her...the fire Marty had started with one smouldering look.

'*Scuzi, signor, signorina.*'

The moment was broken as the *maître d'* looked worriedly at them both.

'You are a doctor of medicine, no?'

'Yes.'

'There is trouble down the street. Many people are hurt. Little children.'

Marty and Natalie instantly stood. 'Whereabouts?' Natalie asked, and the man looked at her. 'I'm a doctor, too,' she added, as though to reassure him. They started moving towards the door.

'At the neighbourhood centre. They were having Christmas celebrations.'

'Have the emergency services been called?'

'Yes. We ourselves have called. I will take care of your belongings.' Before they left, Natalie bent and took off her shoes.

'They're going to be a hindrance,' she said, holding them in one hand.

'That's my Nat,' Marty said, before taking her free hand and heading down the street, the smell of smoke filling their lungs.

'What's the plan?' she asked.

'If the emergency services have been called, we'll just assist where we can.'

'We have no bandages, no oxygen, no supplies at all. I'm not trying to be picky,' she added. 'I'm just stating facts.'

'I have a kit in my car, but it's too far away.' He shook his head. 'We'll manage.'

'Improvise,' she said, different scenarios going through her head. She grabbed her hair and twisted it into a knot that didn't need any pins to hold it in place. The smell of the smoke was becoming stronger. In the distance, sirens began to wail and the area was darker than the block they'd just left.

'At least the cavalry isn't going to be long,' Marty mumbled as the neighbourhood centre came into view.

'If they can get through this Christmas traffic.'

'That's what the sirens and flashing lights are for.' He grinned at her, then coughed a little. 'No unnecessary risks.'

'Same goes for you.'

He gave her hand one last squeeze before letting go and crossing the road. People were everywhere, kids were screaming, everyone was talking and it seemed no one was making sense. They split up, trying to determine who needed help and in what order.

Natalie put her shoes back on and started sorting people into groups. Some had suffered smoke inhalation, others were just scared—and rightly so. There were cuts and bruises, and thankfully a few people who lived in the area brought out medical supplies.

Natalie saw a little boy of about two toddling off down the side of the centre, crying for his mother. She quickly raced down and gathered him up, but as she picked him up she saw a little girl at the window of the centre, crying and banging on the window.

Her heart stuck in her throat for a moment and when the little boy's mother came and took the boy out of her arms Natalie quickly looked around for a way in. This side of the centre was in flames. Through the thick smoke she saw a door to the side and without another thought went inside.

The smoke stung her eyes and she coughed as she dropped to the floor. It wasn't as bad down here and she crawled along the corridor and around into the room where she'd seen the little girl.

The door was jammed and Natalie knew the handle would be hot. She swivelled onto her back and braced herself as best she could, her feet in the middle of the door. She bent her legs and kicked. The little girl screamed. Natalie coughed but didn't give up. She kicked again and again and finally the door opened.

The flames were getting closer but she also heard the sirens of the fire truck and realised the crews had arrived. She coughed and tried to call to the girl but couldn't. She turned again and headed into the room, the little girl coming up and clinging to her.

Natalie tried the base of the window but it was stuck fast. They'd have to go out the way she'd come in. She pulled the girl onto the floor and spoke into her ear.

'Stay right beside me. We're going to crawl...' She stopped and coughed. 'Crawl like snakes through the grass. Ready?'

The little girl looked at her with scared eyes but nodded.

'Let's go.' They crawled out of the room and into the corridor, but the fire had now taken hold of the ceiling above and was blazing furiously.

They made it almost to the door when an ear-splitting crack ripped through the air and Natalie had one second to look up before realising what was about to happen. She covered the girl with her body just as she heard deep male voices shouting around her.

In the next instant everything went black.

CHAPTER TWELVE

'NAT! Nat? Honey, it's me,' Marty called as she was wheeled into A and E. She only vaguely heard him as she felt very drowsy.

'Marty, I need you out of the way,' the triage sister said.

'No. I'm staying with her.'

'Then you wait to the side and let us do our jobs.' She pointed sternly to the corner but Marty didn't know if he could let go of his darling Nat's hand. 'Please, Marty,' Sister said, and he realised he needed to do as he was told...but he didn't like it.

He watched as the staff worked on Natalie. He hadn't been at this hospital long but he knew that in all hospitals, when it came to one of their own, the treatment they were given was the best of the best. The head of the burns unit as well as the plastic surgery unit would both be called to come and assess Natalie.

'Keep that airway clear. Natalie? Can you hear me?' the A and E registrar called. The ambulance officers had established an IV line and administered high-flow humidified oxygen through a non-rebreather mask.

Natalie mumbled something incoherent, which at least showed the staff she was mildly aware of what was going on around her. They hooked her up to an electrocardiograph and monitored her vital signs, cutting away her clothing and removing her jewellery. One of the nurses came and handed Marty the earrings and bracelet she'd been wearing. Tenderly he turned the bracelet over in his fingers, remembering how long it had taken him to choose from all the bracelets in the shop. It had cost him quite a bit, but back then fifteen dollars had seemed a lot. In some ways he wanted to throw it out and buy her something more expensive, more delicate, but as soon as the thought passed through his mind, he knew he'd never do it.

This bracelet was their link from their past to their future. It was precious—to both of them—and although they may have grown up, the sentiment around the gift was still the same. He glanced up, watching the staff giving her the care she needed.

170

They would get through this and triumph—they had to. He was desperate to show her how much he loved her, how much he'd listened to the words she'd said all those years ago in Fiji. How ironic that when she'd said he would one day find someone who was absolutely perfect for him, he hadn't realised it would be her. Sure, the attraction had been there but in every way Nat was his soul mate and regardless of what lay ahead of them, both immediately or in the future, they would conquer it together.

Natalie tried to open her eyes but it hurt too much. She shifted her head against the pillow and relaxed. The beeping sound wasn't her alarm, which meant she could sleep for longer.

'Natalie?'

She frowned at the sound of Richard's voice. What was he doing in her bedroom? She tried again to open her eyes but for some reason it hurt too much. The beeping sound became louder and she felt her head begin to pound in synchronicity. She screwed her eyelids even tighter, deciding it wasn't worth it. She didn't need to open her eyes to speak.

'Richard?' Her voice sounded so strange. 'What are you doing here?' She choked on the last word and within a second felt soothing ice-chips being spooned into her mouth.

'You were hurt. Remember?'

Natalie tried hard to remember, but the sound of someone else coming into her room and talking to Richard was too much for her to handle and she gratefully drifted back to sleep.

The next time she stirred was when someone pressed a kiss to her mouth. She frowned. 'No. No. Go away, Richard.'

Marty was struck with such intense jealousy at the other man's name on her lips that it took him a few seconds to realise she'd told Richard to go away. 'It's Marty,' he murmured near her ear, and amazingly she sighed with relief.

'Good. You're allowed to kiss me.'

Her words warmed his heart. 'You'd better believe it. Me and no one else.' He chuckled.

A moment later she said, 'It's bright,' as she tried to open her eyes.

Marty instantly stood and closed the blinds. 'Better?'

'Yes. What are you doing here?'

He paused for a moment before asking, 'Where do you think I am?'

'In my bedroom. Richard was here, too, or was I dreaming?'

Marty knew many staff members had been up to visit her so it wasn't out of the ordinary for Everley to be one of them. 'You're in hospital, Nat.'

'What?' She struggled to sit up but he eased her back.

'Stay still, honey. You're doing just fine. I've been making sure they look after you.' He grimaced. He'd bugged her admitting doctor so much he'd been told to cool it or he'd be banished from the ward.

'What happened?'

'Do you remember the fire?'

'At the neighbourhood centre.'

'That's the one.'

Her eyes came open and she slowly focused. 'The little girl?'

'She's safe and recovering in our ward. You saved her life, Nat.'

'I don't remember getting her out.'

'You protected her. The firefighters said you were both really lucky.' He shifted so he was sitting on the edge of her bed, both of his hands clasped around her left hand. 'I aged a thousand years when they brought you out. I thought I told you not to take any unnecessary risks.'

'I'm sorry.'

'No more Dr Heroine—*ever*.'

'I'll do my best.'

Marty paused and she realised he was trying to get himself under control. Finally, he spoke. 'A ceiling beam came down, hit you on the head and knocked you out. Thankfully, the section of beam that hit you wasn't on fire at that stage. You did manage to breathe in quite a bit of smoke, but your lungs are now fine and clear.'

'Which unit am I in? Burns?'

'Yes. Your right arm and hand are burnt and you have a few burns on your face.'

Natalie's eyes widened at this news. 'My face?'

Again he paused before saying, 'And...and they had to cut your hair.'

Tears welled in her eyes and drifted down her cheeks and he let go of her hand so she could touch her hair. As she felt the jagged cut, the tears increased. Marty took a tissue and carefully dabbed them away. 'Don't, Nat. Don't cry. You're here. You're alive. It's all good.' As though he needed to prove it to her, he pressed his lips to hers. 'I was so worried but now...now it's all going to be all right.'

She nodded at his words, sniffing and pulling herself together. 'What's the time?'

'Sun is just setting. Why?'

'I want to see my doctor. Who am I under?'

'Janelle.'

At this news, Natalie relaxed. 'Janelle is the best.'

'That's St Gregory's for you. Always reserves the best doctors for their staff.' He kissed her again. 'I'll see if she can come and see you.'

'Thanks.' Natalie sighed and closed her eyes, desperate for some shred of control.

'You know, I owe you a lot more birthday kisses,' he said softly in an attempt to cheer her up.

Natalie's eyes snapped open. 'My things. My shoes, my present...' She looked down at her bandaged arm. 'My bracelet.'

'All safe. I have your jewellery and Beth has the other things, although your dress was sort of ruined.'

Natalie nodded, trying to put on a brave face. 'Again. I don't seem to have much luck when I dress up. From now on I'm going out in my oldest clothes.'

Marty chuckled. 'You're amazing, Nat. You give out so much, to your patients, to your friends. The child you saved will be forever grateful. I know her parents are and they're eager to meet you properly, but Janelle has said not until you're stronger.'

Neither of them spoke as the reality of her situation started settling over Natalie. She may have saved that little girl but at what cost to her own life? She needed to talk to Janelle, to find out how bad her burns were. Even so, it wasn't as though she'd be rushing back to work any time soon. With the way she looked now, would Marty want to continue pursuing a relationship with her...if that was the way they'd been headed?

She closed her eyes, trying to block out the many questions running through her mind.

'Tired?' he asked softly.

'Mmm.'

'Pain?'

'A little.'

'I'll get the nurse.' He kissed her then reluctantly let her hand go and headed off. Natalie was both distraught and thankful when he left. His explanation of events had shocked her. She couldn't believe she'd been brought to St Gregory's as a patient, but Marty wouldn't lie to her.

Everything had been going so well between them and now they were faced with this!

Tears rolled down her cheeks again as she drifted into a fitful sleep.

For the next few days, Natalie lived from one event to the next. There was the ward round, breakfast, visitors, treatment, lunch, hairdresser visits, more treatment, more visitors, more food, more...more...more and all she wanted was to curl up in a little ball and weep.

The head of clinical psychology came to see her and explained that depression, especially at this early stage, was quite normal. Natalie had no idea that depression could be so lonely, even when you were surrounded by people.

Marty was definitely the brightest spark of her life and he was always so loving and attentive with every visit, bringing in cards and pictures the children in the paediatric ward had made. He told her what was happening in the ward and the plans that were coming together for Christmas Day.

He sat on her bed, then patted his stomach. 'What do you think? Do I still need that extra padding?'

Natalie pretended to ponder the question for a moment before nodding. 'Might be best.' She ran her hand over his chest, loving the fact that she had the right to touch him in such an intimate way. 'You're all firm, hard muscle.' She said the words slowly, watching as his gaze darkened. As she'd known he would, he leaned in and kissed her, his mouth letting her know just how much he desired her.

'I can't wait until you're discharged,' he murmured.

'Going to carry me up the stairs to my bedroom again?'

'Ha! There's nothing wrong with your legs, Nat. You can walk.'

'Huh. Some knight in shining armour you turned out to be.'

'Is that what you want, honey? Someone to rescue you?' The teasing light had disappeared from his eyes and his tone was serious.

Natalie felt as though he could see deep into her soul—all the way to the depression she'd been doing her best to hide from him.

'There's a sadness in your eyes and I wish I knew what I could do to help.'

Much to her chagrin, tears welled in her eyes and she squeezed his hand. 'You do the most. Just being here, your visits, help.'

'Do they?'

Natalie closed her eyes and carefully rested her head back on the pillows, still getting used to her new, bob-length hairstyle. She brushed the hair back behind her ear with her left hand, trying to put off for as long as she could the conversation she knew they had to have.

When a tear escaped and trailed down her cheek, Marty tenderly brushed it away and that opened the floodgates. 'Aw, honey,' he whispered as he gathered her closer. He wasn't sure what to do but just holding her worked for him and he hoped it worked for her, too.

'I don't know if I can do this,' she finally said, her voice breaking and another few sobs shaking through her body.

'Do what?'

'*Us!*'

'Us?' He seemed surprised and pulled back to look at her. 'What do you mean?'

'I just don't know what's going to happen to me. Janelle's happy with my progress but things have just... Oh, I don't know.'

'Hey, hey. We'll work it out.'

She nodded, not sure she believed him. She *wanted* to believe him—in fact, when he was with her, she felt as though she could do anything, but when he left, doubts began to set in, especially through the long, lonely nights.

'I think,' she said softly, 'that I just need some time.'

'Time?' he asked cautiously.

'Time to just think and figure things out.'

'Meaning?'

'Meaning I'm going to ask for no visitors tomorrow.'

'Christmas Eve? Probably a wise decision. The entire hospital is getting ready for Christmas Day and tomorrow promises to be worse than the last few days.'

'I mean *no* visitors, Marty.'

'You don't want to see me?'

'I need to work things out.' When he opened his mouth to protest, she quickly went on. 'My life has changed—dramatically. Janelle thinks I might need skin grafts and they take a long time to recover from, and who knows when I'll have full movement back in my arm. I won't be able to work and...' She trailed off, feeling a fresh bout of tears welling up.

'Shh.' He kissed her lips, silencing her for the moment.

'And I have months and months of rehabilitation coming up and you don't need that,' she added softly when he'd finally released her mouth.

'*I* don't need it?' He frowned. 'What do you mean?'

'I...I...' She worked hard to control her breathing. 'I need to think.'

'About *me?*'

'Marty, I can't do this to you. I can't put you through all this.' She indicated her right arm.

'Why not?' he demanded.

Natalie's breathing increased and she tried hard to swallow over the enormous lump in her throat. 'I have a long journey ahead of me—'

'And I'll be there with you every step of the way.'

'I don't want you to look back with regrets, and besides...' She stopped, her lower lip wobbling as she failed to hold onto her emotions. 'I'm not pretty any more.'

'Oh, honey.' He shook his head, then kissed her again.

'You deserve one of your pretty girls to hang around with, not me. I don't want to be a burden to you. You've been through a rotten relationship before and I don't want that to happen to you again.'

'It won't happen again.' Frustration welled up in him and he wanted to blurt out that he loved her, that everything was going to be fine and that he wanted to marry her. He'd had the proposal planned perfectly for Christmas Day and he desperately wanted to surprise her. Besides, with the mood she was in right now, she'd probably refuse him and there was no way he was going to chance that. 'You and I are good together,' he said. 'And besides, ever heard the saying beauty is only skin deep? It's very true. I'm not as superficial as that anatomy text book you used to date. I'm here for the long haul and you probably won't believe me when I say that you are *very* pretty, but it's true.'

'But my life has just been changed. I've been dealt a different set of cards and I don't know where everything fits. I'm confused and scared and I need time to figure things out. You're the one who said I like being in control and that's very true, but right now I feel so completely out of control that I need to figure out a plan.'

'Do you think I'm going to leave you?' Marty watched her eyes carefully and saw her look away.

'Marty, it's not going to be easy. It's also no way to start off a relationship.'

'Sure, but you know me. I love a challenge.'

Natalie closed her eyes and shook her head, not sure whether to laugh or cry. 'You always know the most perfect thing to say.'

'And don't you forget it,' Marty teased, then grew serious. Carefully, he cupped her face in his hands, his gaze tender and caring. 'I'll give you space tomorrow but only tomorrow. It won't be easy but I'll respect your wishes. Just tell me one thing.'

Natalie held her breath and waited for his question.

'Do you love me?'

He sounded unsure, which wasn't like Marty at all. In that one instant Natalie realised how much power she had over him. She held his gaze, hoping he'd see the truth in her eyes.

'Yes.'

Marty exhaled the breath he'd been holding, his gorgeous smile spreading across his lips and melting her heart once more. 'Then that's all I need. That will help me through tomorrow.' This time, when he bent to kiss her, there was a new promise and a new hope that coursed through them both.

'Come on, Marty,' the nurse said as she walked in. 'Oops. Sorry.' She didn't leave but instead crossed to the foot of the bed. Marty reluctantly released Natalie. 'It's time for you to leave.'

Marty nodded, not looking at the other woman. He only had eyes for his darling Nat. He brushed another kiss across her lips. 'Christmas morning can't come soon enough,' he murmured.

When he left, the doubts started to raise their ugly heads again and when she woke up on Christmas Eve, depression had once more settled over her. She didn't eat much at breakfast or lunch, instead closing her eyes and wallowing in self-pity, telling herself she had every right to do so.

When Janelle came around to review her, Natalie was wiping her eyes and blowing her nose.

'You look a sorry sight,' the doctor said. 'I understand you've asked for no visitors or phone calls today.'

Natalie nodded.

'Think that's wise?'

'Who knows?' she blurted as a fresh bout of tears began.

'Who indeed?' Janelle replied. 'Let's take a look at your arm.'

It was almost a relief to focus on what was happening rather than sifting through her thoughts.

'You're missing him, aren't you,' Janelle stated.

'Who?'

'Oh, as if you need to ask. The whole hospital is buzzing with rumours that you and Marty are a couple. As the new bachelor to the hospital, he didn't last long. He's already called the nurses' station quite a few times this morning, checking up on you, and he's asked me to contact him after my review.' Janelle chuckled. 'Marty Williams is *definitely* off the bachelor roster. It's quite clear that he loves you very much.'

'It is?'

Janelle merely laughed again as she carefully examined Natalie's arm.

'This is looking very good, very good indeed. In fact, I don't think we're going to need skin grafts after all. It's healing very nicely all by itself. Naturally, you'll have scarring but in two, three years' time you'll hardly be able to notice them.'

Natalie watched as the nurse carefully rewrapped her arm in the special burns dressing.

'Really?'

'I'm not in the habit of lying to my patients, Natalie, especially when one of them is a colleague.'

Natalie breathed an amazed sigh of relief. 'Thank you, Janelle. That is the best Christmas present you could have given me.'

When she was left alone, Natalie thought over her situation and realised it wasn't as bad as she'd initially thought. She was still in for a lot of treatment and rehabilitation but she knew she would cope. She had the support of Beth and Davey and her mother...and Marty? If she let go of him, she'd not only be recovering from her injuries but from a broken heart as well. Janelle had said that he loved her but she'd yet to hear those words from his own lips. It was clear he cared for her and he'd said he would be sticking around to help her, but in what way? As her friend? Boyfriend? Was he willing to take another chance at marriage? She had no idea where their relationship was going.

Taking a deep breath, she vowed to find out. Tomorrow, Christmas Day, would be a day of discoveries…and hopefully they would be discoveries that would make her happy for the rest of her life.

By the time the evening meal was served, she had a completely different outlook. She loved Marty and was determined to show him they belonged together. That night she slept a lot better and in the morning, with help from the nurses, she managed to shower and carefully wash her hair.

'I'm beginning to like my hair this length,' she told the nurses. 'I don't need to worry about putting it up to keep it out the way.'

Natalie waited impatiently for Marty to come and was very surprised when Sister Dorset walked into her room just after breakfast, pushing an empty wheelchair.

'Good morning, Natalie. Merry Christmas.'

Natalie simply stared at the other woman. Had Sister just called her Natalie? 'Er…good morning, Sister.'

'Ready for your first Christmas surprise?'

'I…um…I guess so.'

'Right. Out of bed, then.' Sister Dorset helped Natalie up, brushing away the burns unit nurse when she came in to see what was going on.

'I'm fine, Nurse. I'm taking Dr Fox down to Paediatrics and I'll have her back in an hour.'

'Of course, Sister,' the nurse replied, and with that, Natalie was effectively transferred into Sister Dorset's care.

They didn't speak a word until they were in the lift when Sister Dorset said, 'That's quite a young man you have there, Natalie.'

'Marty?'

'Yes. Dr Williams has proved himself in many areas in a short space of time. He's trustworthy, honest, caring and good with the children. Not only that but he obviously loves you very much.'

'So everyone keeps telling me.'

The lift doors opened and Sister slowly pushed her along the corridor. 'He came down to the ward the day after your accident looking at least ten years older. He told me he could see you were depressed and he wasn't sure what to do or how he could help.' She paused outside the doors to the paediatric unit. 'I told him to be himself and follow his instincts.' Sister nodded. 'Yes, he's quite a man.' A smile twitched at her lips as she said, 'Why, if I were thirty years younger, you'd have a run for your money.'

'Sister!' Natalie was surprised and shocked to hear Sister talking like this.

Sister Dorset actually chuckled. 'It's Christmas, Natalie. Enjoy the more mellow side of me while you can. I also think it's only fair to tell you that I know of the little bet you and Dr Williams had going.'

Natalie coloured. 'Oh, Sister. I'm sorry. There was no harm meant and—'

'It's quite all right. Reminded me of the fun I used to have when I was just a student nurse. I only want to say that your young man has earned himself the right to call me by my first name, as have you—but only when we're off duty, if you don't mind.' She opened the door to the ward. 'And perhaps today.' She smiled at Natalie again, before pushing the chair into the ward.

'Well, this is certainly a day for discoveries,' Natalie muttered quietly to herself as Sister took her down to the playroom, which was full of children and parents. Some children were in wheelchairs, others in their beds, some on chairs and others on the floor. The craft tables had been pushed aside and the Christmas tree had been brought in, its lights flashing merrily.

The children all cheered when Natalie was wheeled in and several came over to wish her a merry Christmas and give her a hug. Tears swam in Natalie's eyes but for the first time since the fire they were tears of happiness and love.

Then the sound of jingling bells filled the air and the children went into hyperdrive as they realised what was happening.

'It's Santa,' some of them whispered, and even the older children were excited.

'Ho! Ho! Ho!' said a deep voice, and a moment later Santa, in his baking-hot velvet suit, appeared in the doorway. A loud cheer went up and some of the children rushed to hug him while others sat and stared.

'Merry Christmas,' Santa called, then looked around the room. 'Now, are there any children here who have been good?' he asked.

Again a loud cheer went up and the noise was deafening. Natalie's heart filled with love and it bubbled over as she watched Marty making the children so happy. She'd once thought that he would make a wonderful father and now she knew for sure. Hopefully he was going to be the father of *her* children.

He gave out presents, personally labelled for each child that was there. Then he gave out small Christmas food baskets, beautifully wrapped, to the parents. It wasn't until all the presents had been given out that Sammy, who was lying in his bed, which had been pushed next to Natalie, said, 'But Dr Natalie didn't get anything, Santa.'

'Sammy, my boy, you're so right,' Santa Marty said. 'And I know just the present to give her.' He dug into his sack and pulled out an envelope. Natalie took it with shaking hands then glanced up at Santa. Then, much to the surprise of everyone in the room, Santa bent and kissed Dr Natalie firmly on the lips—beard and all.

A few of the parents clapped and the staff certainly did, but Natalie heard one child say, 'What about Dr Marty? I thought he liked Dr Natalie?'

Natalie smiled at him then looked back at the envelope. With trembling fingers she opened it and pulled out a string of paper dolls. All had been decorated with smiling faces and a message had been written across their bodies. It said, WILL YOU MARRY ME?

Natalie's breath caught in her throat and she looked up at Santa adoringly. 'Why, Santa, I thought you'd never ask,' she murmured, before he kissed her again. Then she whispered, 'You'd better make your exit before the children guess you're not the real Santa.'

'Good point.' He straightened. 'Ho! Ho! Ho!' he said again. 'Santa has a lot more boys and girls to see, so you all have a very happy day and remember to be good next year.' After a few more cuddles he was gone, and ten minutes later Dr Marty came back into the room, disappointed he'd missed Santa but interested to see what the children had received.

'Santa kissed Dr Natalie,' Sammy said immediately.

'Did he now?' Marty raised his eyebrows and smiled at Nat. 'Should I be jealous?'

Natalie returned his smile. 'Perhaps. Looks as though you might have competition.' A few of the parents laughed. 'Santa even proposed.'

'Hmm. I can see I'm going to have to fix this.'

At that moment Sister Dorset bustled in and declared it was time for Dr Natalie to return to her own ward. Natalie promised to come and see them all the next day and, after giving Sammy a special Christmas hug, allowed herself to be wheeled back to the burns unit.

'Are you tired?' Marty asked her.

'A little.'

'Uh-oh.'

'Why?'

There was a knock on the door and Beth, Davey, Lisa and Cassie came into the room. Marty pulled out a piece of mistletoe from his pocket and kissed the other women in the room on the cheek. Then he held it over Natalie's head.

'Do you honestly need mistletoe as an excuse?'

'Probably not, but I thought it might be kind of romantic for our first official Christmas kiss. After all, I have to compete with Santa.'

Natalie laughed. 'Plan on giving me a plethora of kisses?'

'Absolutely.' With that, he lowered his head and all her doubts vanished into thin air once more.

'They're at it again,' Beth muttered. 'I thought this was supposed to be a party.'

'So it is. Bring in the trolley,' Marty said, and Natalie was surprised when Sister Dorset once more walked into her room, this time wheeling a hospital trolley full of presents and food.

'Thank you, Aggie,' Marty said, then turned and winked at Natalie, showing her he'd won their bet. Then he handed around Santa hats, placing one carefully on Natalie's head and then a kiss on her lips.

'Reminds me of the day we met up again.'

She smiled.

'I like your hair like this. Have I told you that?'

'Really? I think I like it, too.' Natalie raised her left hand self-consciously to her head.

'You're beautiful,' he whispered.

'Thank you, you charming man.'

'Marty ''Charming'' Williams. That's me. Regarding our bet, I'll collect on my winnings later. Right now, it's party time.' And to prove his point he popped a party popper into the air, the tiny streamers coming down and landing on her bedcover.

They had presents, chocolates and lots of Christmas goodies such as turkey and plum pudding. They were all wearing ridiculous Christmas hats and blowing whistles when there was a knock at the door.

'Ryan! You made it,' Marty called, and gave his cousin a hearty slap on the back. 'Let me introduce you to everyone.' He did, and Natalie noticed Ryan had the same Casanova charm as his cousin. All the women in the room seemed to swoon as Ryan smiled at them, except for Beth, but then Natalie remembered Beth and Ryan had already met.

'I take it everything turned out the way you planned?' Ryan asked her quietly.

'Well, almost.' She indicated her arm.

'But you're happy?' he quizzed her.

'Very.'

'Good.' Ryan bent and kissed her cheek. 'You're perfect for him. You always were.'

Natalie smiled at him but Marty interrupted. 'Hey, hey. She's my woman.'

'*Your* woman?' Natalie raised her eyebrows warningly and everyone laughed. Marty's answer was to press another kiss to her lips.

'You'd better believe it, honey,' he whispered.

They continued with the party until the sun had set, with many staff members dropping in at one time or another. By the time the last person left, Natalie was exhausted. Marty came and sat down on her bed and kissed her.

'Had a good day?'

'Wonderful.'

'You look wonderful. Do you know that?'

'Thank you.'

'I'm not just giving you platitudes, Nat.'

'I know.'

'Do you? I can still feel reservations between us and I want to assure you they're unnecessary.'

Natalie bit her lip, wondering if she could change the subject. 'Aggie, eh?'

He smiled. 'I have her well and truly eating out of my hand.'

'You are so conceited.'

'Yeah, but you love me.'

Natalie sighed. 'Yes. Yes, I do. I've been fighting it for so long.'

'Really?'

'I think I started fighting it when we met up in Fiji.'

'Now you're joking, right?'

'No joke at all, although there was no way I'd admit it to myself.

I found it difficult enough to admit I was attracted to you back then.'

'Curious about me at school, attracted to me in Fiji and in love with me now.'

'Yes.' She sighed again.

He leaned in closer. 'You do know that I've been totally smitten by you since we first met up again?'

'What?'

'Oh, yes. First in deepest smit and then in deepest love.'

She smiled at his incorrect English, then focused on what he'd said. 'You love me?'

'Of course I do.' He sounded surprised at her question.

'But, Marty, are you sure?'

'Yes.'

'But...' She paused but knew she had to continue. All her doubts needed to be washed away. 'What about all the girls you like to date?'

'I've already told you I didn't kiss a single one of them.' He crossed his heart. 'I arrived in town, ready for a little fun, and found you.'

'Not fun at all.'

'On the contrary. Finding the girl of my dreams means a *lot* of fun ahead.'

'The girl you were curious about.'

He smiled. 'You were everything I ever wanted but you were already going out with someone.' He shrugged. 'So I decided to spread myself around but after the first week I knew it was useless. I wanted to spend time with you and I could see that Everley wasn't right for you.'

'Arrogant *and* conceited.'

He shook his head. 'I'm just a man who knows what he wants, and I want you. I've won our bet fair and square, Nat, and now you have to accept my proposal.'

'Which is?'

Marty once more handed her an envelope. She took it and said, 'Another marriage proposal? I've already had one today, you know.'

'Mmm. So you've said. It's not a proposal. It's your annual Christmas card.'

'Oh.' Natalie opened the envelope and took out the card. She stared at it for a moment then threw back her head and laughed. 'Is that us?'

'Yes. I found the picture in one of our school year books and scanned it, thinking it would make a wonderful card for you. I also wanted to give this back to you.' He reached into his pocket and pulled out her bracelet.

'I love this bracelet,' she murmured. 'And I love you.'

She accepted his kiss before he pulled back, saying,

'But wait...there's more!' He pulled another present from his pocket, a small square box and handed it to her. 'Please, note this is not wrapped in Christmas paper. It is not a Christmas present, neither is it a belated birthday present, and I demand that you rip the paper. I don't think I could stand the suspense.'

'I'm going to have to,' she said holding up her bandaged hand. 'Being nice and neat requires all ten digits working.'

'They're working. Five of them are just wrapped up, that's all. Let me help you.' They pulled the wrapping paper off together and then Marty opened the box. A beautiful gold ring lay inside, a square-cut turquoise in the middle and two diamonds on either side.

'It's beautiful *and* my birthstone.'

'Can I put it on you?'

'Marty, wait. I know you love me and you know I love you, but what if...?' She paused. She needed to say this, needed to know he accepted the difficulties they were now facing. 'What if the road ahead is too rocky for us? As I said, it's not a good way to start a relationship.'

'I know you might be scared, especially given your parents' rocky marriage and then their divorce, but we're not them. I may have the same colouring as your father but I'm not him, Nat.'

'I know. I've always known you were nothing like him but still...I'm scared.'

'But we're not starting a relationship, my darling Nat. We're continuing. We started our relationship over fifteen years ago. It may change direction now and then but we'll always be together. For years I've been looking for my home...the place where I fit, and I fit with you, Nat. You and no one else.'

'But, you know, the grass is always greener on the other side and all that. You've been footloose and fancy-free for so long. Is settling down what you really want?'

'Yes, it is and I'll tell you something about that grass. It *isn't* greener on the other side. The grass is greener where you water it and I want to plant a patch all the way around us and keep on watering it for the rest of our lives.' He placed a hand on either side of her face, his thumbs gently caressing her small bandages. 'You belong to me and I belong to you. We always have and now we can go forward together and build a wonderful life.'

Fresh tears were gathering in Natalie's eyes. His words had made every last doubt disappear and in that moment, even though she'd thought it impossible, her love for him increased.

'I am so hopelessly in love with you, Marty Williams, and I want to be with you for ever.'

A slow smile spread across his lips and, after kissing her, he placed the ring on her finger. 'Of course, you do realise we're going to need to have at least four children for a decent Twister competition.'

Natalie groaned then laughed. 'Four?'

Marty nodded. 'The girls will have your beauty and the boys will have my charm.'

'A lethal combination.'

'And they'll all have your stubbornness,' he continued.

'And they'll all have your warped sense of humour.'

'And they'll all have our intelligence.'

'And they'll all be arrogant and conceited like their father.'

'All right. Enough's enough.'

Natalie laughed, happier than she'd ever been, and touched his face with her hand. Tenderly she kissed his lips. 'We'll have our work cut out for us,' she whispered.

'I know.' He kissed her back then grinned and raised his eyebrow on a rakish angle. 'But I love a challenge.'

When baby's delivered just in time for Christmas!

This Christmas, three loving couples receive the most precious gift of all!

Don't miss out on *Precious Gifts* on sale 2nd December 2005

Available at most branches of WHSmith, Tesco, ASDA, Borders, Eason, Sainsbury's and most bookshops

www.millsandboon.co.uk

FREE!

4 Books
and a surprise gift!

We would like to take this opportunity to thank you for reading this Mills & Boon® book by offering you the chance to take FOUR more specially selected titles from the Medical Romance™ series absolutely FREE! We're also making this offer to introduce you to the benefits of the Reader Service™—

- ★ **FREE home delivery**
- ★ **FREE gifts and competitions**
- ★ **FREE monthly Newsletter**
- ★ **Exclusive Reader Service offers**
- ★ **Books available before they're in the shops**

Accepting these FREE books and gift places you under no obligation to buy, you may cancel at any time, even after receiving your free shipment. Simply complete your details below and return the entire page to the address below. You don't even need a stamp!

YES! Please send me 4 free Medical Romance books and a surprise gift. I understand that unless you hear from me, I will receive 6 superb new titles every month for just £2.75 each, postage and packing free. I am under no obligation to purchase any books and may cancel my subscription at any time. The free books and gift will be mine to keep in any case.

MSZEF

Ms/Mrs/Miss/Mr ....Initials.................
BLOCK CAPITALS PLEASE

Surname ....

Address...

....

....Postcode.....................

Send this whole page to:
UK: FREEPOST CN81, Croydon, CR9 3WZ